ONE
LAST
UNVEIL

(A TARA MILLS MYSTERY—BOOK THREE)

SARAH SUTTON

Sarah Sutton

Sarah Sutton is author of the TARA MILLS mystery series, which includes ONE LAST STEP (Book #1), ONE LAST BREATH (Book #2), ONE LAST UNVEIL (Book #3), and ONE LAST LIE (Book #4).

Sarah has always been fascinated by the mystery genre and loves to write suspenseful books with complex characters. Sarah would love to hear from you, so please visit www.sarahsuttonauthor.com to email her, to join the mailing list, to hear the latest news, and to stay in touch!

BOOKS BY SARAH SUTTON

TARA MILLS MYSTERY SERIES
ONE LAST STEP (Book #1)
ONE LAST BREATH (Book #2)
ONE LAST UNVEIL (Book #3)
ONE LAST LIE (Book #4)

Prologue

Chloe tossed her house keys onto the kitchen table as she heaved a long sigh. It was only eight thirty in the morning, but she was already tired. She had just dropped her daughter off at the bus stop, and in her usual way, Felicity—her daughter—had made it perfectly clear that she had no desire to follow through with her morning routine. She had kicked and screamed, dumped the contents of her backpack out onto the floor as they were just about to leave the house, and then stomped her feet the whole way to the bus stop.

Chloe poured herself a cup of coffee—she needed it—and then sat at her kitchen table, staring at the newspaper in front of her. She had work to do, but she needed five minutes to unwind. Mornings with Felicity were never easy. She was a selective mute, after all, and was prone to bursts of frustration as a means of expression. But no matter how many therapy tools Chloe tried to use, it never became easier, and she was always left wondering if she could've handled it differently.

She stared down at the headlines. She needed to shift her focus. She wasn't going to wallow in self-pity today. She wasn't going to question if she was a good mom until the thought debilitated her in every other action for the rest of the day. She needed to focus on her podcast. She now had thousands of listeners. The authorities were finally tuning in. And it was now stirring a rustle in the community as residents remembered the series of murders that had been forgotten for years.

Chloe only hoped that the new attention would bring about leads. The more she dived into the case, the more she needed to find answers. People often asked her why she cared so much, why she took such a personal interest in the story, and for a while she wasn't completely sure. She had no connection the victims. But all she knew was that the injustice caused a fire to burn inside her that a criminal walked free.

As her eyes scanned the paper, a headline stuck out amongst the others: *Nashville Police Reopen Silent Stalker Case*. She smiled. She knew her podcast was the root of their interest. It had been brought to her attention within the past few weeks that her listeners had sent petitions, called in theories, and brought to their attention aspects of the cases that had been overlooked. But it was the witness on her podcast that had come forward years later that ultimately reopened the case. Chloe just hoped it would lead to something.

At the thought, a floorboard creaked in the distance. Chloe's eyes darted to the dim hallway, and she stiffened. She could only see a portion of it, just through the doorframe of the room, but she could see it was empty. Fragments of sunlight danced on the bare hardwood floor, filtering in through a window at the end of the hallway. Only the rustle of the leaves outside at each flick of the wind would cause the filtered light to change shape. She relaxed and heaved a heavy sigh. *It's an old house,* she reminded herself. *Floorboards creak all the time.*

She stared back down at the paper and took a sip of her coffee. She began to read, but each time she read a few words, her eyes would dart to the hallway. There were no other sounds, no more floorboards creaking, but there was something about it that made her feel unsettled. *It's the podcast,* she told herself. She had been on edge for weeks, ever since the community started paying attention, ever since the investigation was reopened. It felt as if she had a target on her back. It was the fact that whoever committed these crimes was still out there, lurking amongst them. It sent a wave of fear through her each time she thought it, even though it was also her driving force for pursuing the podcast in the first place.

She hated to admit it, but the past few weeks she had been acting differently. She questioned everyone's behavior, she looked over her shoulder everywhere she was, and she was an anxious mess when it came to her daughter. It was partially why she felt guilty. She had told herself from day one that she wouldn't let her interest in this case interfere with her daughter's life. She didn't want her having fear, or any understanding, for that matter, on what her mother was looking into. But Chloe knew she did. It was inevitable. Felicity had seen her fidgeting anxiously as she watched the news, as she got up each time at a commercial break to scan the backyard, making sure everything was just as she left it, and each time she would check that every window was locked.

At the thought, her eyes moved once again to the doorframe. *The window.* She had opened it last night. She closed it, but now she couldn't recall if she had secured the lock. She recalled the creaking floorboard. It suddenly burst in her mind like a warning. *I'm just being paranoid*, she tried to tell herself, but she was now at the edge of her seat, her eyes locked on the hallway and her mug gripped so tightly in her hand, it hurt.

Deep down, she knew it wasn't just paranoia. It was a natural response that she knew she had every right to feel. She knew everything there was to know about the Silent Killer—that he brutally stabbed his victims, that he left odd, cryptic messages behind, and that he almost always entered the homes of his victims through an unlatched window.

Chloe's heart drummed. She knew that if there were any reason for him to come out of hiding, to strike again, it would be because of the recent attention to his crimes—the attention that *she* had caused.

She took a deep breath as she slid her clenched fingers from her mug and stood, careful not to let the chair scrape and sound on the tiled floor. She inched to the doorframe as she tried to steady her breathing. *Stop being paranoid*, she told herself again. *Just lock the window and be done with it.* She stuck just her head out into the hallway, peering at the window at the end. There was nothing there, just the sun filtering in through the trees and lighting the darkened home. She relaxed and smiled. *I'm being ridiculous*, she told herself as she moved toward the window, now not focused on the weight of her feet at each step.

She squinted at the sunlight dancing across her vision as she reached for the latch on the window. She quickly locked it and heaved another sigh. *All that panic,* she said to herself as she shook her head. The podcast was certainly getting to her. She reminded herself that it was unlikely the killer would come out of hiding now. Whoever it was would be twenty years older, after all. But in the back of her mind she still knew that it was indeed possible—that some serial killers lay dormant for years, only to resurface again.

Chloe forced the thought from her mind as she turned from the window, but just as she spun fully around, a strange sensation ran through her. She could've sworn she saw movement in the dark bedroom next to where she stood. She stiffened. A shiver ran down her spine. This time it was more than paranoia—it was an instinct. She knew her eyes wouldn't lie. She had seen something. She could feel eyes peering at her. Her blood ran cold.

The floorboard creaked again, and she turned her head sharply, peering into the dark room. She gasped for air. Silhouetted against the closed curtains, she could see him—the shape of a man—and she knew exactly who it was. It was the one she had feared all along.

She turned on her heels, her pulse drumming in her ears. She could see the front door, if she could only make it. But he was right behind her. His hand clawed at her hair until he grabbed hold, jerking her head back. She spun around. She was ready to fight, but then a pain burst in her abdomen. She looked down at blood pooling on her shirt, at a knife being pulled from her open wound.

She fell to the floor as he stood over her. He was a large man with broad shoulders, but she couldn't see his face, which was covered by a ski mask.

"Please, I have a daughter," she pleaded. It was all she could muster, but she knew deep down that it meant nothing to him.

He tilted his head sideways, as if studying his prey. And then he fell to his knees, the knife held high until it plunged once again into her gut.

She gasped for air that wasn't there as one last thought formed in her mind: Felicity. No one would be at the bus stop to greet her after school. Tears formed at the thought of her walking home alone, her finding her mother like this. She wished for a miracle.

But at each thrust of the knife, at each tear of her wound, her thoughts slipped further away, and her world darkened around her.

Chapter One

Tara stared at a table of photos against the wall in Dr. Eisenburg's office as she fidgeted with her hands in her lap. She had been to this office many times, but not in quite some time, and she had forgotten how uncomfortable it always made her at first. She had promised John she would go again. She had promised herself.

But as she stared at the pictures of Dr. Eisenburg's family, she remembered why she never liked sitting in this room and why she always felt guarded. It had been over a year now, and old photos on Dr. Eisenburg's table had been weeded out as new ones took center stage. One Tara had never seen before was of her daughter graduating, another of the whole family on a ski trip. Tara always wondered why she put them there. She assumed it was her way of saying, "I have a family too, I'm not just a psychologist," but what Dr. Eisenburg failed to realize was by highlighting the normalcy in her family life, she was also highlighting the differences.

"Tara." Dr. Eisenburg's voice rang in the silent room, and Tara turned her attention away from the photos. Dr. Eisenburg peered at her just over her glasses, which had slid to the edge of her nose. She sat across from her in a large leather chair, smiling. "I said how's being engaged," she asked.

"Uh, oh, it's great—really great." Tara forced a smile as her eyes moved to the ring on her finger.

She didn't dare meet the doctor's eyes. She knew her lack of desire to speak on the subject seeped into her words, tainting them with the sound of unhappiness. She had tried to hide it as best she could, but she knew she revealed more than she wanted to. As she peered up at Dr. Eisenburg, it was clear she was waiting for Tara to elaborate. Her eyes were still focused on Tara, as if she still had yet to finish a sentence. It was what she always did when she sensed Tara wasn't speaking the full truth. She would never ask outright but rather present an opportunity for Tara to say more. It was a therapist technique, Tara assumed, and it usually worked, but not today. Today, she wasn't ready.

It had been a few weeks since John proposed, but they still had yet to decide on a date. She knew it was her own fault things had not moved forward, and it was only a matter of time before John would grow frustrated. In fact, she was beginning to sense that he already was, and she felt badly. She would never want him to think it was because of him, but she still had yet to tell him the truth—that it was because of Mackenzie James, the unknown woman who had been visiting her father in prison. Ever since she received the letter from her, telling her to stop digging, it had taken center stage in her mind more and more. It was something she wanted to get to the bottom of before she focused on the wedding, but it was also something she had yet to tell John about.

"So what brings you in today?" Dr. Eisenburg finally asked. It was clear Tara wasn't going to speak until spoken to, so Eisenburg opened the floor once again.

Tara took a deep breath. What really brought her in was not something she would admit out loud, that it was to make John happy, to hold true to her promise. Instead, she said exactly what John would want her to say. "Nightmares," she started. "I'm having them again."

It was true; she was. Ever since she received the letter in the mail, its meaning had turned into an obsession that tortured her at all hours, including at night. It had woken her up many times—nightmares of Mackenzie James standing over her bed, watching her, of her father standing over her mother's body with Mackenzie there. Each time, Tara would bolt upright in bed, a scream escaping her lungs on instinct and John switching the light on in panic. She had to tell him about them; it was inevitable. But for some reason she still couldn't yet tell him why, that it all stemmed from the letter.

Eisenburg curled one side of her mouth and nodded as if to say she understood, even though Tara knew very well that she didn't.

"What about, exactly?" Eisenburg asked. She already knew Tara's history—that her father murdered her mother, that she had witnessed it as a child, and that it had tortured her until adulthood—but it was her technique never to make assumptions. She wanted Tara to spell it out herself for both of their sakes, and it was something Tara always hated.

Tara took a deep breath. "My father again," she started. "And my mother. Same nightmares I've had." She cleared her throat awkwardly as her eyes moved to a clock hanging over the table of pictures.

"Do you know why you might be having them again?" Eisenburg followed Tara's gaze as she spoke, as if to remind her to stay focused.

Tara forced her eyes in front of her and shook her head. She couldn't admit why—that it was because of another unresolved piece of her past.

"Well, we know why you had them last time," Dr. Eisenburg replied. "Do you think the reasoning could be the same?"

Tara looked down at her hands. She knew exactly what she was referring to. The last time Tara had the nightmares, she learned that it was due to a repressed memory. They stopped the moment Tara admitted to herself what they meant—that she suspected someone else was in the room the night her mother was murdered, that she had seen her father whisper something to the corner of the room, an area Tara couldn't see from the hallway she stood in. But this time, she knew it was different.

Tara shook her head once again. "I've been honest with myself," she admitted as she stared blankly into the distance. "But maybe it's because I still haven't figured out who was in the room that night," she added.

It was a thought that reoccurred in her mind constantly, and she had no doubt that it was the root of her nightmares. She didn't yet know what Mackenzie James had to do with her past, but she couldn't shake the feeling that she was somehow connected to that night.

Dr. Eisenburg leaned back in her chair as she crossed her legs confidently. "But then why would they stop, only to reoccur?"

Her words made Tara's clarity fade into a cloud of confusion. It was a question that she hadn't even considered, and now that it was posed, she didn't have an answer for it either.

Tara looked up, meeting Eisenburg's eyes. "I'm not sure." Her reply faded into silence as she rolled the question around in her head. "It's been bothering me more and more, I suppose," she added.

Eisenburg fixed her sliding glasses onto the bridge of her nose as she gave Tara a warm smile. "Have you told John any of this?"

Tara felt her face grow hot. Her eyes drifted once again to the ring sitting heavily on her finger. "I don't want to keep burdening him," she muttered. "I owe it to him to focus on the wedding—on us for a change."

"But can you?"

The question hung heavy in the room. "I have to," Tara replied. John had been so supportive toward her as she delved into her past and as her career as an FBI agent in the BAU sent her away on assignments with little notice. For the first time, they had something entirely positive to focus on. She knew if she told him about Mackenzie James, it would hang like a dark cloud around this special time.

"Do you, though?" Eisenburg clasped her hands in her lap as she sat up straighter. "I know your instinct is to protect him, but when the nightmares stopped last time, they didn't just stop when you admitted to yourself why they were occurring. You admitted it to John as well."

Tara knew what she was suggesting, but she was still not ready to tell him.

"What if it only makes your nightmares worse again?" Eisenburg asked.

Tara hadn't considered that, and the suggestion made her feel a sudden lack of control. She couldn't allow what happened last time to happen again—the nightmares progressing into panic attacks that affected her job. Last time, she had almost lost a suspect. If it happened again, she knew it would be the last time. She would either end up fired or dead. The thought sent a shiver through her.

Dr. Eisenburg spoke again. "Marriage is just as much about protection and love as it is about trust, and you can't have trust without honesty." She paused and stared deep into Tara's eyes as if to make sure her words were truly sinking in. "If you keep this buried, it's only going to snowball into something bigger."

Tara sighed and turned her gaze to the floor. Eisenburg's words twisted her stomach into a knot. She was right. Last time Tara had tried to keep something all to herself, it only spiraled out of control until it was forced out of her. Would that only happen again? And would John be even angrier if he found out that Tara never told him about Mackenzie James's letter? Would he lose trust in her? Tara met Eisenburg's eyes. "I know, you're right," she said.

Eisenburg nodded. "So what do you think you're going to do?"

Tara took a deep breath. It wasn't right keeping this from John. They were getting married, they were going to share a life together, and she knew deep down that it meant she needed to be more open with him. "I need to talk to John," she replied as she glanced once again at her ring.

She was going to tell him about the letter and about whom she thought it was from. But it wasn't the letter that Tara feared sharing with John the most. In fact, it wasn't the letter at all. It was what it meant to her—what she planned to do because of it. Tara touched the diamond on her ring, pressing her fingers nervously against the prongs. She needed to know who Mackenzie James was and why she was visiting her father. The desire pulsated inside her. She was closer than ever before to unveiling who was in the room the night of her mother's murder. She could feel it, and she could also feel that Mackenzie knew something. The letter only confirmed it. And that was why Tara feared telling John. She was going to do exactly what the letter warned her not to. She was going to keep digging.

Chapter Two

Tara stood in her bedroom doorway, staring at the wooden dresser in front of her bed as her heart began to pound. Ever since she buried the letter in her drawer, she had only glanced at it in secret, when John wasn't around. She would study the words, the writing, looking for any possible clue. But now, for the first time, she would be taking it out for good and showing it to John.

He wasn't home yet, but she knew she didn't have much time. She had spoken to him once she left the therapist. He was at band practice, but he had left around the same time as her. Any moment and he would be walking through the door. Tara's stomach churned.

Tara's eyes rose to the mirror above her dresser to see her reflection. She was still in what she wore to work, a polo shirt and black pants. Her straight brown hair was tucked neatly behind her ears and hanging just below her chin. But as she looked at her eyes, she could see the toll that the last few weeks had taken. They were dull and bloodshot from exhaustion, from

14

the nightmares, from the letter that had occupied her mind at all hours. Her green eyes looked piercing through the redness. But as she stared at the mirror, she knew she had not been completely honest with herself. It wasn't just the letter that tormented her. It was keeping it all from John. Each day that had gone by, each day that she kept it a buried secret, she knew it would be harder to tell him and for him to understand. By doing so, she thought she was protecting him. But she now knew that she wasn't. She could only protect John by protecting their relationship, and secrets certainly didn't do that.

Tara took a deep breath as her eyes fell to the dresser once more. She moved closer, pulled open her drawer, and dug under her socks to where she had carefully hidden the envelope. She felt her fingers touch the paper as her eyes fell upon her name and address written quickly in blue ink across it. She scooped it up, the envelope cool in her warm, sweaty palm as she pulled out the piece of paper within and unfolded it. The words *STOP DIGGING* stared back at her, and a chill swept through her, the same way it did when she opened it for the first time.

I can't do this, she said to herself. *I can't tell John.* Her mind tugged at her decision as fear flooded her body. *Is this the right time?* she wondered. After all, they were planning a wedding. This was supposed to be a time filled with blissful happiness. It was a time to celebrate *them.* But this letter would make everything about her. It would make John worry again. It would mean that she would be opening the door to her past even wider. It would disrupt everything.

15

"Tara?" John's voice rang through the hall as the front door shut behind him, sending a jolt through Tara's body.

His keys clanked on the island counter. The sound of his footsteps grew closer. But Tara couldn't respond. The envelope sat too heavy in her hand.

"Tara?" he called again.

She quickly pulled open her drawer, about to bury the envelope once more, but then a thought made her freeze. *I can't keep more secrets. He's about to be my husband.* She knew perfectly well that she couldn't start their marriage on a lie. How could he trust her fully if she hid things from him? She *had* to tell him. It was the right thing to do.

"Didn't you hear me?"

Tara spun around to see John. His perfectly combed-over hair that he had left for work with that morning was now slick with sweat and gel. His shirt was unbuttoned halfway down his chest. His sleeves were pushed up, revealing his muscular forearms. It was always after band practice that Tara would remark at how handsome he was, but not today. Today, the playfulness was far beyond her reach. He stood in the doorway, confusion plastered on his face. Tara's stomach swirled with nausea.

"What's wrong?" he asked as his eyes fell to the envelope clenched in Tara's hand. "What is that?" His expression morphed into concern, then fear as his mind ran wild.

"Everything's fine," Tara finally replied, realizing that she had been silent too long. "I..." she stopped herself. She hadn't prepared for how she would tell him. *Just show him,* she said to herself. "I got this in the mail," she added as she handed over the letter.

John looked down at it, his eyebrows knitted, as he stared at the writing on the envelope, as he looked for a return address that wasn't there. He pulled out the paper within it, unfolded it, and then his head shot backward. "Stop digging." The words rolled off his lips as he read them, trying to make sense of what he was seeing. After a moment, his eyes raised to Tara's. "You think it's from—?"

He didn't even have to finish his sentence before Tara nodded. There was only one person who could've sent it, and John knew it too. "Mackenzie James," Tara confirmed.

He looked down at it again. He sighed. Tara knew he didn't want to admit it, but the letter confirmed that Mackenzie knew something, that Tara had a reason to dig deeper into her past. He once again met her eyes. "This sounds like it's getting dangerous now." It was the exact response that Tara feared. He was going to push her to do exactly what the letter wanted, and her heart sank. "Why would she suddenly send this now?" he asked as he stared down at the letter once more, trying to make sense of it.

Tara's eyes fell to the floor. She knew this question was coming. "She didn't," she replied. She looked up, meeting his eyes. "I found it in the mail after I confronted her—after you proposed." It was the main reason Tara suspected the letter to be from Mackenzie James in the first place. Just before it arrived, Tara had staked outside of her father's prison in upstate New York, waiting for the woman who was visiting him. It was that day that Tara met Mackenzie

17

James face-to-face. But their encounter only left Tara with more questions. It was as if she feared her. She refused to tell Tara anything and then sped off in her car. A couple days later, the letter arrived. There was no doubt in her mind who it was from.

"Why would you hide this from me?"

Tara's thoughts fled at the sound of John's anger. A mix of pain and fury swirled in his eyes. His hand now clenched the letter tightly.

"We just got engaged, I—"

"You what? Let me guess. You were protecting me?"

John's question hung heavy. He knew her too well. She didn't even have to tell him her reasoning, and she knew her explanation wouldn't make it easier for him to digest.

"I've never lied to you," he added. "Is it really that hard to expect the same from you?"

Tara didn't respond. Her heart was wracked with guilt. He was right; he never lied to her. It was one thing she loved about him, that she could always trust him fully, that she could always count on him. The thought that she didn't give him the same sat heavy on her conscience.

"When are you going to realize that I don't need you to protect me? You're about to be my wife," he continued. "We can't keep things from each other, Tara. All it does is cause issues we don't need."

He slapped the letter on the bed in anger, but Tara didn't know how to respond. He was right, and she didn't know why she always felt this need to protect him—if it was a reaction to some subconscious guilt she felt from not being able to save her mother—but he was right. He didn't need her to protect his feelings. He knew who she was, what her past was, and yet he still wanted to marry her.

"And what, were you planning on digging deeper into this behind my back too?" He threw his hands up in frustration. "Are you going to speak?" He stared at her.

Whenever Tara saw John this upset, it always seemed to take her by surprise. It was a side of him she seldom saw, and she knew that when he reached that point, he wasn't just going to let it go.

Tara barely met his eyes. "I thought about it," she admitted. John let out a grunt in response with a shake of his head. "But I didn't," she finished. She sighed as she took a seat on the bed, scooping up the letter, fidgeting with it. "I'm sorry. I should've told you. I just—" She paused, meeting his blue eyes that now held traces of compassion, and then looked back down at the envelope held tightly in her hand. "We just got engaged. I wanted to enjoy that with you. I can't keep dragging you down again with all my baggage."

"And I don't know how many times I have to tell you," he snapped back. "Your baggage is my baggage." He sat down next to her and heaved a frustrated sigh. "But you have to believe it yourself," he added.

He was right. Tara had trouble seeing her issues as anyone's other than her own. All her life, she had kept everything pertaining to her mother's murder to herself. The only person she would discuss it with was her grandmother, with whom she lived after the incident, but they still seldom spoke about it. It was too difficult for both of them. And because of that,

Tara often felt the need to handle things on her own—not to involve others' feelings. Getting married was certainly something she would need to adjust to.

But John's reaction caused uncertainty to well up within her. Every time Tara withheld information from him to protect him, he would always end up pitying her once he learned that it stemmed from her tortured past. But this time was different. He seemed fed up, tired of walking this road again. Tara instinctively grabbed his hand, lacing her fingers in his.

"I promise, I won't hide anything from you again."

For a moment, John's hand tensed, as if he were going to pull it away, but then he let it relax in her grasp. "You make a lot of promises. I just wish you were better at keeping them." He stared off in front of him, trying hard not to look at her.

"I'm trying, John. I didn't do it to hurt you."

Tara's words were met with silence. She knew her words were losing their meaning, and it twisted her stomach. But she also knew he had every right to feel that way—she had said them before.

John looked back down at the envelope in Tara's hands. "How did she get our address anyway?"

Tara shrugged. That was a question she had pondered as well. The only person they shared in common was Tara's father, but Tara assumed he wouldn't have given it to her. Last she had met with him, it seemed as if he didn't even want them to know about each other, so putting them in contact seemed unlikely.

John turned toward her. "It doesn't scare you at all?"

"It makes me want to find out what she's hiding. I feel like I'm so close, John. I just need to keep pushing. I—"

"This sounds dangerous, Tara," John interjected. "She's threatening you." He stared deep in her eyes as if to make sure she understood his words.

"I can handle her, John. After all, I'm an FBI agent."

"But this is on your own; it's different."

Again, silence filled the room. For so long, John had supported Tara in uncovering her past. In fact, he had said on multiple occasions how admirable it was—that it took someone with great strength to face the darkest point of their life. But right now, Tara didn't feel supported. She was growing frustrated. She had to see this through, and John knew that. It was the only way she could find closure in her past—the only way the nightmares would stop for good.

"You know I have to do this," she finally said.

John's eyes were fixed on the floor. "I know." The words slipped out of his mouth in a whisper. "I just wish we could just focus on the wedding—on us."

Tara felt a tug on her heart. Maybe she was being unfair to him. This one moment in time that they had to focus on each other, she was admitting that she may pick up and leave to go hunt down her demons at any moment.

"We haven't even picked a date," he added with a forced chuckle, until his voice faded. "Would we be able to have the wedding first?" He looked into her eyes. "Just enjoy us for a moment? And then I'll do whatever I can to support you and help you get to the bottom of this." His eyes fell on the envelope.

Tara placed the letter next to her on the bed as she turned fully toward John. She couldn't disappoint him again. He had supported her through everything she had ever wanted to do, and he deserved to want her to himself fully for once.

"Of course," she finally muttered. A smile grew wide on John's face as he leaned in and kissed her.

But just as Tara pulled away, the letter caught her eye once again, and an unsettled feeling swirled within her. *What did I just agree to?* Could she really go that long without answers? Even though they hadn't yet picked a date, they knew they weren't getting married until next year. And to make matters worse, it was only a matter of time before she would be assigned her next big case, and who knew if that would cause them to push the date back further.

As Tara raised her eyes to meet John's, she forced a smile as one more thought surfaced: *Did I just make another promise I can't keep?*

Chapter Three

Tara's finger curled around the trigger as she aimed her Glock 19 9mm pistol and let off fifteen mags straight into the chest of her target dummy. She lowered her gun, inserted another round, and took aim again, until she once again emptied the clip.

It was 7:00 a.m. on a Tuesday morning, an hour earlier than she'd normally arrive at headquarters. But Tara needed to clear her head. She quickly fixed her unruly hair, retying it into a bun before she loaded her gun once again. It had been a long night, and every aspect of the way she looked today reminded her of it. It was the letter and the promise she made to John. Each time she closed her eyes last night, the letter surfaced in her mind and regret bubbled up as the promise echoed in her head. She had to keep it. She owed it to him. And she knew that acting on her desires to track down Mackenzie James again would only cause tension between her and John.

Tara raised her handgun and let off two shots straight into the forehead before taking a deep breath. A sense of injustice boiled within her. It was the same feeling that had brought her to work early and to the shooting range. She hoped that some stress relief would bury it once and for all, but it was clear now that it was rooted too deep. It seemed that by being fair to John, she in turn had to be unfair to herself. *Don't I deserve answers?* she asked herself as she took aim and pulled the trigger. She finally felt as if she had reached the curtain to her past. All she had to do was take a few more steps forward to pull it back. She knew if she waited too long, it would just make it harder. More curtains would only hang behind the one within reach. She needed to keep digging while it was fresh, before Mackenzie had time to bury anything else now that she knew Tara was on to her.

Tara lowered her gun as her eyes moved to her go-bag sitting on the stool next to her. She slid her hand into the front pocket. She could feel the coolness of the envelope sitting within, sending a wave of guilt and urgency crashing upon her. She wasn't sure why she'd brought it. Part of her wanted to study it more, to try to track down where it came from with her resources at headquarters. But part of her wanted to toss it. It would only send her down a rabbit hole she wasn't sure she had the time or energy for right now.

Tara's eyes lifted to the clock hanging on the wall. It was now almost seven thirty. She pulled off her goggles as she shifted her focus. It was time to head into work. She normally arrived at the office nowadays by eight. Work had been slow after the beach killer case she solved just over a month ago. Her day-to-day now mostly consisted of paperwork or helping other agents with interviews, obtaining search warrants, or any other tasks that needed another set of hands. She knew it was Reinhardt's way of giving her a break. It was the second time he had done so after she solved a big case, and she was beginning to see the pattern. Even though her current work lacked the excitement she often enjoyed from her career, she was beginning to like not having an assignment. She liked being home. She liked having a set schedule. And she liked not having work as the center of her life for once.

Tara exited her alcove and went to the front desk, where she slid her pistol and safety equipment to a retired female officer, thanked her, and turned toward the exit. At this time of day, the range was a popular spot, which was clear from the ever-revolving door and increased foot traffic. It was another reminder to Tara that it was time to leave. She was bound to run into someone she knew, and she didn't seek the gun range for conversation.

"Mills!" Just as Tara pushed open the door of the exit, Camila Lopez came scurrying through and smiled. "How you been? Working on anything interesting?"

Tara forced a smile. It seemed as if everyone wanted to know what she was working on nowadays. It was a common question among her colleagues. She shook her head. "In between cases right now."

Camila was a senior special agent in the BAU, the same division Tara worked in as a newly appointed special agent herself. Over the past couple of months, Tara's reputation had grown favorably. She was still new to the force, but she had helped to solve two big cases within the past year, and agents were certainly noticing her—including Camila. It was only a couple of weeks ago that Camila asked her to lunch with a couple other agents. It was then that she learned that Camila had been working for the bureau for ten years and had once been the partner of Frank Warren, Tara's current partner.

"What about you?" Tara asked.

Camila pushed her graying frizzy bob behind her ear. "Working on a cold case," she said. "It's slow moving right now, so just trying to get a couple rounds in to think."

Tara nodded. Thinking seemed to be a common use for the gun range.

Camila checked her watch as she turned on her heels, making her way to the counter. "You better enjoy it," she added, her voice trailing through the air. "Before you know it, something's going to fall in your lap."

Tara nodded and said her goodbyes as the door closed shut behind her. Camila was right. Any moment now, Tara's life would abruptly change, and it didn't sit well with her. She had her wedding to think about. She had the letter. A new case would only push both out of her focus. And if she were to keep her promise to John and wait until after the wedding to dig into her past, a new case would only push that end goal further from the near future. As Tara stepped out into the fresh air, she hoped today would not be the day. She wasn't ready yet.

Leaves danced across her path as she made her way through the corridor. The early autumn air was crisp and refreshing, and the wind brushed against the bit of sweat trickling down her neck from the gun range, sending goose bumps to prickle in return.

Just as she reached her building, her phone vibrated in her pocket. She stopped right outside the entrance, but as she stared down at the screen, the number flashing across was not one she recognized. It was her work phone, and she rarely got calls that weren't stored unless she was on a case, which she wasn't. She placed the phone to her ear.

"Is this Agent Mills?" A stern deep male voice spoke urgently.

"It is. Can I help you?"

The man took a deep breath. "I got your phone number from Rehoboth PD. You helped to solve that beach killer murder, if I'm not mistaken?"

"Yes, I did," Tara replied. "And who is this?"

He cleared his throat. "My apologies. This is Chief Meyers calling from the Nashville, Tennessee police department. I think I have a case that might interest you." Tara took a seat on a nearby bench. "Have you ever heard of the Silent Stalker?"

Tara thought for a moment. She had. It was one of the cases that she had studied at the academy. He was active in the late nineties to early 2000s and had murdered close to a dozen women in the Tennessee area over the course of a decade. He was known for his carefully planned attacks—entering homes with no sign of forced entry, often through an unlatched window. But she wasn't sure why someone would be calling her about a case from so long ago.

"Yes, those cases have been cold for a while," Tara replied. From what she remembered, the last known victim was murdered close to twenty years ago, and the case went cold soon after.

"It did," the chief affirmed. "Until recently. There's a podcast that started about a year ago. It's sparked a lot of attention in the community, and we opened up the case again."

"You think you have new leads?" Tara asked. She knew podcasts were a great way to resurface new leads. Often they would bring forth new witnesses or new theories from web sleuths that got a kick out of solving these crimes themselves.

"Possibly," he replied. "But that's not exactly why I'm calling." He fell silent for a moment as Tara waited for him to elaborate.

"The woman who started the podcast—Chloe Waterman—she was found murdered in her home yesterday."

"Oh my god." Tara stiffened. "And what, you think it's related?"

"I've worked in this department many years. I actually started in the force right in the middle of the Silent Stalker's rampage." He paused briefly, as if thinking of how to word what he was about to say next. "I've been to a lot of crime scenes in my day, and I've grown a pretty thick skin, but this one made my skin crawl. It was the same feeling I got when I was assigned the Silent Stalker's cases." A shiver ran down Tara's spine. "I saw you solved that tough case in Rehoboth," he continued. "If this guy is striking again, we're going to need all the help we can get."

Tara let his words sink in. It was an unusual call—an unusual case. It did happen, where serial killers would lay dormant for quite some time, only to resurface years later. Usually it was because a case was getting too hot or there was a shift in their personal life that helped alleviate their urge. But twenty years was an abnormally long time for a serial killer to stay dormant. The killer would be much older.

"You really think it's the same killer?"

"I'd be surprised if it wasn't."

His words hung heavy between them. "I'll see what I can do," she finally said.

Moments later, Tara stared down at her now silent phone. It sat like a weight within her palm. She was surprised that of all people, the chief thought to call her. It showed that she was not only making herself known in her department, but in law enforcement as a whole, and she felt a surge of pride. But the feeling soon washed over her and receded. She had to tell Reinhardt, and she already knew what he was going to say—that she should take the case.

Tara stood up and turned toward the entrance of the building as she thought back to what Camila said to her at the range. *Before you know it, something will fall in your lap.* The words echoed in her head. She knew Camila was right, but she also didn't expect it to happen so soon, and it made her stomach churn. As she pushed open the glass doors, she contemplated what she would tell Reinhardt. She knew deep down she wasn't ready. Tennessee was over six hundred miles from Washington, D.C. This was exactly what she didn't want right now—to be taken away from home in the midst of planning a wedding. It would delay the process, which would in turn delay her pursuing Mackenzie James for information.

Tara pressed the button of the elevator and waited as butterflies burst in her belly. She had never turned down a case before. In fact, she didn't even know if she could. She was still so early in her career. But as she waited for the elevator to descend, she wondered if she just might.

Chapter Four

Tara sat opposite Reinhardt, who sat at his desk speaking to Chief Meyers on speakerphone. She had already filled him in on what she knew, but once he realized how large a case it could be, he had called the chief back to hear it all for himself. His face was stern as he took in all the details. His eyes moved under his knitted eyebrows from the phone to Tara and then back again. When the conversation was finished, Reinhardt hung up and lifted his head to Tara as he clasped his hands, resting his forearms on his desk.

"Well, he very clearly wants you," he said. "This is going to be a huge case, if the killer really is who he thinks he is." Reinhardt's voice was stern. He sat back in his chair, placing his hands behind his head as he stared up at the ceiling. "It could always be a fluke, though, some copycat. Twenty years is a long time for a killer to remain dormant."

It was the exact thought Tara had before. As big of a case as it seemed, pieces of it made it seem unlikely. The chief had informed her and Reinhardt that Chloe Waterman was murdered in the same way as the victims of the Silent Stalker in the early 2000s and nineties who were brutally stabbed to death in their homes, but that wasn't enough to link them in her mind or Reinhardt's. The only aspect that did was the podcast, which could be an odd coincidence, a copycat, or the killer truly resurfacing to maybe stop someone who could have been getting to close to answers.

"Are you up for it?" Reinhardt was leaning over his desk once more, staring directly at her.

Tara let the question sink in. It was not one she was expecting. In fact, she had never been asked if she was up for anything; it was just assumed that as a new hungry agent, she would take whatever fell on her lap. She never had a choice. She always understood that part of the job was not having choices on what cases she took. But now she was presented with one, and it caught her off guard. She had already set in her mind that if it were an option, she would turn it down. But she never actually thought it was a possibility. And now that it was presented, Tara wondered if turning it down was a bad look for her career.

"Do I really have a choice?" she asked with a slight chuckle and a small smile. She was being facetious, but part of her truly was seeking an answer.

Reinhardt raised his brows and smiled, as if surprised by her remark. He once again leaned back in his chair, his hands resting on the back of his neck. "Well, you always have a choice, Mills." He paused briefly. "But don't let it get to your head that you're becoming some big shot around here. You are still a rookie."

Tara's heart sank, but his response was already what she expected. His answer was clear. She did have a choice, but there was only one *acceptable* choice. He was right; even though she had solved two big cases, she had been a special agent for less than a year. She certainly was nowhere near done proving herself. And it was clear from his response that turning it down would not look good for her.

For a moment, she thought about John, about the wedding, and about the letter. This would completely turn her focus. But she also knew that this was her job, and this was exactly what she signed up for. *Maybe it'll be a fluke,* she thought. *Maybe it's not really the Silent Stalker after all.* The thought made what she was about to say a little easier to stomach.

She took a deep breath and plastered a smile on her face.

"Of course I'm up for it," she finally said.

Reinhardt's smile grew wider as he reached for his phone. "I'll let Agent Warren know. He'll meet you at the airport. You should go home and pack."

Tara nodded before standing and heading for the door. But as she left Reinhardt's office, she wondered, what if it truly was the Silent Stalker striking again? An uneasy feeling washed over her as another thought burst in her mind. *This could be the biggest case of my career.*

***

Tara crammed her folded clothes quickly into her duffle bag as she heard the shower shut off in the distance. She had arrived home moments ago, but John still didn't know she was there. It was still early. He was still getting ready for work, and any moment now he would walk out of the bathroom and Tara would have to explain that she was leaving. She felt sadness bubble up inside her.

Once again, her work was taking center stage. He would understand, of course, but Tara also knew that he wouldn't be able to help being disappointed. They hadn't even looked at wedding venues yet, and there was certainly no way they would be able to if Tara was all the way in Nashville. It was inevitable that they would have to pause on the wedding planning. But it wasn't just the wedding planning Tara was concerned about. It was the letter, her past that still held unanswered questions. She kneeled down by her go-bag and slid her hand into the front pocket until she felt the envelope. As difficult as it was, she knew that for now she had to put any search into her past to rest. *Maybe it's a good thing.* This case was forcing her not to look for answers at the moment, and maybe that was what she needed in order to keep her promise to John. She listened carefully for a moment to John rustling about in the bathroom before she pulled it out and quickly stood up, tucking it back into her drawer. She didn't even want him to know that she had taken it with her to work, that she was still contemplating digging deeper into her past before they even wed. It wasn't even worth the conversation now, because once again her focus had shifted.

"Why are you home?"

Tara spun around to see John with a towel wrapped around his waist, clean-shaven, the smell of aftershave wafting across the room. His face fell as his eyes moved to the duffle bag, and Tara's heart sank.

"I got assigned a new case."

"Where?" He couldn't hide his anguish. His face was still all emotion, only his lips moving, as if trying with all his might to hold back what he wanted to burst out and say.

"Nashville."

John's eyes fell at the nod of his head as he took a seat on the bed. For a moment, he was silent, unsure what to say. "That's far." The words slid off his lips. Tara nodded. "Is it a big case?" His eyes rose once again to meet hers, hope swirling within them.

"I'm not sure. It could be." Tara sat down next to him, both of them staring at the carpet below their feet. "I won't know for sure until I get there. We have our suspicions that it might not be as big of a case as it seems. If it's not, I'll be back pretty quick."

John nodded. He already knew what Tara didn't say. That if it were a big case, she would be gone a lot longer. He continued to stare down at his feet. He didn't ask questions. He never did. He didn't want to know the details. Nor did Tara want to share them with him. He knew himself well enough to know that it would only stir needless worry and that Tara was always reluctant to share. They had both learned to protect him from the details of any case.

Tara looked over at her bag sitting on the floor. She knew she would have to leave soon. She was meeting Warren at the airport at 10:00 a.m. She reached for her phone in the middle of the bed to check the time. It was almost nine.

"You need to go, don't you?" John asked. He stood up, checking the time as well. "I got to head to work anyway."

Tara nodded as she grabbed her bags. She was surprised John didn't bring up the wedding, but she knew it was on his mind. It had to be. "I can start calling venues and schedule times to look at them for when I'm back," Tara added.

John let out a slight grunt and rolled his eyes as he buttoned up his shirt. "You don't even know when that will be."

He was right; she didn't. "I'll make the appointments for a couple weeks out. That way we have them. We can always move them if needed." She was trying desperately to make him happy. But he only forced a smile and remained silent as he finished getting dressed.

"Are you mad at me?" she asked. "You know I—"

"I know," he interrupted. "You're doing your job." He slid his feet into his shoes, tied them, and then planted a kiss on her cheek. "I'm not mad at you. I can't be," he added before turning to the door. He glanced back at her one last time until his eyes darted away from her. "Now go do your job," he said with a nod. His words seemed forced, laced with stifled emotion.

Tara forced a smile as John exited the room and then the apartment, leaving her in total silence. Butterflies fluttered in her belly. She couldn't help but feel uneasy at the way John left. As understanding as he was, it was clear that Tara's job was beginning to take a toll on him and on their relationship. But she also knew it wasn't just her job. It was her lack of presence when she was here, her mind always somewhere else—on Mackenzie James, on her nightmares.

Tara sighed as she hoisted her duffle bag over her shoulder. She glanced one last time at her dresser drawer. It was clearer to her now more than ever. She was spreading herself too thin. She couldn't focus on work, on her wedding, and her past. She pulled her eyes away from the dresser and focused down the hall, forcing one foot in front of the other.

She switched off the lights in the kitchen and pulled open the front door, but a moment of doubt stopped her from stepping through. She knew it was going to take everything inside her not to try to figure out who Mackenzie James was, but then the thought of John, of the case, pushed forward in her mind. *It will only have to wait for now,* she reminded herself as she stepped into the hallway outside her apartment. The door slammed shut behind her.

Chapter Five

Richard Mills stared down at the slop on his food tray and swirled it with his fork. It was morning, and as hungry as he was, he still always had trouble stomaching the poor excuse for oatmeal they always served him. He had forgotten what real oatmeal tasted like, but he knew this wasn't it. It tasted stale, even when soaked and boiled, and it always amazed him that the prison was even capable of serving stale oatmeal, given the long shelf life. But then again, he knew to always expect the absolute worst here. He scooped a bit on his fork. He took a bite and swallowed it quickly.

"Your visitor coming today?"

Richard looked up to see Jim Peccini sitting diagonally across from him with his elbows on the table as he held his fork in his fist and shoveled oatmeal into his mouth. Dribbles stuck to his salt-and-pepper beard. Two other guys sat on either side of him, Justin Levi and Peter Wang, their heads down as they scarfed down their food.

"What do you think?" Richard shot back. It was a stupid question. Almost everyone in this prison knew he had the same visitor every day. Mackenzie had made her presence known nearly every day since he started his life behind bars, over twenty years ago.

Jim knitted his brows in a scowl as the others smirked at their breakfast. Richard knew Jim didn't like when he was smart with him, or anyone for that matter, but that was exactly why it gave Richard joy. It was the reason Jim was in this place—a bar fight that turned into a bloody brawl, paralyzing a man for life from a stab wound in his back, all over because he was "smart" with Jim. Now Jim was eight years into serving a ten-year sentence for second-degree attempted murder.

But Richard knew that Jim would never act on his anger—not in here. He was up for parole in a matter of months, and Richard liked to use that to his advantage. Even though they were "friends" by prison standards, they didn't quite like each other enough not to mess with one another. They each needed to stay entertained somehow.

"Anyone visiting you today?" Richard asked. "When's that chick you've been writing to going to show her face?"

Jim winced. Everyone knew he had been writing to a woman for months now, an ex-girlfriend who reached out, but each time she had promised to visit, she never ended up coming.

"She's got her kids. She can't come," Jim replied through his teeth.

"Or maybe her husband won't let her," Justin joined in.

Peter and Richard erupted into laughter as Jim's jaw buckled. They all had their suspicions that she hadn't come to visit for the very reason that she was married or dating someone. Richard knew Jim didn't want to admit it, but it was clear he had his suspicions too. In fact, Richard was certain he almost let it slip once, when he seemingly let his guard down for just a glimpse in conversation, but then quickly bit his tongue. It was what they all did here. They could never get too close. They joined together like packs of wolves for protection, but they were still dogs, and their environment was still unforgiving. No one could be trusted fully.

"When are you going to tell us who that girl is who visits you everyday?" Jim shot back.

Richard grew quiet as the laughter around him simmered. It was a question they always threw at him, but one that never got easier at avoiding. "I told you, she's a friend."

"Pretty close friend, huh?" Jim asked, but Richard didn't reply. As far as anyone knew, she was a friend, and that's how he wanted to keep it.

Suddenly all three men's eyes raised over Richard's shoulders as their faces morphed questioningly. Richard smiled. It was perfect timing, and he relaxed. He knew exactly who it would be before he even spun around.

"Richard Mills?" the voice of a corrections officer soared over his shoulder. "She's here," he added. "Your visitor is here."

***

40

Mackenzie James's bloodshot eyes peered tiredly at Richard through the glass. Her frizzy hair was wild around her face, the top glistening under the fluorescent light, revealing that it needed a wash. Her appearance had been similar each day that she had visited over the past few weeks, except for her body, which seemed to shrink in size, while her clothing got larger. At first, she was able to hide her frailness under clothing, but now her collarbone jutted out sharply. Many times, Richard had wanted to ask when she last ate, but he held himself back. He knew she would not take kindly to any form of accusation.

It was early for her, nearly nine o'clock. Lately she had refused to come during her usual time, noon, and she still had yet to admit why. He had his suspicions that it had something to do with Tara, his daughter. After all, her change in routine only began after Tara had visited him, after he told Mackenzie to be careful, and after she nearly had a meltdown. It was a mistake to tell her. He knew it then, and he knew it now as her lack of sleep hung under her eyes like a shadow. Her earlier arrivals had brought to light how little sleep she had been getting, now that she couldn't make up for it once the sun met the horizon—when her demons finally took their turn to sleep.

Ever since she learned that Tara had visited him, something in her changed, and it worried him. She seemed more exhausted than usual, her mind constantly drifting elsewhere, her gaze glossed over with fear.

He picked up the phone and held it to his ear for moment before he spoke.

"How are you doing?" he asked cautiously.

He knew she wasn't doing well, but he was hoping that for once she would open up, reveal the reason for her sudden downward spiral. Every part of her revealed a desperate cry for help. If they weren't separated by glass, he was almost certain she would have an odor to her.

"Fine," she uttered without emotion. "Have you heard from Tara?"

It was the same question she had asked every day for the past few weeks. Her mind was fixated on it. Richard shook his head. "I told you, she's not coming back," he said. He hated to repeat it. Each time, it sent a wave of regret through his body, until reality settled in. For so long he had longed to see her, and now that he finally had, he had to push her away with only a glimpse. But deep down, he knew he didn't deserve any more of her. It was his fault that life and the situation at hand unfolded the way it did.

Mackenzie narrowed her eyes skeptically, and Richard sighed. He knew she didn't trust him. She had trouble trusting anyone. But of all people, he knew he deserved her trust. He had done everything in his power to prove that to her. Anger welled in his throat, but he swallowed it and controlled his voice carefully. "You know you can trust me," he responded.

She loosened her gaze slightly and smirked. She was still doubtful, and it infuriated him more, but he was careful not to let his frustration show.

"Why do you keep asking me that anyway?" he questioned. He knew why she didn't want Tara to visit. It was important for both their sakes that Tara didn't dig up the past or learn of Mackenzie's identity.

It was the exact reason why Richard ended her visit abruptly when she told him of her nightmares. They had sparked a curiosity in her, and he couldn't risk engaging in conversation about the past.

Mackenzie's eyes fell. It was the same response as the last few times he had asked her. Still, she refused to answer.

"You don't need to worry about her," he added. "She's gone."

Her eyes stayed fixed on the ground a moment longer until she lifted her head. "I know," she replied as a cynical smile seeped onto her face.

It was the same smile he had seen before. The same smile that caused the blood to drain from his brain as his body went numb. It was a smile he feared because it was the look of unpredictability. Richard stiffened. "What aren't you telling me, Mackenzie?" He stared her dead in the eye, the way he always did when he needed her to speak the truth.

Her smile faded as her eyes darted around her. She then lowered her voice into the phone. "She needs to mind her own business," she replied.

"What do you mean?" Richard asked. He could tell she wanted to say something that she couldn't due to where they were. They could never be too sure who was listening.

Mackenzie sighed, tucking her frizzy curly hair behind her ear. "She wanted to know who I was," she added. "In the parking lot."

Richard shot his head back in confusion. "You saw her? When?" His jaw clenched in anticipation.

Mackenzie's eyes darted around her once again before she leaned in closer to the glass. "She was waiting for me outside when I came to visit one day."

Richard immediately knew what day she was referring to. It was the day Mackenzie never showed, the day that marked her pivotal change. After that day, her visiting hours changed and exhaustion began to spread over her like a disease.

"She was demanding who I was," Mackenzie added. "She somehow knew I was visiting you."

Richard's heart raced, his hand pulsating from his grip on the phone. "But how—"

"I'm not sure."

He didn't even need to finish his question. They both wondered the same thing. How did Tara even know about Mackenzie? He had never mentioned her, and he had made sure that they never met. If she had learned of her, it was not his doing, and he was the only connection they had.

His eyes drifted to the corner of the room as he remembered learning of Tara's occupation. He had learned after her visit that she was not the accountant she had led him to believe. She was an FBI agent. It had swirled through the conversations of the correction officers, which eventually spiraled through the prisoners and then to him. At first he didn't believe it, but then it all made sense. The incessant questioning, the focus on her mother's murder, trying to dissect a memory. This only confirmed that she was digging into her mother's case.

The tips of his fingers dug into the phone as his gaze landed once again on Mackenzie. He hadn't told her. He couldn't. That information would only make her panic, and a panicked Mackenzie was dangerous.

Her eyes moved to his tight grip, and he instantly relaxed his hand on the phone. He couldn't let her see his fear. Instead, he shrugged.

"She probably saw you visiting me one day," he started. "I don't think she's coming back. Plus, you changed your visiting hours." He tried desperately to reassure her, but her face only tightened in anger. She knew exactly what he was doing.

"I know she's not coming back," Mackenzie replied as she narrowed her eyes once again.

Her words sent a jolt through his body like a warning. She had done something, he could feel it. "And why is that?" He held his voice steady.

"I sent her a letter," she admitted as she broke eye contact, drifting to the corner of the glass window. "She's stepping where she doesn't belong. I needed to let her know."

"Mackenzie…" Her name rolled effortlessly off his tongue. It was exactly what he feared. Panic swirled within him, but he simmered it into a shake of his head, as if to say only that he were disappointed. His thoughts raced. He was too late; she had already panicked and done something rash.

"Where did you send it?" he asked, trying to hold his voice steady. As far as he knew, Mackenzie didn't have her address. He had purposely kept that information far from her grip.

"Her apartment," she replied, sending another wave of confusion and panic through Richard's body.

"But how did you—"

"Get her address?" Mackenzie finished his question with a smirk of satisfaction. "I have my ways."

Richard didn't know how to respond. He knew she was right; she did have her ways. She was always one to get what she wanted, no matter the task or consequence. It was an aspect of her that always made him nervous, especially now. If he was right, if Tara was investigating her mother's murder, it was only a matter of time before Mackenzie would make that discovery. Which meant that it was only a matter of time before Tara was no longer safe.

Chapter Six

Tara watched from the window as the aircraft marshaller stretched out his arm, directing the plane to the runway. The plane moved away from him, in his intended direction, until he was no longer visible. Tara's stomach sank as she pulled her eyes from the window and stared at the seat in front of her. *This is it. There's no going back now.* She had accepted the case. The letter was tucked away in her drawer. Her wedding plans were on pause, and she was pretty sure John was getting fed up with her. It was becoming a pattern that he seemingly came in last in her list of priorities. The thought made her stomach twist into a knot. She didn't blame him, but at the same time she had never intended to make him feel that way. In fact, everything she was doing—digging into her past, trying to get past the trauma, and building her career— was just as much about building a future with John as it was about helping her live a fulfilling life.

The plane picked up speed, and Tara's head shot back into the headrest, forcing her into the present moment. She closed her eyes briefly and took a deep breath. *I'm here. I need to focus on the case*, she reminded herself. Her eyes opened to the sound of a phone powering down, and she turned to Warren, who sat next to her, shoving his phone in his pocket.

As he felt Tara's eyes peering at him, he lifted his head and smiled at her. A piece of his combed-over silver hair brushed his eyebrow. Tara hadn't seen a whole lot of him in the past few weeks. At times, they had worked small cases together, but it was a change from the consistent time they spent together when a large case unfolded. Tara knew he was dating Dr. Harris, the forensic anthropologist who helped with their last big case and who Tara later learned Warren had a history with. It was during the last case that Warren also admitted he had cut Dr. Harris off prematurely, that he had difficult getting close to a woman, and that it was all due to a tragic car accident that took the life of his wife and daughter years ago. But things had changed. Just as Tara admitted her mother would want her to get to the bottom of her murder if it meant freeing Tara from the chains that held her back from full happiness, Warren admitted that his wife would want him to find happiness again too.

As Warren smiled at her, she could see a newfound gratitude for life beaming back at her.

"How's Dr. Harris?" she asked.

He beamed wider. "She's great." He nodded. "Things are going really well."

There was something about seeing Warren fully happy that made the air feel fresher around them. His skin glowed, and the bags that usually hung under his eyes were nowhere to be seen. He looked well rested.

He looked satisfied in his skin. It was as if he had gained a few years in his face— something only pure joy and purpose would bring. It was clear he was no longer haunted by his demons. But as happy as Tara was for him, she couldn't help but feel envious yet frustrated with herself. She had it all. She had a fiancé that loved her. She was a rising star in her profession. Yet she still felt bogged down by her past.

Tara forced a smile. "I'm so happy for you."

"I was supposed to make her dinner tonight. Bought ingredients and everything," he added as he shook his head and pursed his lips. "I even practiced making a whole meal last night." He chuckled. "Had to cancel, of course. Luckily, she understands."

Tara nodded. Dating someone in a similar profession definitely had its benefits. Dr. Harris was subjected to the same spur-of-the-moment cases as they were. She sometimes too had to fly on a whim, and she most certainly understood canceled plans.

The thought made her think of John, of the frustration that he expressed before she left. It made her heart sink. He had always tried his best to understand when Tara had to pick up and leave. He always tried to push his own feelings aside because he knew she had a very important job. But as Tara watched the smile on Warren's face still linger, she realized something. He would never fully understand because the same responsibilities weren't placed on him.

"You all right?" Warren asked.

She had been staring at the seat in front of her for a moment too long. She turned to Warren. His eyebrows were knitted in concern. She nodded and let out a smile.

"Did you meet her kids yet?" she asked, trying to take the focus off of her and back onto their conversation. This was about Warren, after all, and suddenly she felt guilty for seeming distracted.

He chuckled again, his eyes moving toward his lap, where he held unopened case files. "Not yet," he replied. "She did mention that they wanted to meet me, though. I have to say, I'm a bit nervous. If the kids don't like you, you don't stand a chance." He shook his head again.

Tara was surprised. They seemed to be moving much quicker than anticipated. Every time she spoke to Warren within the past few weeks, they had a date planned each and every night. But even though the number of dates was escalating, she wouldn't have expected him to even consider meeting her kids yet. Dr. Harris had two grown children, both in college, a son and daughter. It was only a few weeks ago that Warren had told her that him meeting them was never even a discussion. He felt intimidated by the idea. He wasn't sure if them being older made it easier or harder. They weren't young and impressionable. Warren didn't have to worry about them growing too attached and then the relationship not working out. Nor did he have to worry about being viewed as a negative addition after a troubled divorce. But they were older, they had their own opinions, they understood relationships, and they ultimately had views on what their mother needed.

"So what changed your mind?" Tara asked.

Warren shrugged with a sigh, clasping his hands together in his lap. "I got to stop letting fear hold me back. I'm getting too old for that; I'll miss out on too much."

Tara smiled. She liked this new Warren, and she knew that his new outlook on life had a lot to do with Dr. Harris. What she learned about her so far was that she was the adventurous type. She was a marathon runner, had a passion for skydiving in her twenties, and loved to travel. The idea that "you only live once" was certainly adopted from her influence.

Tara patted Warren on the shoulder. "You'll do fine. What's not to like?" She was like a child giving a parent a pep talk about something she had no experience with. She had never dated anyone with children, and she most certainly didn't know what it was like to date someone with *adult* children. All she did know was that Warren was a good guy, and unless they already had a preconceived notion to dislike him, they were bound to see that too. Warren smiled and nodded. It was clear he appreciated the gesture.

A flicker of the sun caught in Warren's eyes, and he squinted as he looked toward the window next to Tara. She followed his gaze. The plane was now fully in the sky, and through wisps of clouds, she could see Washington, D.C., growing smaller until the buildings looked like specks below them. They were leaving home, leaving all just as it was. It was a reminder that what lay at home would soon be a distant focus for both of them. She just wondered for how long.

Tara turned back to Warren, and for a moment they made eye contact until her eyes fell to the case files in his lap. His gaze dropped as well. It was as if they had the same thought.

"Do you think it really is the silent stalker?" she asked. It was the ultimate question that would define the length of this assignment and how large this case would be.

Warren stared down at his lap, his gaze lingering until he lifted his head, staring off into the distance. "I find it hard to believe after so much time has passed," he replied. "Serial killers do become dormant sometimes and then start again, but twenty years?" He shook his head. It was a rhetorical question. "My guess is a copycat. But we'll see what we're dealing with when we get there." He turned to Tara and sighed. "If I'm wrong, which I hope I'm not, we're in for a long haul." His gaze once again drifted to the window, his face glowing at the touch of the sun.

Tara turned as well. The city was now nowhere in sight. Whatever land lay below was hidden by a blanket of white clouds that stretched to the edge of the blue sky. Tara hoped Warren was right, that it wasn't what Chief Meyers suspected, and that the Silent Stalker was still in the past. *If it's true, if it really is the Silent Stalker*—Tara couldn't finish the thought. The clouds suddenly felt like barriers that she wanted to break through to see her home. The plane suddenly felt so small, Tara completely at its mercy. But it wasn't just the plane—it was the case. If the Silent Stalker was back, she knew she wasn't going home for a long time.

***

Tara stared down at the case files in her lap as Warren turned onto another street. She had been scanning every page, every picture that was held within the Silent Stalker case files. She had done the same on the plane, the images now burned in her mind of bloodstained floors, of victims with multiple stab wounds, of his signature message written in blood on the walls of the homes of his victims. *A heart to mold until it crumbles.* The message echoed in her mind. She had remembered but then forgotten about that one element of the cases until she reviewed the files. It was the same message in every home, for every victim. *It means something, but what?* she wondered. She had no clue. The message had never been released to the public. The only information that was released was that there was a message left on the walls with the victims' blood; what it said remained a mystery. It was a usual tactic by law enforcement to keep some information to themselves. In doing so, it could be used to their advantage when interrogating a possible suspect.

Tara closed the file on her lap and turned to Warren. "What do you think it means?"

He shrugged with a sigh, knowing right away what she was referring to, something that was already on his mind. "Your guess is as good as mine right now," he started, still staring at the road ahead of him. "What we do know is that the victims are all suburban mothers. It could have something to do with that."

Tara nodded; he was right. The word *mold* somehow made her think of motherhood as well, and it would make sense that it was connected, given that all the victims were mothers.

"We shouldn't get too ahead of ourselves, though," he added. "We don't even know if this case is truly connected yet."

Tara nodded again, placing the case file on the dashboard. Again, he was right. They didn't even know if this case was connected, and until they saw this crime scene, which could be entirely different, it was useless to formulate theories.

Tara stared out the window, studying each suburban home as they drove past. She had never been to Nashville before, and she was taken aback a bit by the serene quiet of the suburban neighborhood they drove through. It was hard to imagine that a brutal murder had occurred there. Each house had a long front porch, some with rocking chairs, picturesque against the greenery. It was a quiet middle-class neighborhood in East End Nashville. Theirs was the only car on the street. The only person she had seen was a man walking his dog. It was hard to believe that a crime had happened so close, that this picturesque neighborhood was where a woman was brutally stabbed to death. But it was also hard to believe that the neighborhood was always this quiet. It felt as if fear lurked in every corner, that people were tucked away, glued to the news, unsure of whom to trust. The air tasted bitter. And even though it was in the mid-eighties, which was typical for late September, Tara still felt a slight chill run up her spine.

Warren turned on to the next street, and Tara's eyes moved to the windshield as she stiffened. Up ahead, she could see the swarm of marked and unmarked police vehicles, people moving about like ants. As they veered closer, the yellow tape came into view, pulled tightly across a white porch of a craftsman-style home. The house was quaint, a sage green that blended behind the two ash trees planted perfectly symmetrical on either side of the front lawn. The flowerbeds under each window gave pops of color with black-eyed susans and dahlias. On the porch, two rocking chairs were placed on either side of the door. It all looked so serene, but then she remembered what lay inside, and a sickening feeling rose.

Warren pulled up right in front, just behind the forensics van as two individuals in forensics uniforms stepped over the tape and down the steps to the cobblestone pathway. They held what looked like evidence bags. Chloe Waterman had been murdered yesterday—her body found last night—and they were now finishing up combing the scene. Neighbors were cautiously watching from their properties. To the right, a family of two parents and two male teenagers stood on the porch. They spoke hurriedly to each other as they stared at the house. The boys' backpacks looked like they were tossed onto the porch as they ran up it in a hurry, calling to their parents, trying to find out if there had been any new information since they left for school that morning.

A middle-aged man with broad shoulders, wearing a police uniform, glanced briefly at the family before staring at a woman in front of him and nodding. He stood tall, his hands on his hips, exuding a level of confidence only a seasoned veteran would have. His head was bald, an attempt to make him look younger, but Tara could still see the outline of a receding hairline that was beginning to grow in.

Tara opened her door and stepped out.

"We don't have any information at this point, ma'am. This is an open investigation," the man in the uniform said. The voice unmistakably belonged to the man Tara had spoken to earlier, Chief Meyers.

The woman let out a frustrated sigh. "I just need to know if we're safe. Should we be worried?"

"We are making sure that the community is safe," he replied. The woman wasn't satisfied. She wanted more information. She opened her mouth, about to bark back, but he spoke first. "I will let the public know as soon as I can release more information. But for now, I can assure you that your family is safe. The area is under surveillance by the Nashville PD."

She stood there a moment, questioning if she should push further, but then she sighed again, realizing it was no use. As Tara and Warren approached, Chief Meyers raised his gaze and smiled, instantly recognizing them. The woman turned around, her dirty blond bangs touching her knitted brows. Once she spotted them, she thanked Chief Meyers, excused herself, and walked briskly across the street as if in a hurry to relay any information she had received.

"Chief Meyers." Tara turned her head to face the uniformed man as he held out his hand.

Tara shook it. Her hand felt small in his, and his shake was firm. He had a half smile on his face that carried his mixed emotions. He was relieved to see them, but what he had seen inside that home was like a rip current, pulling him under. It was laced onto every inch of his face.

He looked up, over at the family standing on the porch of the home next door. He turned to Tara and Warren, nodded in the direction of the driveway, and began to walk toward it. Once they were out of earshot, he spoke. "They took the body away last night. A forty-year-old female. Her name is Chloe Waterman," he said as his eyes briefly moved to the door and then back between Tara and Warren. "But we tried to preserve the scene the best we could before you got here."

Tara nodded. "Who found her?" It was one detail that hadn't been discussed on the phone earlier.

At the mention, his jaw buckled, and he swallowed hard. His eyes veered off to the side, as if he couldn't even face his own words. "Her six-year-old daughter," he said. "Got home from school yesterday. Her mom wasn't at the bus stop, so she walked home and found her."

"Oh my God." Tara instinctively put her hand to her mouth. She shared a quick glance with Warren, who suddenly looked colorless. But then he knitted his brows as a question crossed his mind, the same moment as Tara's.

"Didn't you guys get the call last night?" Warren asked. They had learned earlier that day that the 911 call had been made around 8:00 p.m. If the daughter had found her after school, that most likely would've been between two and three in the afternoon.

Meyers sighed as his eyes fell to the ground briefly before lifting his head. "Her dad, the husband, was working late that night. He came home and found her hiding in the closet." He squeezed his eyes shut in agony.

"Shit." Warren shook his head in disgust.

Tara didn't speak. A strange feeling had washed over her. It reminded her all too much of her mother's death, of Tara hiding in the closet as her father killed her. It reminded her all too well of finding her mother's dead body. The same world-ending pain hit her like a punch in the gut, the same confusion and disbelief hardened her surface. Her heart sank. A child had witnessed the same life-changing pain. She knew that the kid's future would be forever altered. She would always carry that pain within her, and it would somehow play a role in every choice she made in life, whether she was aware of it or not. *I have to find who did this,* she said to herself. If she were going to help this girl in any way, it would be to get her mother justice. The need surged through her body.

"Do you think she saw any of what happened?" Tara asked.

The chief shook his head. "I don't think so," he began. "The medical examiner seemed pretty certain that the murder happened in the morning. She wasn't dropped off from the bus until 2:15 p.m."

Tara nodded. "Did you speak to her?"

He sighed. "We tried. The girl's a mute," he admitted with a shrug.

Tara shared a quick glance with Warren. They both knew that was going to make the case a bit more difficult. The one individual who might have seen something was incapable of speaking.

Meyers continued. "We were able to ask her some yes or no questions with her dad present, and she'd shake or nod her head, but she couldn't talk to us. We didn't learn anything new, though. I really don't think she saw anything."

"And the dad?" Tara asked.

"He was at work. We checked; he was in that day."

Tara's eyes moved to the house. She envisioned the girl coming home from school, confused that her mother didn't greet her at the bus stop, only to find her blood on the floor, and then her mother's body. The thought made Tara sick.

Chief Meyers followed Tara's gaze. "I'm sure you both want to take a look," he said as he turned to porch and began to walk toward it.

Tara and Warren turned on their heels, the family next door studying their every move as they strode across the lawn and then up the porch. Tara took a deep breath. It never got easier entering a crime scene. She always thought that it would, that a murder scene would be easier to stomach with increased exposure and experience as an agent. But it still made her just as sick to her stomach as the first crime scene she ever witnessed. She knew now it wasn't a feeling that would ever go away. It was unnatural to view bodies in such a way or to see the remnants of someone's last moments. It went against every human instinct.

The house was dimly lit and it took Tara's eyes a moment to adjust. It was a quaint, beautiful home, with wooden beams that stretched along the high ceilings. Fractured sunlight danced along the floor, casting shadows on a bloodstained wall in the living room. Tara's stomach churned at the sight of it and at the once-white rug that was now permanently marked with large pools of blood. Tara stepped farther into the room to see blood spatter dried and darkened on the foot of the gray couch next to the door and on the legs of the handcrafted wooden coffee table. There was a short trail of it from mid-living room to a few feet from where they stood, as if Chloe had tried to pull herself to the front door. She had almost made it—the realization pulled heavy on Tara's heart. But then a pink unicorn backpack caught her eye. It lay a few feet to the left of the front door on its side, as if it were quickly slung off someone's shoulder in a hurry. Her thoughts drifted once again to the daughter, and her mind went numb.

Tara's eyes drifted to the walls around her, searching for a message upon it, but there wasn't one, and skepticism swirled into her mind at Chief Meyers' theory that the Silent Stalker was the culprit.

Tara turned to Chief Meyers. "Any sign of the murder weapon?"

The chief shook his head. "There was a knife missing from the knife block, though. We're not sure if it means anything."

Tara nodded. It was unclear if the knife was missing before the killing or if it was the murder weapon. They would need to speak to the coroner first to see what type of knife was used and if it matched the one missing from the block. But if that were the case, it could tell them that the murder might've been committed by someone in the home and that it might not've been premeditated.

"What makes you think it's the Silent Stalker?" she asked. She already knew the main similarities— the stab wounds, the female victim attacked alone in her home, and then of course the podcast—but she also knew that the silent stalker had his signature:

leaving a riddle in blood in the room of his victims. It was one of the single most important details that would connect the silent killer to the crime, because what he had written was never released to the public. At Tara's question, a forensics evidence technician combing the carpet looked up at the mention but then buried his head once again in his work.

Chief Meyers caught the glance and cleared his throat, trying to lighten the air, as if he was afraid of the effect of his theory. His eyes fell as he stared at the bloodstained floor for a moment and winced. His eyes instinctively turned to Tara, and he steadied his gaze.

"I worked those cases back in the early 2000s," he started. "I haven't seen a crime scene like this since then, with no sign of forced entry, no fingerprints. Whoever did this knew what they were doing." He suddenly reached in his pocket, pulling out his phone and holding it out for Warren and Tara to see. He had an app store open, and a podcast titled *Unveiling the Silent Stalker* shined in bright yellow letters across a cover of an eerie stock image of a man standing in the distance of a desolate road. "This was the victim's podcast. She was the host," he added. Tara stared at the phone once more, noting that the podcast had over twenty thousand reviews. He pulled the phone back. "It recently started gaining a lot of attention, it opened up the cold case around here; it helped open some new leads. So far nothing has amounted to anything, but it just seems oddly coincidental that she then shows up dead."

Tara shared a glance with Warren. He was right. It was quite a coincidence, and she had to admit that the crime scene was oddly similar, but it still wasn't enough to rule out a copycat.

"Did the killer leave his signature?" she asked. Meyers shook his head abruptly, knowing exactly what she was referring to without any hesitation.

"He didn't," he confirmed. His eyes moved between Tara and Warren, scanning the skepticism on their faces. He then sighed. "Look, I know it could always be a copycat, but I wouldn't be doing my job if I didn't speak my suspicions."

Tara and Warren both nodded. They understood, and they respected him for it.

"Were any windows unlocked?" Warren asked. He and Tara scanned the room around them. There were two windows on either side of them in the room they stood in, and Tara could see another straight ahead, at the end of a long hallway.

The chief shook his head. "Everything was locked, except the hallway window, but it was closed. It's being dusted for prints."

Tara's eyes then drifted once again to the backpack. "Where's the daughter and father now?"

"They are at a family friend's house."

"They're not with other family?" Tara asked. That was usually where victim's families turned after tragedy.

Chief Meyers shook his head again. "They don't have any family around here. They're originally from the west coast."

"You have an address?" She knew speaking to the daughter might be impossible, but she wanted to try, and if anyone could give information about the days leading up to the victim's death, it was her husband.

Chief Meyers texted her an address. "Good luck. His name is Rick Waterman," he added as he placed his phone back in his pocket. "We already picked the father's brain. He's at a complete loss of who would do this. And well his daughter—" His eyes drifted momentarily to her backpack. "It's a lost cause."

Tara thanked him. It was always possible that something was overlooked, that the right question wasn't asked. She had seen it done many times before. And if anyone could relate to the daughter, or get information out of her, it was Tara. They were now unfortunately both connected by a similar tragedy. Tara peeled her eyes away from the backpack that she hadn't even realized they had drifted toward. Warren was already holding the door open, and as she turned back toward him, she met his eyes. He closed them briefly and nodded because he knew it too—if anyone could talk to the daughter, it was Tara, but it wasn't going to be easy.

Chapter Seven

Tara stared at figures moving in a window as Warren pulled the car into the driveway of the Tudor-style home. They were in Donelson, only a neighborhood over from East End, the one they had come from, and was similar, except the house was of a different style. Steeply peaked roofs and overlapping facing gables made the house look like it belonged in a storybook and contrasted with the modern-day farmhouse of the home they came from.

As Warren parked, Tara saw the figures stop. It was a man and woman, she could see now, silhouetted in the window. They were talking but with heated emotion as the man flung his hands into the air at every other word in desperation. As the car stopped, the man looked out the window and then moved away from it, out of view. The woman followed.

"Could that be Rick?" Warren asked as he caught her gaze.

She felt the same skepticism and confusion. The woman must've been the family friend he was staying with. But there was something odd about their

64

interaction. It almost resembled a couple arguing—the way he flung his arms in frustration, how close they stood. It was an argument that would only be seen between two people that knew each other intimately.

"Or her husband, maybe," Tara replied.

Warren gave a skeptical smirk with a shrug as he stepped out of the car. Tara followed as they walked up a brick pathway to the door. Warren knocked.

Voices behind the door grew quiet, silenced by a whispered hush. The door opened, revealing a tall, middle-aged woman with pin-straight jet-black hair that fell just past her chest. She had a full face of makeup that looked like it had been on for quite some time. Her mascara was smeared under eyes, and her lips only had remnants of a deep red. Her eyes were swollen and red and were instantly noticeable against her pale porcelain skin.

"Can I help you?" she asked with a sniffle.

Behind her, a man sat on a couch. It was the same man Tara had seen in the window. His face was buried in his hands, his elbows resting on his knees.

Tara held up her badge, and the woman instinctively stepped back, glancing at the man sitting behind her. The man looked up. His eyes were just as swollen, but instead he had tears streaming down his face. "I think they're here for you," she said to him before holding the door open wider. She waved her arm for them to step into the home.

The man stood up as Tara and Warren entered. "Rick?" Tara asked. He confirmed with a nod. "I'm so sorry for your loss," she added as she took a seat on a chair across from him. Warren echoed her words, but the man didn't respond. He stared blankly at her, as if the word "loss" was one he still didn't quite comprehend.

His eyes drifted to the woman that had opened the door. She closed it gently and then stood awkwardly by it as she stared longingly at Rick, tucking her long black hair behind her ear. He nodded at her as if to tell her he was okay.

She forced a smile. "I'll be upstairs if you need me," she added as she headed to the stairs.

Warren was quick to speak. "We'd like to talk to you too, if you don't mind."

The woman stood for a moment, her hand on the bannister as she shared a look with Rick, and then cautiously moved to the couch. She sat down next to him but was careful not to sit too close.

"I didn't get your name," Tara said.

"Fiona," she responded to the ground as she sat back fully in the couch, crossing her arms.

"And how do you two know each other?"

Fiona opened her mouth, but Rick suddenly spoke. "She was a friend of my wife's. I'm friends with her husband. We've known each other for awhile."

Tara nodded as she watched Fiona's eyes glance at him momentarily and then snap back in front of her, as if to make sure no one saw. There was something unspoken in the room. They weren't being fully truthful, Tara could sense it.

"Where's your husband now?" Tara asked.

"He's in Chicago on business. He's an account manager for a software company."

Tara nodded again. It was odd, she thought, that Chloe's husband would come here of all places, seeking shelter and comfort from one of her good friends.

Tara moved away from the topic for now. "Do you know anyone that would've wanted to harm your wife?" She looked directly at Rick.

He shook his head. "Not that I know of," he started, looking up with grief-stricken eyes. "But that podcast was getting a lot of attention. I told her she needed to be careful."

"Why's that?"

He sighed. "For one thing, she was obsessed. It wasn't good for her. She would always come to bed late, up researching. But it was also what she was doing. Digging into an unsolved case when the killer was still out there." He shook his head. "She had to have angered someone. I mean, she was calling up old witnesses, getting interviews. She even re-sparked an investigation." His voice trembled at the end as he grabbed hold of his stubbly chin, pulling at his face in disbelief. "I should've done something more," he added with a whimper.

The woman next to him inched closer and stroked his back in an effort to comfort him. He quickly shot her a look, and her hand fell, as if instantly realizing she had gone a step too far. Her face flushed.

"He's right, she was terribly obsessed," she added, an effort to deflect attention away from her actions.

Again, their interaction seemed odd to Tara. It was as if they were holding back, as if they were careful not to reveal how close they actually were.

Tara looked right at Rick. "Where were you coming from when you found her and your daughter?" She already knew what he had told Chief Meyers, that he had come from work. That he had walked in and found his wife dead on the floor and his daughter hiding in the closet. But Tara wanted to hear it for herself. She needed to see his reaction.

"Work," he confirmed without skipping a beat. "I work for an insurance company as a sales manager." He shared a quick glance at Fiona as if seeking reassurance but then suddenly shifted his focus, turning his eyes sharply to Tara. It was as if he were second-guessing his every move. *Odd,* Tara thought. To be acting in such a way when he had just lost his wife. The thought of how he was being perceived should be far from his mind.

"And what time was that?" Tara asked.

"Around seven. I work late pretty often," he added.

"Did she ever mention to either of you that she was afraid?" Tara asked.

The woman shook her head instantly, but Rick hesitated. Tara probed further.

He sighed. "She never said outright that she was afraid, but she seemed it at times. She would never tell me why. I wondered if someone was following her." His eyes fell to his hands clasped tightly together in his lap. He stared at them as he squinted in disappointment at himself.

"What made you think that?" Tara asked.

He shrugged. "She just always seemed to be looking over her shoulder, checking windows. At one point she even mentioned she wanted a security system."

Tara shared a brief look with Warren. "Did she say why?"

He shook his head. "She wouldn't tell me anything," he replied, tears welling once again. "She was like that. She never wanted me to worry. But something was off." He paused a moment, trying to steady his emotion. "I should've done more," he said again. His voice shook.

Tara continued to ask more questions—if Chloe ever seemed afraid of someone she interviewed, if she began to avoid any place in particular, if he ever noticed someone lurking. But each question was met without a lead.

Suddenly his eyes darted to the ceiling above, and Tara's followed. Footsteps treaded across the floor, then a door slammed. He winced.

"My daughter," he confirmed. "This has been very hard for her, as you can understand." Tears dropped to his feet.

Tara nodded as her stomach churned. It was the girl who had found her mother's body, who hid in the closet in fear. She closed her eyes briefly, steadying herself. She understood more than he'd ever know—the total devastation, the fear. She knew all too well the hole that would forever be in his daughter's heart. She understood that she would forever try to fill it and always fail.

Tara looked back up at him, now at the edge of his seat, tension pulsing through his body. He wanted to run to her. "Are we done here?"

Tara paused a moment. "Would we be able to speak with her?" The man let out a frustrated grunt, but Tara continued. "I understand how difficult this is for all of you, but if she saw anything, if she could help in anyway, it might help bring closure."

He rolled his eyes. "Don't you think she's been through enough?" Tara was about to speak, but he continued. "She's a mute anyway, has been for as long as she was old enough to talk. It's no use."

Tara was about to insist it was for good reason, that even though the moment would be painful, it was all in an effort to help her heal. If anyone understood that, it was Tara. But before she could even open her mouth, sobbing trailed down the stairs and swirled around them all, sucking the air out of the room.

"I can go check on her," Fiona said. She began to get to her feet, but Rick shot her a threatening gaze, and she instantly sank back into the chair.

He stood. "Do you mind?" he asked Tara, but he didn't require a response as he moved to the stairs. He then stopped at the bottom, turning fully toward Tara and Warren. "I think we're done here," he added.

Moments later, Tara and Warren stood in the driveway. She could see that Warren was itching to speak, but it wasn't until they reached the car and sat inside that he opened his mouth.

"Something's not right with that situation," he said as he put the keys in the ignition.

Tara nodded. He was right. It was the same thought that echoed in her mind. There was something odd about the relationship. Rick Waterman seemed awfully close to his wife's supposed friend. At times, it seemed as if there was an unspoken conversation between them. They were hiding something.

"You think they're having an affair?" Tara asked.

Warren's eyes stayed locked on the house, on the sheer curtains of an upstairs window. "I'd be very surprised if they weren't."

Tara followed Warren's gaze. She could see a shadowy figure moving behind the curtain. It was the father, moving about in the room his daughter was in. "You think he's guilty?"

Warren remained silent for a moment, as if considering the thought. "Of an affair? Definitely. Of murder, well..." They watched the shadowy figure move to the window and close thicker curtains so nothing could be seen. "We'll need more proof. I say we head to the morgue."

Tara nodded as he began to back the car out of the driveway, but her eyes stayed focused on the now dark window. She thought of the girl, of her pain of losing her mother, of having an unfaithful father. *Is he capable of murder?* The thought made Tara's heart burst into flames. She was going to get that girl justice, no matter what it took. She pulled out her phone and opened the podcast store. She searched *Unveiling the Silent Stalker,* and Chloe Waterman's podcast was the first result. *Maybe answers are closer than we think.* If Chloe was so focused on her creation, maybe it held some answers. She downloaded the first episode and placed her phone in the center console for both her and Warren to hear.

Chapter Eight

Tara and Warren listened intently as the car neared the morgue. They had listened to part of the first episode that had been posted over a year ago but then skipped to the most recent, trying to understand her final moments. It had been posted less than a week ago and was focused on the now opened cold case and what she had brought to light.

Tara read over the case files as Chloe reiterated where the investigation stood. It was all because of one interview that the investigation was reopened. An old neighbor of one of the victims who was fifteen years old at the time of the murder. She had taken her dog outside in their fenced-in backyard before bed. It was 11:00 p.m. and the neighborhood was quiet, but she had heard a rustling in the backyard of her neighbor's property, and out of curiosity, she had looked through the fence. A young man, wearing all black, was quietly turning over a recycling bin. He pushed it right under a window and then tiptoed around the house, disappearing into the night, leaving the recycling bin propped against the window. Two days later, Mrs. Garcia was found brutally stabbed to death in her home by her mother, who had been watching her son and came to drop him off. It was believed that the attacker came in through that very window where the fifteen-year-old girl had seen a man prop a recycling bin days before.

"But it wasn't just the fact that she witnessed him preparing for his kill; it was the glimpse of his face that reopened the case," Chloe said on her podcast.

She was correct, Tara said to herself as she read over the case files. The teenager had described a man in his mid to late twenties, tall and thin, clean-shaven. She had caught a glimpse of him as he turned back toward the road and a streetlight beam slid across his face. All those years, she had been too afraid to come forward until she was an adult and caught wind of the podcast and had called in. It led to a composite sketch of what the man could look like now, twenty years later. Tara stared down at it. He would be in his forties now, which showed in the drawing. Wrinkles lined his forehead. Slight bags hung under his eyes, hairline receding.

"How could they possibly determine an accurate composite sketch?" a woman asked on the podcast. She was a guest, Serenity Jackson, a fellow sleuth, and she had the same question that formed in Tara's mind. The teenager only saw a glimpse of the man, and she had waited twenty years to describe him. The accuracy was questionable, and while forensic artists were skilled, a twenty-year age gap was difficult to render in a sketch.

Chloe agreed with Serenity as they shared a few words, and Serenity chuckled. They seemed to have a good relationship, a friendship, and Tara had noted that she was a frequent guest.

"She spoke in episode one too, right?" Tara asked, now looking at Warren, who stared at the road intently, his eyebrows knitted, focusing on each word.

He nodded. "Could be friends," he said as he pulled into the parking lot of the morgue. "Her husband would probably have her contact information."

He was right; they needed to talk to her. If Chloe was closed off from her husband, it was likely she had confided in someone why she was afraid. A close friend would be the ultimate confidante. And if this woman was on Chloe's most recent podcast episode, then she had been in her presence around the same time that her husband had noted her odd behavior. A close friend that could potentially hold information about their marriage.

Warren put the car in park, and Tara grabbed her phone, turning the podcast off. Speaking to Serenity Jackson would be their next move, but first, they needed to see the body.

***

Tara and Warren stood in the morgue, facing the metal coolers lining the walls. The coroner had just pulled out Chloe Waterman's body. A white sheet was draped over her, but Tara could still see her feet and perfectly red painted toenails peeking out from the edge of the sheet.

The coroner took a deep breath and stared at them. He was middle-aged, Tara guessed in his fifties. He was bald but had thick black eyebrows that grazed the top of his glasses. He had already explained to them that he had been doing this a long time, but his face said differently. He had a furrowed brow; his skin had grown paler since they entered the room. He had the look of someone who had just seen their first dead body.

"Brace yourselves," he said as he reached for the sheet. He began to pull it back slowly, as if he were second-guessing his decision. "I think this is the most brutal murder I've dealt with. It's enough to give you nightmares."

He pulled back the sheet completely, and Tara instinctively stepped back as her stomach churned. He was right. It was brutal. Stab wounds were on every inch of Chloe's abdomen. Her arm looked as if it were partially detached. Her and Warren both unwillingly stepped forward, examining the rest of her body. Even though Chloe's eyes were now closed, Tara could still see the utter horror on her face. Her long brown hair was matted with blood. Tara looked toward Warren, who stood cold-faced, as if trying to hide how sick to his stomach he was, but Tara could see the color draining from his face. He looked back up at coroner, unable to look at the body anymore.

"He stabbed her twenty seven times," the coroner said with a look of utter disgust. "She was most likely already deceased about halfway through."

"How does that compare with the Silent Stalker victims?" Warren asked.

The coroner nodded as if to say he had the same question. "I looked at the reports," he said. "Similar. They were all stabbed between twenty to thirty times."

Tara's stomach churned at the thought of the daughter finding her mother in such a state. Even Tara only caught a glimpse of her own mother when she was killed. She was too preoccupied with hiding from her father even to process what she had seen. But this girl had seen her mother like this alone. She had hid in a closet, scared, alone, unable to speak, without knowing if help was on its way. The thought made Tara's eyes well up, but she stiffened, sucking back her emotion until she could hold her composure.

"Do you know a time of death?" she asked.

He nodded. "I'd say mid to late morning. Between nine and eleven."

"Any sign of sexual assault?" Warren asked, but the medical examiner shook his head. It was a detail consistent with the cold cases.

"And the murder weapon?" Tara asked.

The coroner draped the sheet back over the body, and everyone in the room relaxed slightly.

"This case is almost identical to the cold case victims, except when you focus on the murder weapon. It was definitely a knife," he said. "But it wasn't *the* knife."

"How so?"

The coroner sighed. "The cold case victims were all consistently stabbed with a straight-edge knife." He glanced at the body. "Her killer used a jagged-edged knife."

Tara and Warren glanced at each other. She could see the same question reflected in his eyes. *What does it mean?* Could it mean that it wasn't the same killer? Or could it only mean that the killer had traded one murder weapon for another after twenty years? Both were possible.

Tara knew enough about forensics to know that knives did not have unique characteristics that would distinguish one brand from another. It was one of the aspects of a stabbing case that made it more difficult than a firearms case. With firearms, barrels had unique grooves that traced a bullet to them and then to a manufacturer. With a knife, you needed the actual weapon in order to trace where it came from. But Tara knew they might have a chance.

She turned to Warren. "The knife block," she said. A slight smile formed on his face, and he nodded. She didn't need to explain. He too remembered what Chief Meyers had said. *A knife was missing from the knife block.* They might be able to identify what knife was missing from that block by looking up the manufacturer details of that block and seeing what knives it came with. It would mean that the killer had not entered with a murder weapon, which would increase the possibility that it was not premeditated or it was someone that was already inside the house.

At the thought, a chill ran up Tara's spine as she thought of Rick. They needed to know how close he actually was with Fiona. Tara turned to Warren, but he was already thanking the coroner for his time. He then focused on Tara.

"We need to talk to Serenity Jackson," he said.

Chapter Nine

He sat in his car, his tired eyes closed, his head resting on his headrest as he listened to the podcast. Chloe's voice sailed through the speakers of his car, and he smiled to himself. He felt at ease hearing her voice, knowing that she was gone. He had listened to each episode of the podcast numerous times. He could almost recite each theory, each guest as they entered. He could almost recite her words before she spoke them. Theories about him were everywhere now, everyone was talking about him, and it sent a thrill through his body.

He had forgotten how good it felt. The control, yet the release of his anger. At first, he didn't want to kill her. He wanted to live a normal life, but she was asking for it. He gritted his teeth at the thought. It was her fault. She had become too invested, she had focused all her energy on it, and it consumed her. Every waking hour, she had dug deeper, becoming more obsessed. It was her obsession that killed her. And it was her obsession that rekindled his.

He opened his eyes and stared down at the knife in his hand. The black handle felt cool in his palm as he held it tightly, bringing it steering-wheel height and turning it every which way. The sun peeked in through his window, and he squinted each time it caught on the knife and reflected into his eyes. But each time it did, a sense of power washed over him. It was a power he hadn't felt in quite some time—that he was in control. For so long, he had lived in the shadows, letting the current of his life direct him. But now he was controlling the narrative once again.

The podcast continued to play, and adrenaline pulsated through his body as he anticipated what was next to come. Serenity Jackson's voice sounded through his speakers. Her soft, perfect voice that accentuated every word. It hissed through the car, making his skin crawl. She was the exact type of person he hated. She was just like Chloe. They were both better off dead.

At that thought, his deep-sunken eyes stared out of the windshield as he pulled down the visor, shielding his eyes from the sun, casting a shadow over them. Up ahead, a few houses down, he could see her—Serenity. Reusable grocery bags were wrapped around her wrist. She slung them across her shoulder and lugged the groceries from her car as she carefully walked up the stone steps of her home in her wedge booties. His blood boiled as he saw her.

He had been keeping an eye on her for days now, studying her every move, understanding her habits. He was getting close to seeing a pattern. It would soon be time to make his move. Serenity shuffled into her home and closed her door, and he knew it was time to go. He smiled to himself because he knew he would see her again soon. They would soon come face to face. At that thought, he turned his car on and drove away.

Chapter Ten

Tara and Warren stood on the steps of Serenity Jackson's home. They had spoken to Chloe's husband, and he had given them Serenity's contact information. It only took one quick call, and she had invited them to come stop by. Tara knocked, and as she waited, her mind wandered to the murder weapon. The knife still had not been found, but Chief Meyers agreed to look into the knife missing from the block. He would call them back as soon as he learned of anything.

Clunky shoes sounded across the floor, moving closer until the door swung open. A beautiful woman stood in front of them. Her jet-black hair was in tight, thin braids that cascaded over her shoulders and flowed just below her breasts. They contrasted against the flowing yellow blouse that hung on her small, short frame that was evident by her tight jeans and wedged leather booties that attempted to make her look taller. She forced a smile, but sadness hung in her eyes, making it hard for her to look at them directly.

She opened the door wider. "Please, come in," she said as she waved her arm into the house.

Tara and Warren stepped into her living room, which was filled with natural light from a large bay window and an overhead skylight. Beautiful wildflowers decorated the room in vases on end tables and above a white brick fireplace mantel. She moved over to a pale yellow couch and took a seat, motioning for them to sit across from her. She stared at them, eager, her face full of sadness.

"You and Chloe were close?" Tara asked.

The woman sighed and nodded. "I met Chloe when she first moved here ten years ago. We were in a book club together and just really got along." Tears began to well up as she looked away. "I can't believe she's gone." Her voice shook as her words trailed off, becoming stuck in her throat.

"I'm so sorry," Tara said. Warren echoed her words, but the woman only nodded.

She took a deep breath, ready to dive back in. "I helped her a lot with her daughter," she added as she reached for a tissue on the coffee table. It was an odd place for them, but Tara assumed they were there for this very reason. "Her daughter is a mute, has been her whole life. And, well, it's been tough for Chloe at times. She was a stay-at-home mom. Then she started that podcast to give her a sense of independence. It was really good for her for a while..."

She trailed off, but Tara knew what she was insinuating. It was the same impression that Chloe's husband had given, that the podcast had become an unhealthy obsession.

"She became obsessed with it?" Tara asked.

Serenity nodded, pursing her lips. She sighed. "I think the more her life spiraled out of control, the more she buried herself in it." She shook her head.

Tara exchanged a quick glance with Warren. The words hung heavy. *Her life spiraled out of control.* It was the first time that they were given an impression that something had gone wrong in Chloe's life recently. They were on the brink of something. They could feel it.

"Spiraled?" Tara asked.

Serenity knitted her eyebrows in confusion as her eyes moved between Tara and Warren. "Rick didn't tell you?" she asked, but before Tara could respond she continued, "The separation. He didn't tell you they were getting separated?"

Silence fell in the room as Tara and Warren glanced at each other. Tara shook her head. Rick had never mentioned it, but now Tara was extremely suspicious as to why. Fiona suddenly stuck out like a splinter in her mind. Tara recalled the closeness between them and that they both seemed to be trying to tame it in front of Tara and Warren. It was suspicious then, but now Tara was certain something more was going on between them. *But why were they hiding it?*

"Do you happen to know why they were getting separated?" Tara asked.

Serenity raised her eyebrows, shocked that this was all new information to them. She leaned forward, crossing her legs and resting a hand on her knee. "He must not have known that I knew," she said, shaking her head. "They hadn't really told anyone about it yet, but Chloe is my best friend, so of course she told me."

She stopped for a moment, then remembered Tara's question. "They fought a lot. Having a mute daughter definitely put strain on their relationship, but that wasn't the final straw." She paused for a moment, seemingly questioning if she was going too far.

"Any information you have will help," Warren jumped in.

Serenity nodded with a sigh. "Well, Chloe was almost certain he was cheating, with a friend of ours, Fiona." It was the woman Tara had met earlier—the family friend. It was now without a doubt. Serenity continued, "She saw flirty texts between them once. He tried to deny it, but it was pretty clear. He was getting home at odd hours, missing dinner." She shrugged. "It sounded pretty obvious to me."

Warren interjected. "Was the idea to separate recent?"

Serenity thought for a moment, her eyes drifting to the corner of the room. "A couple weeks ago," she replied. "We went out for coffee, and she was just inconsolable."

The husband was beginning to look increasingly suspicious, but Tara still didn't see a motive for murder. After all, they were getting separated. He was getting what he wanted. He wasn't in a marriage. He was going to be able to be with his mistress. But then Tara's mind focused on the daughter.

"Who was the daughter going to live with?"

Without skipping a beat, Serenity replied, "With Chloe, of course." At her words, a sadness swept across her face once again, and she reached for a tissue. "At least, that was her plan anyway," she added with a shake of her head.

Tara could feel that they were on the cusp of something important. "And why is that?"

The woman sighed again, and for the first time, a look of fear crossed her face. "Chloe was concerned about his lack of sensitivity to her daughter's needs. He'd get very frustrated at times, from what Chloe told me."

Warren leaned forward. "Did he ever hurt her?"

Serenity's face fell as she shook her head. "If he did, she never told me." She pushed her braided hair behind her ear as another wave of emotion washed over her, but she grabbed hold of herself, tensing her body, and spoke again. "All I know is she threatened him for full custody. I overheard her on the phone with him about a week ago."

Tara and Warren exchanged another look. An agreed separation that he clearly wanted was not enough for a motive, but threatening to take his child away certainly could be. *Could he have used her interest in the podcast to throw law enforcement off?* Tara wondered. *To make it look like it was the Silent Stalker?*

Tara pushed for more information, whether she knew how Rick reacted, if she knew why exactly Chloe threatened him. But each question was answered with little information. Chloe had been very tight-lipped about it all, which left Tara even more suspicious.

After exhausting their efforts, Tara and Warren thanked Serenity for her time. But as they stood up to leave, she spoke again. "If you don't mind," she started, dancing delicately with her words. "I'd like to pick up where Chloe left off with the podcast." She paused for a moment. "I just know how much it meant to her, so if you have any information that she left behind regarding it, I would like to honor her and finish it."

Warren stepped in. "As of now, it's evidence," he replied. He narrowed his eyes in concern. "And it's in your best interest to stay away from that podcast for now. It might've been what put a target on Chloe's back."

Her face fell, a look of defeat and fear washing over her, but Tara knew she understood. She nodded and led them out.

Once Tara and Warren stepped outside, they immediately turned to each other, walking briskly to the car. They both knew what their next move would be. They needed to find out why Rick withheld the information about his separation. He was clearly hiding something. And at that thought, Tara suddenly questioned his alibi.

"I think we should check with his work, make sure he was really there," Tara said as she opened the passenger door. Warren nodded. Chief Meyers said they had already checked his alibi, but she needed to hear it for herself, and so did Warren.

"We'll go to the station, call him in for questioning. We'll check his alibi then."

Tara nodded as Warren started the car. As he pulled out of the driveway, Tara wondered if this truly was a copycat case, and if they were nearing the end of it.

***

Tara and Warren sat eagerly as the phone in front of them rang on speaker. They were at the station in a small private room. They sat at a desk that was the only piece of furniture. The walls were blank except for a whiteboard that had no writing on it. Chief Meyers had given them the phone number of Rick Waterman's boss. He worked for an insurance company in Nashville and had been there for the past eight years. The phone rang momentarily before a man's voice picked up. It was deep and raspy, as if he had smoked too many cigarettes. Tara could hear shuffling in the background, as if he were packing up for the day.

"Dwight Walsh?" Tara asked.

The shuffling ceased. "Who's asking?"

Tara introduced them as she heard the thud of a briefcase being placed on the ground.

"I already spoke to police," he responded. "Rick was in that day. He was here until seven. I'm not sure what more help I can give you." His voice fell. "How's he doing?"

Tara could hear the sincere concern in his voice. "As can be expected," she replied before asking him a few more questions. Had Rick missed any days leading up to the murder? Had he been acting strange at all? Did anyone ever visit him at work? But each question was immediately shut down.

"Look, if you need me to attest to his character, Rick is a good guy. He would never do this."

His words were sincere, but Tara knew that a boss would only know one side of an employee. "We're just covering our bases," Tara replied. "Did he leave at all during the day?"

"I think he left for lunch, but other than that, no," the man responded. Tara glanced at Warren. If he had left for lunch, it would put a hole in his alibi unless he went somewhere where someone could vouch that they had seen him.

"Do you know how long he left?" Tara asked.

The man thought a moment, but he couldn't recall. "I don't really keep tabs on my employees like that. As long as they do their job, they can come and go as they please." His words were chipping away at Rick's alibi. He was silent a moment but then suddenly spoke as a thought popped into his head. "Our receptionist might know. She sits in front of our office. She sees everyone who comes in and out of here."

Tara thanked him. He asked her to hold as he transferred her to the receptionist. Moments later, a young, soft voice came through the phone.

"This is Jessica," she confirmed. Her voice shook slightly. Tara was certain she had never spoken to the FBI before, and the thought made her nervous.

Tara asked her a series of questions, the same ones she had asked Rick's boss. But each question led nowhere.

"Do you remember him leaving for lunch that day?" Tara asked.

"He left early. I'm not sure I'd call it lunch," she said. "Sometimes he steps out in the morning to meet a client and grabs lunch when he's out to eat in the office." She thought for a moment. "He usually comes in around seven thirty. I think he left around nine."

"Do you remember when he came back?" Tara asked.

She didn't even need to think. "He was gone a few hours, which isn't too unusual."

Tara pushed her further, and she continued, "He probably came back around noon."

The medical examiner had said that her time of death was between nine and eleven. Tara had already looked up the distance between the home and his office. It was about a ten-minute drive. It was certainly possible that he could leave work, confront his wife, murder her, and have plenty enough time to get back to his office.

Warren jumped in. "Did you notice anything different about his appearance?"

She thought for a moment. "Well," she started but then stopped. There was hesitation in her voice. "Look, I don't want to get anyone in trouble. I mean, he's a nice guy. I really don't think he would do something like this."

"We're just trying to put the pieces together," Tara replied. It was clear that Warren's question sparked a memory she knew would not paint him in a good light. They were on the brink of something. Tara could sense it was at the tip of her tongue.

The girl sighed. "Well, all I can say is he had a different shirt on. I just assumed he spilled something on it. I remember because when he came in, his collar wasn't folded correctly. I stopped him to let him know, and it occurred to me that his shirt was a different color."

Tara thanked her. It was all the information they needed. There was a major hole in his alibi now. He had been unaccounted for roughly three hours, he had changed his clothes, and he withheld the information that he and Chloe were getting separated. After they hung up, Tara turned to Warren.

"It looks like Rick has some explaining to do," she said.

***

Just outside the interrogation room, Tara and Warren stood in a long, narrow hallway, separated from Rick Waterman by only a door. He had been called in for questioning to recount his story once again. But little did he know that he was now a key person of interest. Tara itched to step inside, but they stood in between the door and Chief Meyers, who had just revealed that he had some information to give them on the knife, which they needed to hear first.

He stood in front of them with a furrowed brow that hovered over his tired eyes that had seen a lot for one day, even in Nashville.

"It was a Ginsu block in Chloe Waterman's kitchen," he started. "Every knife in the set was there except one with a jagged edge. We asked the medical examiner, and he confirmed that it could've certainly been used on the victim."

"No way to know for sure?" Tara asked.

Chief Meyers shook his head, his face falling into defeat.

He didn't need to explain. Tara already knew why. They couldn't trace a specific knife to the body without the murder weapon being present and having traces of the victim's blood on it. Right now, they had neither. They also wouldn't be able to link the knife to the killer without the killer's DNA or fingerprints being present on the murder weapon too.

But Chief Meyers' revelation did tell them *something*. It told them that whoever had murdered Chloe Waterman most likely got the murder weapon from within her home. It could say something about intent. It could say that it was most likely not a planned attack. It could say that the killer potentially lived within the home. *Could Rick have come home during work hours and then suddenly in an act of rage reached for the weapon and murdered his wife?* Tara wondered. *Or could he have come home, fixated on the thought of killing her, and then gave in to his impulses?* It was all possible. Very possible. After all, he had already withheld the information about his separation or that they fought about parenting of their daughter. Tara turned to Warren. He looked at her with suspicion, his body tense, already leaning slightly to the door. Chief Meyers' words had only cemented their theory further. The only thing left to do was confront Rick head-on and see how he responded to their questions.

Meyers looked between them and then at the door. "I'll leave you two to it," he said with a nod. "Good luck." He turned down the hallway, leaving Tara and Warren alone. It was now getting late, but the station was still bustling. She could see officers at the end of the hallway, their voices trailing down it as they spoke to Chief Meyers as he approached. She imagined that it would be bustling late into the night until this case was solved.

She turned to Warren. "Rick better have a good explanation," she said as her eyes drifted to the door.

Warren nodded as he took a step forward. He turned the doorknob and pushed it open in one swift motion. Rick jerked in his seat as they entered, startled. He peered up at them, squinting under the fluorescent light that beat down on him from the ceiling. His eyes were red and puffy, as if he had spent some time crying. It seemed genuine, but Tara also knew that anyone who was smart enough would make it appear that way. Or it could simply be because he felt remorse.

He sat at a wooden table with two chairs placed on the opposite side of him. The rest of the room was empty. The walls were blank except for a two-way mirror. As Tara and Warren sat down, his eyes moved briefly toward it and lingered there.

"Why am I here?" he asked. "I already gave you all the information I have. My daughter needs me." He let out a frustrated sigh as he leaned forward, throwing his hands up.

Tara leaned forward in her chair and clasped her hand together on the desk. "Is Fiona watching her?"

He leaned back in his chair, throwing his hands up once more. "Why does that matter?"

He didn't even suspect that they knew about the affair. *Serenity was right, he probably doesn't know that Chloe told her*, Tara thought.

"Why didn't you tell us that you and Chloe were getting separated?" Tara asked.

He shot his head back instinctually, as if he had just been slapped. He opened his mouth to speak, about to protest, but then he closed it, rethinking his next move.

"I don't see why that's relevant," he replied. He slunk into his chair as he crossed his arms like a shield above his chest.

Tara continued, "And Fiona, she's not just a friend, is she?"

Color suddenly rose up Rick's neck as his forehead began to glisten with a thin layer of sweat. He had realized why he was here, that he was now a prime suspect. He remained silent for a moment, carefully deciding what to say.

He shrugged, trying hard to show a sense of ease, but his body had a reaction of its own that highlighted his fear. "I guess so," he started. "We haven't made it official yet, which is why I didn't say anything, but we have been seeing each other."

He knew better than to deny it. He knew that they had already caught him. Denying it would only dig him into a deeper hole, making him look guiltier. His eyes darted between Tara and Warren. "Who told you all this, anyway?" There was anger boiling in his words, but he only let it simmer, careful to control how he appeared. His question only affirmed what Serenity had told them, that he didn't think anyone knew about the separation. But as he looked between Tara and Warren, realization sparked in his eyes. His eyes fell to his feet as he shook his head. A burst of air left his lips. "Serenity," he said under his breath. He looked up once again, meeting Tara's eyes. "What else did she tell you?" He leaned forward, placing his elbows on the table, and stroked his forehead hard briefly. "Look, she doesn't like me. Me and Chloe had some fights. Serenity was always her shoulder to cry on. Of course she's going to paint me in a bad light."

"We never said anyone painted you in a bad light," Tara replied

He sighed, slouching back into his chair, his arms outstretched on the table. "Why am I here?" he asked, growing desperate as tears began to well up.

Tara studied his face. His emotion didn't seem forced, but Tara still couldn't be too sure as to why he was showing it in the first place. *Is he guilty and afraid of his fatal outcome? Or is he just distraught at losing his wife and the mother of his child and exhausted?* Tara contemplated both questions as she stared into his eyes.

"Did Chloe threaten sole custody?" she asked, leaning forward.

Rick knitted his brows, a look of disgust crossing his face as he realized why he was really here. "What the hell are you trying to accuse me of? What, you think I'd kill her over that?" He let out a grunt, throwing his hands in the air.

"It's got to make you pretty angry, I'm sure," Tara replied. "Why did she threaten it anyway? Did you do something to your daughter?"

His body jerked forward. "Absolutely not," he shot back. He gripped the table hard but then quickly loosened his hands, sitting back once again. He had quickly realized the contradiction in his body language, that he was defending his lack of aggression by getting overly agitated. He sighed. "It's tough with my daughter. She's a selective mute. She has a severe anxiety disorder that has caused her muteness. We've tried everything from therapy to meditation." He took a deep breath.

It was the first time Tara had heard that she was only a selective mute, which would mean that she did speak, just not all the time. The revelation made Tara regret not being able to speak to her, but she wondered if that was Rick's reason for not letting her. Maybe he was afraid of what she would reveal.

Rick continued, "She gets frustrated and won't communicate. It's been difficult for me at times, and I haven't always handled it in the right way." He looked down at the table, and Tara watched shame wash over him that seemed genuine.

"In what way?" Tara questioned.

He shook his head, still unable to lift his eyes. "I yelled at her a couple times. I scared her, but that's it." He looked up, meeting Tara's eyes and shifting between her and Warren as if searching their faces for a reaction. "My daughter is already predispositioned to anxiety, me yelling at her doesn't help, and Chloe lost it, said I was damaging our child." He leaned forward again, placing his elbow on the table and cupping his scruffy chin. He pulled at his face in frustration.

Once again, Tara searched his face for any sign of an act, but all she saw was genuine disappointment in himself. The man before her was being ripped to shreds with regret. Tara stared at him. He looked like a balloon about to pop. It was as if the pain had filled him to the brim until there was nowhere else to go but to pour out of him. He looked away, covering his eyes with his hands as he began to sob.

"This is crazy," he said as his voice shook. "I know what you're accusing me of, and it's not right.

I'd never hurt her. My wife or my daughter." He choked on his words. "Even if things weren't good between us, she was a good mother. I would never in a million years do that to my daughter."

Tara looked at Warren. He was either not guilty or a very manipulative liar. His emotion seemed all too real. But there was one last question Tara needed to ask.

"Where did you go when you left work for three hours?" Tara asked.

He wiped the tears away as he looked up at her. It was as if her question had twisted a knife in his gut, stirring a new pain. The color drained from his face as he held his breath. He stiffened. It was as if he was about to jump into an ice-cold body of water.

"I was with Fiona." The words burst out of him like air from a popped balloon. He keeled forward, overcome by a pained cry.

***

Silence hung heavy as Warren reached for the phone between him and Tara. They had just spoken to Fiona, who had in fact backed up Rick's alibi. She had confirmed that he was at her house during his break from work, but Tara and Warren already knew that she would confirm it. They were in a relationship. It was unlikely she wouldn't vouch for him, so there was always the possibility that she would lie.

Tara looked at Warren, whose eyes were still fixed on the phone, squinting into a hard stare the way they always did when he was deep in thought. She knew what he was thinking. He had doubt that Rick was guilty.

"You believe him, don't you?"

Warren looked up, breaking out of his trance. He leaned back into his chair, looking up at the ceiling, cupping his neck with his hands. He sighed. "Don't you?"

Tara nodded. "Unless he's a skilled actor. He seemed like a man just overcome with guilt and grief," she added. But then she thought of his daughter. She understood why he wouldn't let them talk to her after all she had been through, but she couldn't help but feel slightly suspicious. It was also new knowledge that she was only a selective mute. *Was that a slip? Did he not mean to tell us that?* After all, he had kept the separation a secret and that he and Fiona were more than friends. It made her wonder what else he could be holding back.

"It's hard to trust him, though," Tara said.

Warren raised his brows and nodded. "He certainly chose not to share quite a bit," he confirmed as he turned toward her. "Do you believe that he just thought it was irrelevant?"

Tara shook her head. "Maybe partially, but I think he knows we'd want to know."

Warren sat up in his chair, leaning his arms on the table and studying the wall. "He could've just been overtaken by shame and didn't want to have to say it," he replied.

Tara had thought about that too. After all, he had cheated on his wife with her friend. It was what had led to their separation. But to make matters worse, he had been with his mistress at the same moment his wife was being murdered. It was enough to rip anyone's conscience apart. But then Tara had another thought.

"Why would he stay at Fiona's house after the murder?" It seemed odd to her that if he were so overstricken by guilt, he would seek comfort in the one person who was tied to that guilt.

Warren shrugged. "He doesn't have any family around here. It sounds like he doesn't have anyone else to lean on."

Warren was right; he most likely didn't. Any family they had lived halfway across the country, and Tara didn't get the sense that they had a big social circle. She remembered how Rick and Fiona were acting—standoffish toward each other. At first when Tara heard about the affair, she had thought that their reaction toward each other was an effort to hide their relationship. But now she wondered if it was more than that, if it was also because Rick didn't want to be close to her, that the thought was too much to bear after what had happened to his wife.

But even though Tara and Warren had their doubts, there was one piece of it all that they needed to look into: his daughter. She was the one who found the body, and after all that Rick had kept hidden, not allowing them to speak to his daughter seemed somewhat suspicious. Tara hated to admit it. She didn't want to make the girl relive what she saw, but she knew they at least had to try to speak to her. Tara looked at the clock hanging on the wall above them. It was now around seven in the evening. There was no way they would be able to speak to her now, and Tara knew the poor girl had already gone through enough today. She looked at Warren. "If there's anything else he's hiding, his daughter would probably know," she said.

Warren nodded, his eyes drifting to the clock as well. "We should pick up in the morning," he replied as he stood up. Tara followed, but as they moved toward the door, an unsettled feeling washed over her. They both had their doubts about Rick, and as Tara reached for the door, she wondered if that could mean the killer was still out there.

Chapter Eleven

Tara shoved a forkful of lasagna into her mouth as her body ached for more. She hadn't realized how hungry she was until room service had delivered her dinner and she caught the first scent of her food. She had barely eaten all day, and her body was making her pay for it now, along with her exhaustion. It had barreled into her full force, and she ached to go lie in her bed. But she couldn't just yet.

She had to call John. She hadn't spoken to him all day. He hadn't texted her. She had only texted him once today, when she had landed to let him know that she had gotten there okay, but he had only replied to let her know that he received it.

She assumed he didn't want to bother her during the case, but she also knew there was something deeper. After all, John wasn't exactly excited about her new case, and she knew he was still upset that Tara had hidden the letter from him. Remembering their conversation made Tara's stomach twist into a knot. Part of her felt betrayed by John's reaction to the letter and to her leaving for this case. It seemed selfish in some ways that he would ask her not to look into Mackenzie James until after the wedding. They both knew it was something she needed for her own closure, and that it was an essential piece of her healing from her childhood trauma. *Closure is important to get before a wedding,* she reminded herself. In some ways it seemed like the opportune time. She of course didn't expect John to see it that way, but she thought that he would want her to seek healing and not put anything on pause that would help her do so.

His reaction to her new assignment then flared in her mind. It was cruel to get mad at her, she thought. *He signed up for this. I have to do my job.* Resentment boiled to the surface as her thoughts spun into a whirlwind of emotions. Her eyes locked on her phone as she questioned if she should even call him, if she should be angry with him. Heat rose to her face. But the longer she stared at her phone, John's face surfaced in her mind with more clarity. She remembered the disappointment etched on his face during their conversation about the letter. She remembered the sadness that seeped into a wilting smile when she told him she was leaving on assignment. At each thought, her resentment simmered.

John wasn't intentionally trying to be selfish. He wasn't trying to make things difficult for her. He missed her. He felt distant. The thought made a sadness swell, and she suddenly longed for him. She reached for her phone and called him.

The phone only rang twice before he picked up. "Tara," he started. He said her name in one long exhale. It was as if he had been holding his breath, and her call was the relief he needed. She could almost see his smile, causing one to spread on her face as well. Silence hung heavy between them. Tara was about to speak. She wanted to discuss how they left things, but as she opened her mouth, he spoke. "How's the case going?"

Her heart sank. She knew what he was really asking was when she was coming home. She ached to give him a positive response, but she couldn't. "We have a possible suspect, but the case is still ongoing. I'll know more tomorrow."

Her words were met with silence. It was as if he were waiting for her to elaborate, to give him a definitive answer of when the case would be over, but she couldn't. And he knew she couldn't say more. It was an active investigation, but he also knew that she didn't like to share too much with him until after her cases were over. It saved him the worry and mental anguish of the details, and he knew it too, which was why he never pushed for them. He knew it would only cause mental torture over something that was not in his control.

"How was your day?" Tara asked, trying to break the ice a bit before they spoke of a touchier subject. They spoke a bit longer as John recounted his usual workday and band practice, and some office drama that had continued to unfold between two employees he was friends with who had been competing for a high-level client.

When John finally finished, their unspoken conversation weighed heavy between them, until it was ready to burst out of Tara's mouth.

"I really don't like how I left," she finally said.

"I didn't either," he replied without skipping a beat, as if he too was waiting to speak of it. He sighed. "I shouldn't have gotten upset about you leaving. It's just—" He paused, trying to think of how to word it. "Just things have been good for a while, after the engagement. You were always present." He sighed again, this time in frustration as his words brought forth the emotion he was trying desperately to tame. "But then the nightmares came back, then the letter and you going off on assignment. It just feels like I'm losing you again."

"But John, you're not. I'm not going anywhere," Tara replied.

"But you are." John's words were sharp. "I don't mean physically going anywhere. It's mentally that I'm concerned about. Sometimes it feels like even when I'm with you, you're somewhere else completely."

Tara didn't respond; his words burned a wound inside her. He was right; she had been more in the moment right after they got engaged. Any thoughts of her father or of Mackenzie James were pushed from her mind as she tried desperately to hold on to the bliss. She had been solely focused on them, on John, on herself. But he was right. It was the only time that Tara had made any effort to push thoughts related to her past or of a case out of her mind, and it had never occurred to her that it negatively affected him. She suddenly fully understood how he felt, and her stomach swirled with regret.

She knew that feeling well. In fact, she had felt it many times before. Each time Tara's mother promised her a day of fun, or an art project—something Tara loved—that they could work on together, her mind was always somewhere else. Looking back now, Tara knew what it was, and it was almost hard to believe that she hadn't picked up on it at the time. It was written in all of her mother's movements, in the way she would continuously check the time and frantically clean up when they weren't even done. She made a desperate effort to make sure that there was no trace of a mess before Tara's father walked through the door. When Tara was a child, she would get frustrated with her, but now she understood. Her reaction was in fear of what Tara's father would do if he saw a mess. Even though she wanted to just make Tara happy, she had unknowingly caused a negative experience by not being in the moment. Tara's heart ached at the memory. She knew exactly what John felt. It was rejection.

"You're right," she said and sighed. All this time, she had been chasing something else, even when she was spending time with John. It was no wonder he felt distant from her. But as John's feelings came to light, her own still flickered inside her. She knew now more than ever that she couldn't ignore them, even if John wanted her to. But she still could do better by him. "I need to be more present," she started. She took a deep breath, as if ready to plunge into a body of water. "But that doesn't mean that I shouldn't get to the bottom of my past. Any time I put my search on hold, it's going to get harder."

John didn't speak. Tara couldn't tell if he was angry, or if he knew she was right, or both. "I can do both, John. I can plan this wedding, be more present with you, but still figure out my past. It's not right of you to ask me not to do that."

John sighed. Tara was waiting for him to bring up that she had already agreed, that she was breaking another promise, and for a moment it sounded as if he were about to speak, but then he stopped himself. He knew he couldn't protest. He knew he was wrong. "But what if it's dangerous?" he finally said.

"I've dealt with worse. And you and I both know I can't let that hold me back. I need to do this, John."

Again, he remained silent, contemplating her words, deciding whether to push back or meet her halfway. He took a deep breath and exhaled with frustration and defeat. "Where would you start?"

Tara smiled. He was on her side; he was going to support her in figuring out who Mackenzie James was. But then his question lingered between them. She hadn't quite considered it herself. She had been too preoccupied with letting John know about the letter and then the case that she hadn't had a second to even think about what her first move would be. She knew nothing about Mackenzie James other than that she visited her father. If he wasn't going to give any information, she would have to look elsewhere. She had already searched social media. She needed another place to start.

"I could try the old bars he used to go to in town," Tara suggested.

John agreed, but he didn't suggest anything further. It was as if he wanted to do the bare minimum in being supportive. But Tara knew it was out of concern. He was afraid he would push her into a dangerous situation.

"When are you going to start looking into this?"

Tara paused. She knew it would most certainly not be tonight, not until the case was over. She checked the time on her phone. It was already ten at night, and her body felt it. She needed to rest. As much as she wanted to start right now, she knew it was no use. She needed to go to New York for answers, and of course that wasn't happening any time soon. She needed to be well rested. And just as John had reminded her, she needed to stay present. Her attention needed to remain on the case. She just hoped it would be over soon. "As soon as this case is over," she said as her eyes began to feel heavy. She yawned. John sensed that it was time to go.

"Well, rest up," he replied.

Moments later, Tara sat in a silent room, her eyes still locked on her phone lying in front of her on the table. A part of her wanted desperately to pick up her phone, to begin an Internet search looking into Mackenzie James, but she knew she couldn't. She needed to keep her focus, and she needed to sleep. She pushed her urge out of her mind, letting the remembrance of the little girl who had just lost her mother spread from her mind to her body, grasping a hold of her heart. *It's selfish,* Tara thought. *Even to think about myself right now and my personal struggles. There was a child that had gone to bed without her mother, hoping that maybe it was all a nightmare, that maybe she would wake in the morning to her face beaming down.* Tara's heart ached at the thought as her exhaustion weighed heavy on her until it was too much to bear. She needed to rest. She needed to be fully prepared for what tomorrow would bring when they spoke to Chloe's daughter. Tara washed up, slid into the cool sheets of her hotel bed, and exhaustion finally took hold, pulling her into a deep sleep.

***

The warm sun beat down on Tara's shoulders, making the straps of her backpack slick with sweat. She wiped the sweat from her brow, sweeping her hand across her forehead and catching a glimpse of her small, childish hands. It was a lovely day. The birds chirped on the trees in her yard, the sky a crystal blue. She stood on a large, protruding porch with two empty rocking chairs and a mat at her feet that said Home, Sweet Home. *It was late in the afternoon, and the sense of a full day of events weighed down on her. She was exhausted. She was ready to rest. She was ready to see her mother.*

Tara stared at the doorknob in front of her. She wanted to push it open, to step into the comfort of her home, to lie on her couch and have a snack to ease the growling in her belly. But there was something within her that hesitated. Her mother hadn't met her at the bus stop as she normally would, but yet she was home. Her car was in the driveway. She could see the living room light through the sheer curtains. She sensed something, like an animal sensing an approaching storm. Danger lurked in the air like an intoxicating cloud of warning, but she knew she had to step through. She had no one else. No one to run to, no one to check for her. It was the only way.

Tara reached for the cool knob in her sweaty palm and turned it. She closed her eyes, pushing the door open in one swift movement. She waited a moment, waited for a reaction, for someone to speak. She waited for her mother to call to her but was disappointed when she was only met by silence. Goosebumps rose on her skin. It felt as if the air had been sucked from the space around her, and she couldn't take a breath. She no longer heard the birds or felt the sun on her back. The space around her felt warmer; it felt stuffy. She felt like she was in an entirely different space. Her instincts forced her eyes open, and as Tara looked around, a warning burst inside her. She was in the hallway of her childhood home. Pictures of her and her mother decorated the walls. It was dimly lit, just a yellow light shining down on her like a spotlight.

Tara hesitated to look forward; she knew what was there. But her eyes had their own mind, and like a gravitational pull, her gaze was pulled forward. But as Tara stared into the living room, her small child's body went numb. Goosebumps prickled her arms. What lay before her, where she had seen her mother in her own blood, splayed across the living floor as a young child, was a different woman. It was Chloe Waterman.

Tara sprang up in bed, her clothes drenched in sweat. She turned the light on, letting it fill the room as the drumbeat of her heart steadied. It was the same nightmare Tara always had of seeing her mother's lifeless body in the living room, but this was different. It was warped by the case. But Tara knew exactly what it meant. She identified strongly with Chloe's daughter, so much so that she had intertwined their traumas into one. Tara's heart ached for her, to think that Chloe's daughter could be waking to her first nightmare that could potentially continue just like Tara's had well in to adulthood. The thought made her sick to her stomach as an urge to help her find justice surged into her mind. But as Tara lay in bed, another thought pushed forward. Even though getting justice would help, it would still never be enough for Chloe's daughter or for Tara. It would never bring their mothers back, but Tara hoped it would bring them peace. She couldn't even be sure how justice would affect Chloe's daughter, because she still had yet to find it fully for herself. And now, more than ever, she suddenly understood the importance. Finding justice would not only help her find peace within herself, but it would also make her a better agent. It would make her a better agent for this case. And at that thought, Tara knew she needed to try calling her father one last time.

Chapter Twelve

Serenity Jackson sat on her couch as Chloe's voice filled the room. Her eyes were glued to her laptop, where she had Chloe's podcast playing and any bit of research she had accumulated open in different tabs. Each article she had read at least five times, and each time she finished, she would click to the next one and then the one after that. She wasn't sure what she was looking for. She wanted to pick up where Chloe had left off. She wanted to fulfill Chloe's desires. But it was more than that. The podcast was the only tangible thing that held Chloe's heart and soul. It was like a piece of artwork that someone had created and left behind, but a piece of them vibrated through it as you stared at it.

Serenity knew the FBI had warned her to stay away, that it was dangerous. But she couldn't. The podcast was everything to Chloe, besides her daughter. It was her comfort, her constant during a turbulent time in her life. It made her feel effective when she felt like she was failing at everything else. Serenity's eyes filled with tears, and her fingers stopped scrolling. *She deserved happiness,* she said to herself. *She didn't deserve to die.* It was a thought that kept stabbing Serenity's mind torturously until all she could do to find relief was bury herself in Chloe's work.

Serenity couldn't help but think that Rick had murdered his wife and staged it to look like the Silent Stalker. As much as the thought of it being the true Silent Stalker scared her at times, she had a hard time believing it. With all that Chloe and Rick had been going through, seeing Chloe's pain and her concern over her Rick's temperament with their daughter, Serenity couldn't shake her bad feelings about him. Her blood boiled at the thought.

She had already received countless emails from podcast fans and web sleuths that had their own theories that the Silent Stalker was back—that he had resurfaced in an effort to keep buried what Chloe had dug up. It was a more exciting and interesting theory to outsiders. It pained her each time she read an email, sleuths offering their condolences but then immediately pestering her for a theory. Chloe had now become a true crime story for entertainment. It irked her. But each time another comment burrowed deep into Serenity's skin, a need surged within her to finish what Chloe had started. She needed to help solve this case.

She read over the countless articles she had saved when helping Chloe research the case. She had dug up articles from the newspaper the next day each time the killer took another victim. Serenity glanced down at a notepad placed next to her on the couch. In blue ink, scribbled on the paper, she had many pages of notes. It was what she and Chloe had done in their research. They searched for connections in order to formulate theories. They searched for names of witnesses of past suspects and pieced together a timeline that they recited in a story-like form on their podcast. They had dug up contact information of family members, of neighbors, of experts that had been part of the investigation and had those that agreed to speak on the podcast.

Including Chloe, there were eleven victims in total, all mothers, all in their thirties or forties. Each time, the killer had entered the house, believed to be through a window, and brutally stabbed his victims until he vanished without a trace. Serenity had to admit that it was strikingly similar to how Chloe was found, and she had met the characteristics of his victims. She was a mother in her early forties. She had been stabbed to death in her home. There was no trace of the killer. But she also knew that Rick was smart. Chloe's interest in the Silent Stalker case created the perfect opportunity for anyone to make her death look like one of his victims.

At the thought, Serenity's eyes drifted to the seat next to her. It had been on that very couch that Serenity and Chloe sat on Wednesdays while Chloe's daughter was in school, sipping coffee, scouring through articles, piecing together their findings, and planning for upcoming episodes. The couch was a pale yellow, Chloe's favorite color. Serenity could almost hear her voice, complimenting Serenity on her taste as she sank into the sofa, holding her mug of coffee with both hands to prevent any possibility of spillage, as if it were some very expensive piece. The memory brought a smile to Serenity's lips. She had never been too fond of that couch. She had bought it from a catalog and wasn't too sure about it at first, but it had grown on her, all because of Chloe. It was one thing she had loved about Chloe. She saw beauty everywhere. She would make you fall in love with everything you hated about your house, or about yourself. Five days ago, she had sat on that very couch, complimented it as she sat down, and then turned to Serenity to praise her talent for interior decorating. Before that day, Serenity had never even thought of her interest in buying throw pillows and décor as a talent.

Serenity's heart suddenly burned at the memory. Little did she know that it would be the last time Chloe sat next to her or entered her home. Her smile faded as emptiness spread throughout her and throughout the room. It felt empty and cold.

Serenity took a deep breath, an effort to suck in the cry that wanted to burst out of her. She went to lift her notebook, an attempt to bury herself in her work once again, but as she did, her eyes fell upon the phone next her. She had barely looked at it since Chloe's passing. It was the phone they had used for tips. Listeners would call in with possible tips or questions they wanted answered on the podcast. It was hard for Serenity to listen to them. The tips rarely held value, and she didn't want to hear another person send their condolences. For some reason it seemed harder to listen to than to read in an email.

But this time, the phone caught her eye. The screen was lit up. Someone had just called her. There were two missed calls from an identical number, and a voicemail. It was odd for someone to call twice in a row. *Maybe someone really does have a tip*, she

113

thought, her eyes still fixed on the black screen. For a moment she questioned even listening to it, and whether it was worth the possible wave of emotion it would cause, but then she thought of Chloe. *How can I continue where she left off if I won't even listen to a voicemail?* She took a deep breath and scooped up her phone without giving herself a second to think about it.

She pressed *play*, put the phone to her ear, and sank back into the couch. But as the voicemail played, she stiffened. All she could hear were long, controlled breaths. She stared at the phone once more, at the phone number. But she was certain she didn't recognize the number, only the area code, which was local. *It's a prank*, she thought, letting herself relax. *Someone who listened to the podcast is playing a sick joke.* It seemed like the only logical explanation. *I'll block the number*, she said to herself as she rolled her eyes. But just as she was about to hang up, a sinister laugh broke through the breathing. The voice was deep, vibrating through the phone, sending a wave of chills through her body. The laugher simmered, a moment of silence followed, and then a deep voice spoke. "A heart to mold until it crumbles," it said. The sinister laughter grew louder, and then the call went dead.

Serenity looked around the room. She was still alone. She was a single woman. No boyfriend, no current husband. She was a widow. The house always felt empty and lonely, but for the first time she was scared to be alone. She had no one to call. Chloe had been the one person she would turn to if she needed company, and now she needed to face the silence on her own. She took a deep breath. *Just someone trying to scare me,* she told herself again. She had no idea what the words meant. They echoed in her mind, but again she focused on shaking it off. She would tell police, have them track the number, and she turned back to her work, placing the phone on silent once again.

But just as she started to read another article, a floor creaked in the distance, and then the same sinister laugh sailed down the hallway into the room where Serenity sat, sucking the air completely dry. She couldn't move. She couldn't breathe. She couldn't believe her own ears. *I'm hearing things*, she reassured herself. But her instincts told her otherwise. She stood quietly, careful not to make a sound, her eyes locked on the front door. But before she could even think to run, a hooded figure sprinted from around the corner. She began to run to the door, but a sharp, agonizing pain hit her in the back and spread through her body. She fell, the same pain hitting her over and over again until her vision went black.

Chapter Thirteen

Tara held her phone, her finger hovering over the *send* button. It was now six in the morning. She hadn't slept since she had awoken from her nightmare a couple hours earlier, anxiously waiting for the clock to turn to the time that it was now. The prison would accept her call. She just hoped her father would take it.

Tara took a deep breath and steadied herself before pressing *send* and placing the phone to her ear without leaving a second to question herself. Within a few moments, the operator was on the phone asking who Tara was calling.

"Richard Mills," she stated.

The operator clanked her fingers on the keyboard without a word. Tara knew she was checking the call list. Last time, she had not been on it. She wondered now if this was just a waste of time. *Why would he suddenly put me on it? He wouldn't.* Hope leaked away as she sat in silence, growing frustrated with herself and the valuable time she was currently wasting. The typing stopped.

"Just a moment, I'll connect you."

A wave of panic suddenly washed over her. She had never expected that she would actually be able to speak to him. She was about to ask if the operator was mistaken, if she had checked the wrong inmate, but before she could, she heard ringing. Tara steadied her breathing. *This must be a mistake,* she told herself, allowing the thought to ease her anxiety. But just as her mind relaxed, her father's voice sounded in her ear.

"Tara, why are you calling me?" he asked, sounding frustrated.

Tara took a deep breath. She needed to stay strong. "The same reason why you probably put me on your call list. To talk," she shot back.

He sighed. "I did that because I knew you would call, and I needed to tell you to stop."

"If you told me why, then maybe I would."

"You're quite the firecracker now, aren't you? Not the timid little girl I remember." Tara could picture the smirk he had plastered on his face. "I guess that's why you're an FBI agent."

Heat suddenly rose to Tara's face. She couldn't respond. She had wanted to keep that information from him, but she was stupid to think it wouldn't somehow trickle back to him. *Shit.* She figured that the bit of information was now laced in his reasoning for not wanting to speak to her.

"Just like you have your secrets, I have my own. So stop calling," he added.

Secrets. The word burned in her mind. "Just tell me who Mackenzie James is and I'll leave you alone."

"Stop!" he yelled, something within him snapping. Tara instinctively cowered, as if she were a little girl again, her father yelling at her in a drunken rage. She couldn't speak as he sighed. It was as if he regretted his outburst, something Tara had never witnessed. His voice then suddenly became stern, a parent warning a child. "You need to stop," he said again, lowering his voice. He then whispered, "It's dangerous."

Tara was about to protest more, but the phone went dead.

She held the phone to her ear for a moment longer, frozen. *Dangerous*, she repeated. *What did he mean by that? Is Mackenzie James dangerous? Is he protecting me?* The thought sent a wave of confusion over her. Her father had never looked out for her. It was hard for her to believe that he would even care to do so. Warmth spread through her body as she thought that maybe he did care about her. It was as if she was as child again, trying to find any traces of love in his angry outbursts, as if it would make them hurt less. It was an instinctual reaction of survival still harbored inside her, bubbling to the surface at the slightest trigger. But Tara quickly pushed the feeling aside, horrified at the split second she had cared. *Don't be stupid, Tara,* she told herself. *It's what he wants you to think. He's protecting himself.* But at the thought, she couldn't help but ask herself why. He was serving a life sentence. There was nothing more for him to lose. He had to be protecting Mackenzie. It was the only explanation that made sense.

Tara's phone interrupted her train of thought. She looked down at it. It was Warren. It was nearly seven o' clock now, and Tara assumed he was calling to get started on their day. She scooped it up, placing the phone to her ear. Before she could even say "good morning," Warren's words burst from his mouth.

"Serenity Jackson's been murdered."

Tara's heart dropped and her body went numb. That was the woman they spoke to just yesterday, Chloe's friend. She suddenly felt sick to her stomach with guilt.

"While Rick was in custody?"

Warren confirmed, "They let him go this morning, after they found Serenity's body."

A chill ran through Tara's body. They both knew that it could only mean one thing. Rick wasn't the killer, and whoever it was still lurked out there.

"Grab the keys. I'll meet you downstairs," Tara said as she jumped up, scrabbling in her suitcase for clothes.

"There's more," Warren added. There was a warning in his voice, and Tara stopped what she was doing, bracing herself. "Chief says this scene is even more similar to the Silent Stalker cases. He left a signature."

Tara didn't reply. She knew what it meant. She had remembered from the case files that he left a signature of a message on the wall in the victim's blood. Goosebumps prickled Tara's forearms. She knew what the chief was insinuating, and she could sense that Warren believed it too. She finally spoke.

"He's back."

***

Tara sat in the car in silence as Warren neared the house they had been at the day earlier, interviewing the woman that they were now about to see lifeless. An overwhelming guilt weighed heavy on her. They had warned Serenity to stay away from the podcast. But Tara didn't think Serenity was that involved with it to become a target herself. After all, she was a frequent guest, but it wasn't *her* podcast. And to make matters worse, Tara had been focused all night on her own personal issues. *I could've been theorizing. I could've been researching*, she told herself. It was a thought she had over and over again until she felt like she was drowning in it. She couldn't help but wonder, if she hadn't been so focused on her father and Mackenzie James, would she have figured out that Serenity was a target? She had certainly learned her lesson. She wasn't going to let her lack of focus cause another person to be harmed. Once again, she had to push Mackenzie James aside, and this time for good until the case was over.

"You can't blame yourself," Warren said, his hands clenching the steering wheel hard, clearly in a mental battle of his own.

"How can I not?" Tara asked. "We didn't even see her as a target. Who knows if we even made her one by having her talk to us." Her words punched her in the gut once again. She couldn't even say what else made her feel so guilty. She had done it too many times already, and yes, she knew she could trust Warren. But after a while, anyone would question her ability to be on the case.

Warren sighed. "It's hard, believe me, I know." His eyes moved between the road and Tara. "But we're not doing anyone any favors by focusing on the past. If anything, being ridden with guilt will just cloud our judgment. We have to look at this objectively, as hard as that is."

Tara nodded. He was right. Beating herself up was not going to bring Serenity Jackson back, nor would it bring her closer to finding the killer. Guilt was only going to drag her feet in the mud. Tara stared at the road ahead of her. They were now on Serenity Jackson's street. Tara had admired the neighborhood yesterday, but now it had a different feeling. Yesterday, the beautiful farmhouse-style houses and immaculate lawns where children played without a worry demonstrated what a safe neighborhood it was. But today, it was as if a storm was approaching. No one was outside, no children were playing, no one was going for their daily run or walking their dog on the sidewalk.

It felt as if they were driving into the eye of a storm. As they neared the house, Tara braced herself. A few houses down, she could see the police vehicles lining the streets, the reporters staking out outside, waiting for any glimpse or word of what was happening. Warren pulled up behind two police vehicles and let the chief know they were there. Within a few moments, the chief was on the lawn. Like vultures, the reporters' eyes shot toward him.

"Come on, you going to update us?" one brunette reporter asked the chief with frustration as Tara and Warren exited the car. Her five-inch heels clanked against the pavement as she moved closer, making her way around others. She was noticeably short but tried to compensate with her heels and attitude.

"Can you confirm it's the Silent Stalker?" another female reporter asked.

The chief calmly held up his hand. "We'll have a press conference at four. I will address your questions then."

The reporters looked at each other, sharing their disappointment. But they knew it was useless to push harder. The chief couldn't report anything yet.

His eyes then moved to Tara and Warren, and he took a deep breath. He looked even more tired than he had at Chloe Waterman's house. His sunken eyes were now unmistakably bloodshot. This case was certainly taking a mental toll on him, and Tara was certain he was battling the same guilt she felt. He looked back at the reporters one last time as he saw one of them about to speak.

"Chief…" she started. It was the short brunette. She couldn't help herself. She had to make sure she tried one last time.

He put his hand up, signaling her to stop, and surprisingly she did. "Miranda, I will answer your questions at the press conference," he interjected, causing her to cower back. She nodded. They clearly knew each other. Tara assumed she was the same age as the chief, in her late forties. Her hair was a perfect chocolate brown, almost too perfect to be natural, which made her appear younger. But the lines around her eyes and forehead revealed her true age.

The chief walked across the lawn, leaving the reporters in the distance. Warren and Tara followed.

"You have quite the control of the media," Warren mentioned when they were far enough out of earshot.

The chief shrugged with a sigh. "They respect me around here. A lot of law enforcement finds the media a nuisance, but they're just doing their job. And they protect this town too by informing them. Some of them were doing this when I was on the Silent Stalker case twenty years ago." Tara knew he was referring to the woman he had mentioned by name.

When they reached the front door, he finally turned around toward them. They stood on the porch, the reporters' eyes feeling like targets on their backs. "This never gets easier," he said. His eyes drifted to the door. Tara could hear movement from behind it and the flashing of cameras from the forensics team. He pushed the door open, stepping into the living room that Tara and Warren had sat in just a day earlier. But as Tara took a look around, it was hard to believe she had just been there. A hole burned in her stomach as her eyes fell upon Serenity Jackson sprawled lifeless on the floor. Her body, face down, her hands clenched in desperation, clawing at the floor in front of her. The tips of her black, braided hair were drenched in blood that had pooled from the large gashes in her back. She was wearing the same outfit Tara had met her in.

Tara's eyes instinctively pulled away, turning toward Warren, but as she looked at him, his eyes were fixed on something else. Tara followed his gaze, and as she met Warren's focus, the hole burned larger inside her. Just above the pale yellow couch, illuminated from the sunlight shining through the sheer curtains behind them, blood was smeared on the white walls. Tara read what it said as adrenaline pumped through her body: *A heart to mold until it crumbles*. It

123

sent a chill through her. She had read that message before, in the case files. It was the same message that had been seen at each cold case, smeared across the walls in a similar fashion. She remembered the images, and this was strikingly similar. The letters were large, filling up almost the entire space from the couch to the ceiling. It looked as if someone had taken their entire hand, dipped it in blood, and spread it across the wall in long, quick strokes.

Tara turned to the chief, whose eyes were locked on it as well. The sun shined across his face, but he didn't squint; he didn't blink. Even though he had already seen it, his face looked paler. It had drained the color from him, which Tara assumed was the exact reaction he had the first time he saw it.

"Any fingerprints?" Tara asked.

Tara's words broke his trance, and he pulled away, backing up slightly out of the sun, as if now noticing that it was hitting his eyes. He shook his head. "Forensics checked the wall. Whoever it was used gloves. Of course some prints were found around the house, but I'd assume they're Serenity's."

"Who found her?" Warren asked.

The chief sighed. "Her sister. They went out for dinner the night before. Apparently, they do that weekly. Her sister came over to return something she left in her car." His eyes drifted to the body for a moment, a look of sheer sadness washing over him, until he focused back on Tara and Warren. "The sister drove over here," he continued. "That's when she found her and called us."

"Where is she now?" Tara asked.

The chief's eyes fell to the floor as he shook his head. "Poor woman was beside herself. We sent her home." He gave a defeated shrug. "We couldn't get anything out of her, she was too emotional, understandably, but I don't think she knows anything."

Tara nodded, her eyes locked on Serenity's body. She inched forward with Warren following behind. When close enough, they both crouched down. Dark red stains soaked through the yellow blouse Tara had seen her in yesterday. The familiarity of her clothing sent a wave of shock over her until it receded into anger that someone could do this. Adrenaline pumped through her body as Tara's eyes scanned Serenity's back. She had at least fifteen stab wounds in her torso, a couple in her upper back, and Tara counted five on her upper thighs where the knife had pierced her jeans, revealing flesh and fatty tissue. Tara's stomach churned.

"We'll need to know if it was a jagged edged knife or not," Warren said as he stood up. Tara pulled her eyes away from Serenity's body and stood to face the chief. Tara nodded in agreement with Warren's statement. If it were a jagged knife, it was very likely the same murder weapon was used to murder both women.

The chief nodded. "We'll know after the medical examiner can take a look at the body."

Once again, Tara's eyes moved to the lettering on the wall. She had remembered what she had read, that the message was never released to the public, but she also remembered that one person had witnessed it firsthand. She looked at Chief Meyers, whose eyes were now locked on it too. He stared at it longingly, eyes wide with fear. It was as if he were staring at something he had tried hard to forget.

"You look like you saw a ghost," Tara said. "Does it look familiar?" It was written all over his face, but she had to confirm it.

His eyes darted away, falling to the floor, and he nodded. "I wouldn't forget that signature," he started. He raised his gaze, staring straight into Tara's eyes. "It's identical. I'm sure of it."

A silence lingered between them. He meant it; she could see in his stare that he felt in in every piece of his being—the Silent Stalker was back. Tara couldn't help but feel it too. This looked too similar to the cold cases to be a copycat. The message on the wall topped it off. Only someone who knew insider details of the cold case or had written it themselves would know about that lettering.

"We need a handwriting expert to confirm," Tara replied.

The chief nodded. "One's already on it."

"Any clue what it means?" Warren chimed in.

Chief Meyers shrugged. "I've been obsessing over it ever since I saw it for the first time twenty years ago. I couldn't tell you. At first I thought maybe it had to do with rejection. Maybe he was rejected by women and developed some sort of hatred toward them." He shook his head. "But I would imagine there would be a sexual component if that were the case, and none of these victims showed any sign of sexual assault."

Tara thought back to the theory she and Warren had originally discussed, that maybe it had something to do with mothers. Each victim in the cold cases and

Chloe were mothers. However, she wasn't sure about Serenity.

"Did Serenity have children?" she asked.

He shook his head. "She lived alone, no kids as far as we know."

Tara's heart sank. Serenity not having kids completely disproved her theory.

Chief Meyers' eyes moved to the coffee table, and Tara turned to meet his target. Sitting atop the coffee table sat a cell phone in an evidence bag. He inched toward it. "You guys got to hear this too," he said as he put on a glove, pulled out the phone, and played a voicemail on speaker.

A chill burst in the room as long, controlled breaths sounded through the phone, then a sinister laugh. Goosebumps formed on Tara's arms when the voice finally spoke, echoing the same message as on the wall. When it ended, Chief Meyers slipped the phone back into the evidence bag. "It's their tip phone for the podcast. It shows she listened to it," he said. "We're pretty sure right before she was murdered. The voicemail was left at 10:06 p.m., which is right around the presumed time of death." Tara's heart sank at the thought that Serenity's last moments were spent in utter terror before she even knew how threatened her life actually was. But then another thought occurred to her, and Tara's eyes turned to a hallway that led to the bedroom.

"That would mean the phone call was made within the home," she uttered. There was no way the killer had time to make the call, then enter the home with such little time in between. She would've heard him.

Tara had a feeling that he was hidden in the home the whole time.

Chief Meyers nodded. "The closet door in her bedroom was open," he said. "He must've been in there from when she had gotten home from dinner until right after that phone call."

Tara's blood ran cold. "Did you find anything?"

The chief shook his head. "Forensics combed the place for hair, fibers, fingerprints. Everything so far seems to point back to Serenity." He sighed with frustration, knowing very well that the lack of evidence was going to make things very difficult. Not only did it mean that there wasn't any forensic evidence to go on, but it also meant that it was intentional. The killer knew exactly what he was doing.

"Any way to trace the call?" Warren asked.

"It traces back to a burner phone," the chief replied.

It was all they needed to know to confirm that they wouldn't be able to find who called. Disappointment swelled, but then a thought burst into her mind. It was the remembrance of the podcast, of the eyewitness who came forward, which reopened the case. The teenage girl that had seen someone in the middle of the night push a recycling bin under the victim's window and leave the night before she was murdered.

"Did you check the backyard?" Tara asked.

The chief's eyes fell to the floor. He sighed again as he shook his head. "We did, didn't find anything." He looked at Tara and shrugged. Disappointment poured off him. But Tara wanted to see the backyard herself. She and Warren both knew how common it was for something to be overlooked. She turned to Warren. "Let's just take a look."

Moments later, they stood surrounded by a freshly cut, perfectly green lawn. A six-foot cedar fence lined the perimeter that provided ample privacy from neighboring lawns and opened to the driveway through a gate. They had entered through it, following a stone pathway that opened onto a large patio that stretched the entire length of the house. Tara looked around. Teak patio furniture was centered around a stone fire pit that looked barely used. Everything was perfectly placed, clean, and expensive-looking, but it all looked to be where it should be. Nothing looked out of place. Tara scanned the fence. There were three properties that touched Serenity's fence, one on each side. She wondered if the killer could've accessed or escaped Serenity's property through neighboring lawns, but she also knew that no one would be able to jump a six-foot fence. They would need something to step on to, to prop them up. But as she looked around the property, nothing was pushed up against the fence.

She turned to the chief. "Can you get someone to check the neighboring lawns? See if anything was propped up against the fence?"

The chief nodded. She didn't even need to explain. He already understood what she was theorizing.

Tara turned to Warren. He was facing the house, scanning every inch of the home. "She didn't have a surveillance system, did she?" he asked.

The chief pursed his lips and shook his head.

"Have you checked with neighbors?" Tara asked.

Again, the chief shook his head. "Only briefly," he confirmed. "Just a couple neighbors who came out to find out what was going on. No one saw anything."

She looked at Warren, and he nodded. She didn't even need to say it. Interviewing the neighbors would be their first step, after they spoke to Serenity's sister. They needed to check all neighboring homes for cameras.

Silence fell as Tara and Warren continued to scan the backyard. It was a one-story farmhouse with a basement. Two small rectangular windows sat just above the foundation. Tara moved toward them and bent down beside them. They were covered by thin, sheer curtains, but Tara could still make out the basement furniture of couches and television behind them. She checked for a latch, but they were only to provide light into the dark room. They didn't open. She stood up.

"Which is the bedroom?" she asked, referring to the room where the closet was open.

Chief Meyers pointed to a window almost right above her. It was too high for her to reach. She was 5'6". But it was low enough that someone of Warren's height would be able to graze the trim with his fingers. Warren was about six feet. But even with the height, Tara knew that someone would need a lot of upper body strength to pull themselves up into the window, especially if they were doing it sneakily. It was more likely that whoever it was would need some leverage. But as Tara looked under the window, there was nothing nearby or underneath the window. The closest object was one of the teak chairs about five feet away. But then she spotted something. There was a window in the corner of the house farthest from the driveway. Underneath sat a recycling bin with a lid. It was tall, about waist-high.

"What room does this window lead into?" Tara asked. She pointed to it.

"The bathroom," Chief Meyers responded.

Tara looked at Warren. She could see him eyeing the recycling bin as well. It wasn't placed directly underneath, but it was close enough that someone could step onto it and leverage themselves in through the window. It was also an odd place to keep a recycling bin.

"It doesn't make sense," Tara started. "Why someone would put their recycling bin all the way over here, when the driveway is over there?" She pointed to the other side of the house.

Warren and the chief nodded in unison as the chief pulled on his chin in thought. They all knew it was likely someone had put it there, but the question was when. The killer could've moved it there the night he killed Serenity, but Tara thought it unlikely. Deciding what to prop under the window on the spot would be risky. It would increase the odds that someone would hear it or see him, and it would require more thought in the moment, which would require more time at the scene. Tara knew the killer was smarter than that. Her thoughts turned to the podcast, to the witness that had seen the killer planning for his attack many years ago. He had done the exact same thing, placing something underneath a window to give him leverage. He had done it prior to the attack. He had planned. It was another confirmation that the Silent Stalker was back.

Tara stared longingly at the recycling bin. "I don't think this was put here last night."

Another silence fell. She didn't even need to turn to see their faces. Their silence spoke for itself.

"We need to find out who was back here in the days prior," Warren finally replied. Tara's eyes broke their trance as she spun around, meeting Warren's gaze.

"We'll start with the sister," she replied.

Warren nodded as they glanced around the yard one last time. She glanced at the neighboring homes, their second floors peeking out over the fence. After talking to Serenity's sister, they would have to check with neighbors. But even though the podcast had provided an opportunity for an unknown witness to come forward years later, Tara wondered now if it would hurt their case. Yes, it helped further the investigation, but it also gave the killer knowledge that could make him smarter.

Tara pulled her eyes always from the tops of the homes as Warren said his goodbyes to the chief. She did so as well and then followed him across the patio, toward the driveway, where they had parked. But as Tara crept behind him, her eyes fixed on the neighboring homes once more and frustration surged through her body. *This is going to be harder than it has ever been,* she told herself. The killer was wiser and older. He had learned from the information that had come to light. But most of all, Tara knew, he would now take greater lengths to remain unseen. He would blend in with the night.

Chapter Fourteen

Lights flashed from signs along Broadway as Warren and Tara drove through the heart of Nashville. It was still morning, but looking down the street, she imagined it would be hard to tell. People sat outside at restaurants, drinking mimosas and listening to live bands, country music trailing down the streets. Tara had never been to Nashville. It was a place she and John had always wanted to visit, and it was exactly as she had imagined it. Guitars were painted on almost every other store sign along the strip. Bachelorette parties pedaled on bike-powered bars down the street.

She never thought her first trip would be under these circumstances. This place would now be forever tainted by this trip, and it saddened her slightly. But she also didn't know why she would've expected different. She knew her job would take her all over the country, and major cities like Nashville were main targets.

Tara stared out the window as Warren turned onto a quieter street. Tara ducked slightly, looking up at a tall skyscraper in the distance and then down at the

GPS. They were nearing their destination, Serenity's sister's apartment building. She took a deep breath, preparing herself. She knew that no matter how many times she spoke to families of victims, it would never get easier. It would always twist a knife in her gut. But she needed not to let her empathy get to her. She needed to stay objective. She needed to get information. She focused on the recycling bin. She knew that if they could only find out who had put it there, they would find the killer. Tara knew the killer wouldn't make the same mistake twice. He wouldn't move the recycling bin in the dead of night, all dressed in black. He would blend in better than that.

She looked over at Warren. "You think the killer could've posed as someone? A meter reader or something like that?"

Warren nodded, weighing the thought. "It's certainly possible. I don't think he'd move those recycling bins like he did years ago."

Tara nodded. Warren pulled up in front of a large skyscraper. "We'll see if the sister knows of anyone who might've been there in the days prior," he added as they both stepped out of the car.

"If not, let's hope a neighbor has cameras of the street. We might be able to catch a glimpse of who was at her house."

Warren nodded again as they made their way into the building. A doorman held the door open as they stepped into a large marbled floor lobby and into an elevator. Tara pressed the button for the seventh floor. Moments later, they stood in front of Kiara Jackson's door. Tara knocked.

"I'm coming," they heard in between sniffles and above the pounding of feet growing louder. The door unlocked and swung open. A short, petite woman stood in front of them. Her eyes were red and bloodshot from crying, but Tara could still see that she had Serenity's eyes. It was like looking at a younger version of her, except Kiara had a fuller face. She must've been in her mid-twenties. Her black hair was pulled back tight in a frizzy ponytail with a beige headband. She had a face full of makeup. Her lips were burgundy. Tara assumed she had gotten ready for the day and maybe even had plans after stopping at her sister's. But now mascara streaked her face where tears had fallen and created dark shadows under her brown eyes.

She held a crumpled tissue in her hand and used it to wipe a forgotten tear on her cheek before crumpling it once again in her palm.

"Come in," she said as she pressed her back up against the door to hold it open.

She was expecting them. They had called her on the way to allow her time to prepare somewhat. Tara and Warren stepped inside. The apartment opened into a short hallway with a bathroom on one side and the kitchen on the other. At the end of the hallway, it opened into an average apartment-sized living room, but the windows that covered the entire wall opposite the entrance made it feel ten times larger. They were on the seventh floor, and the windows overlooked a large portion of Nashville. Cars looked like ants below them, and it gave Tara an unsettled feeling, like standing on the edge of a ledge. She had never liked heights.

"That's quite a view," Tara said as she took a seat on a couch straight across from the windows.

A slight smile spread on Kiara's face as she stared at the windows, the light catching in her eyes. "I always hated dark, stuffy apartments, so when I looked for one, it was important to me that it had lots of natural light." Her eyes fell to the tissue still crumpled in her palm. She squeezed it tight. "Serenity actually sent me this listing," she added, tears beginning to pool in her eyes. She quickly wiped them away and looked back up at them. "You're going to find who did this, right?"

Sadness welled within Tara. There was a loneliness surrounding her that made the apartment suddenly feel like it lacked air. Right away she got the sense that Kiara didn't have many people nearby. She wasn't sure why, but the fact that she was grieving alone spoke loudly.

Tara turned to Warren. She could see the same sadness in his eyes. They both nodded, and Warren spoke. "That's certainly what we're here for, to make sure your sister gets justice."

"We'll find who did this," Tara added.

Kiara nodded and took a deep breath to steady her emotions.

"Do you know anyone who could've possibly done this? Did she ever mention that she was afraid of anyone?"

Kiara shook her head. "Everyone loved her. I have no clue who would've wanted to hurt her. She never mentioned anything about being afraid."

"Was she dating anyone?" Tara asked.

Again, Kiara shook her head. "She lost her husband two years ago. A motorcycle accident. She hasn't dated anyone since." She grew quiet for a moment, as if to steady her emotions. "That's why I moved here. I was going to school in New York, but after she lost her husband, I moved back to be closer to her about a year ago."

"And your parents?" Tara asked.

"They passed away years ago. My mother was an alcoholic and my dad had cancer." She stared off into the distance, her eyes fixed on the wall.

Tara nodded. It seemed as if Serenity and Kiara only had each other. It was clear that they had their fair share of tragedy, but this seemed to be the ultimate blow for Kiara. She looked broken. Tara's heart ached for her.

"What kind of work did your sister do?" Tara asked. She knew she was involved in the podcast, but she had to have been making an income some other way.

"She was an executive assistant for Johnson Financial, it's a financial firm," Kiara replied.

"Anyone she was close with there? Or spoke to at all outside of work?"

Kiara shook her head without missing a beat. "She worked from home. She really didn't talk to anyone outside of work, and her communications with anyone were mostly through email. She worked there a long time." Kiara paused and looked into the distance. "She worked there even before she and Theo got married, her husband. Probably close to ten years now. The office moved to New York about five years ago, but they allowed her to stay here and work remotely." She used the tissue still scrunched in her hand and blew her nose. Then she sighed. "She never really liked that job much," she continued. "It was good money and flexible, but it wasn't fulfilling. But when Chloe got her into that podcast, it was like a new purpose flooded through her. She was all of a sudden fascinated with true crime, trying to piece together any clues in cold cases."

Tara nodded. It was the same fascination as Chloe and the only connector between them besides being friends. She pulled out her phone, pulling up a picture of the recycling bin. "This may seem like an odd question," she started as she held the phone out in front of her for Kiara to see. She leaned forward. "Did your sister usually put her recycling bins under this window?"

Kiara stared down at the image and knitted her eyebrows. "I mean, I didn't usually pay much mind to her recycling bins," she said, still staring at the image. She looked up. "It does seem like an odd place to put it, though, on that side of the house. Serenity wasn't the strongest person, so I can't imagine that she'd make more work for herself by placing it so far from the driveway and then having to carry it across the lawn."

Tara glanced at Warren. It was the same thought they had earlier.

Kiara's eyes darted between them. "Why? You think someone put that there?"

"We're not sure," Warren interjected. "But if someone did, then they probably put it there in preparation within the days prior."

Kiara's hand instinctively went to her mouth in surprise.

"Can you think of anyone that might've been in her backyard? A meter reader? A handyman? Anyone?"

Kiara shook her head, staring at them in a daze. "Not that I know of."

Tara continued to ask more questions, whether she ever mentioned feeling followed, feeling afraid home alone, anyone odd contacting her from the podcast, but at each question, Kiara just shook her head. "I really wish I could give you more. I want to find this person as much as you do, if not more," she finally said.

After exhausting their efforts, Tara and Warren stood up. Tara glanced around the empty apartment until her eyes landed once again on Kiara. Her swollen eyes were hard to look at without wanting to comfort her, and it was most certainly hard to leave her like that. "Do you have a friend maybe you can call?" Tara asked. "I'd hate for you to be alone right now."

Kiara's eyes fell to the floor, and she nodded. "I haven't told anyone yet. I needed to process it a bit first." She lifted her head, tears pooling again. She took a deep breath, steadying herself. "I have friends in the area, though. I know who to call. I'll be okay."

Moments later, Tara and Warren were headed to the elevator.

"We'll ask Chief Meyers to have the police look into her coworkers. I have a feeling that not much is going to come of it, though, considering the office is located in New York," Tara said.

Warren sighed. He was already reaching for his phone to call the chief, but then he turned to Tara. "In the meantime, we'll check out the neighbors," he said as the elevator doors opened. "Someone had to have heard or seen something, and if we're lucky, they have cameras."

Tara nodded. It was their only hope. But as the elevator descended, Tara wondered if the podcast had made him think smarter, and if this time he made sure that no one saw him at all.

***

Tara and Warren stepped off of a porch and onto Serenity Jackson's street. They had just approached a second home. At the first house, located directly across from Serenity's, no one was home. No one came to the door, and no car was in the driveway. At the second home, next to Serenity's, the woman who answered informed them that she hadn't been home the past few days. Now Tara and Warren surveyed the remaining homes on the street as hope began to fade.

"Let's scan for surveillance doorbells," Tara said. She was referring to doorbells that had video streaming and recording on them. Her eyes wandered across the street, and Warren nodded.

"If a doorbell was to capture anything in front of Serenity's house, it would need to be across the street," he added before stepping out into the road to cross.

Tara followed, scanning the homes, squinting to see their doorbells. They walked past two houses until Tara stopped in front of one located diagonally across from Serenity's. She moved closer, staring at the doorbell, and pointed at it. "Got one." She smiled.

Warren smiled as well, but Tara cold see he was holding back, skepticism laced on his face. He didn't want to get his hopes up. The house was unlike most others on the street, which were American farmhouses. This one was a French Provincial. There was no large, protruding porch. Instead, only three steps led to the front door, which was centered directly in the middle of the perfectly symmetrical home with a steeply pitched roof. A wreath with yellow flowers hung on the blue door.

They walked up to the door, Tara knocked, and within moments the door swung open. An older woman in a sweeping floral dress stood in front of them. She had white hair in a pixie cut, with big diamond stud earrings. She had light makeup on, and Tara couldn't help but notice that the skin on her face was tight, too tight to be natural for someone her age, probably her late sixties. She stared at them, genuinely perplexed. It probably wasn't every day that two complete strangers showed up on her doorstep. Tara held up her badge, and her face suddenly softened.

"I suppose you're going around to all the neighbors," she said, still holding the door open as she pursed her lips and shook her head. "It's a true shame. Serenity was a nice girl."

"Do you mind if we come in?" Warren asked.

The woman looked startled, as if it all of sudden occurred to her that she should've invited them in. She held the door open. "Of course."

They stepped into a large foyer with cathedral ceilings and dark hardwood floors. A chandelier dangled from above them, and a set of stairs descended into the room, where Tara spotted a man standing at the top of them, hand on the banister. He hesitated and then slowly walked down the stairs with confusion plastered on his face. The woman caught Tara's gaze and followed it until her face broke out into a warm smile.

"Tony," the woman started. "This is the FBI. They just wanted to talk to us about Serenity." She turned to Tara and Warren. "My husband."

He continued down the stairs, now without hesitation as his confusion washed away, replaced by seriousness. "Of course," he replied.

He seemed a similar age to the woman, but more natural-looking, which made him appear slightly older. He had large bushy eyebrows that were slightly darker than his silver hair and stubbly chin. He wore jeans and a button-down shirt.

The woman waved for them to follow her as she walked through the foyer to the living room. The man followed behind them. The room opened up into a large naturally lit room. A beige hand-woven rug blanketed the hardwood floor, under a brown leather couch and two chairs. A piano sat in the corner.

Tara and Warren took a seat in the chairs. The couple sat across from them.

"I'm not sure how much help we can be, but we're certainly happy to help in any way we can," the man said as he looked at Tara and Warren and then to his wife, who nodded.

"Did you know Serenity well?" Tara asked.

The woman shrugged and shook her head. "We've been neighbors probably about five years. We were friendly, but I certainly wouldn't say we knew her well."

"Did you ever see anyone over her house? Or maybe just lurking around it?" Tara asked.

The man and woman looked at each other and then shrugged. "No," the man said. "No one odd, at least. We saw her sister many times. Her friend would also come over often. That one that was on the news, who ran the podcast." He looked down with a shake of his head.

His wife swallowed hard as she grabbed her husband's hand. It was as if she was trying to hold down the bile. They were clearly shaken by the whole thing.

Tara asked a few more questions. If they ever noticed Serenity acting fearful. If they ever noticed her acting odd or looking over her shoulder, if they ever spotted someone out of place on their street or lurking late at night. But each time, the couple shook their heads in unison.

"Did you ever notice anyone over that might have gone into her backyard? Maybe someone doing work on her home?" she asked.

Again they shook their heads.

After exhausting their efforts, Tara knew there was one last hope. "We noticed you have a video doorbell. Would you mind if we took a look at the footage?"

The man straightened up. "Of course," he replied without skipping a beat, shifting slightly in his seat and pulling his phone from his pocket. "It's fairly new," he added, searching the app on his phone. "My son bought it for my birthday recently. I've always been interested in technology. I'm still figuring it out a bit. Oh, here you go." He opened the app and navigated to the camera viewing option.

Tara took it from his hand, and she and Warren stared down at it. They could already see Serenity's home across the street. Her entire home was in view, and Tara's heart fluttered. It was exactly what they needed. She rewound the footage to three days ago and then fast-forwarded slowly. She saw people walking by, walking their dogs, children riding their bikes, joggers. But no one seemed out of place. No one looked at Serenity's house; no one had a shifty gaze. Tara fast-forwarded but then stopped to see Serenity pull into her driveway. She stepped out of her car, slung her purse over her shoulder, grabbed a cup of coffee from her car, walked up to her front door, and stepped inside. She was dressed casually in jeans and a t-shirt, and it was still early morning. Tara assumed she had gone to grab coffee before she started work. Tara slowly fast-forwarded. Again, some neighbors walked by in the hours that followed, but no one looked out of place, and Serenity didn't leave her house for the remainder of the day. But Tara didn't yet lose hope. She continued to scroll through the footage until the day of Serenity's murder was in front of them. Again, at the same time as the day prior, Tara watched Serenity leave her house, only to return thirty minutes later with a coffee in hand and entering her home by herself.

Tara fast-forwarded slightly but then stopped and let the video play, eyes glued to the phone. The time across the screen showed 12:05, and Tara watched as Serenity exited her house once again, got into her car, and pulled away. Tara assumed it was her lunch break.

She was just about to fast-forward again when a delivery truck pulled up in front of her home, and Tara watched intently as a man hopped out of the truck with a package in hand and walked up Serenity's driveway, past the steps to her front door.

"Is he...?" Tara started, but then stopped. She was going to ask if the man was entering Serenity's backyard, but she couldn't finish the question. She was too preoccupied, watching the man on the camera. It was as if Warren didn't even hear her. His eyes too were glued to the phone. They watched as the man unlatched Serenity's gate, stepped into the backyard, and was then out of sight. Moments later, he returned to his truck with his package nowhere in sight. He sat in his truck for a few moments, staring down at something in his hand. Tara assumed it was a phone, but then he looked up as Serenity pulled into her driveway. She stepped out of her car with groceries in hand, and he drove away. Tara suddenly looked up, sharing a skeptical glance with Warren.

They both directed their gaze to the neighbors, still seated across from them. The man was leaning forward, elbows on his knees, hands laced together, staring at them with concern. The woman leaned forward as well, her eyebrows knitted. They both knew that Tara and Warren had seen something.

Tara rewound until the driver was clearly in view. He was tall and slender, but it was hard to tell from just the video, which was a good distance away, how old he was or catch a clear glimpse of his face. He wore a company uniform with a matching baseball cap. Tara held out the phone in front of her.

"Have you seen this man before?"

They both glanced down but then quickly looked up at each other in surprise.

"Of course," the husband said. "He has this route quite often. He's delivered packages here a few times too."

"And does he usually put the packages in the back of the house?"

Without hesitation, the woman nodded. "There was a theft problem a while ago where someone was taking packages. He started putting them in the backyard to prevent it."

The man chimed in. "That's why my son also got us the doorbell."

Tara shared a quick glance with Warren. His eyes narrowed, the same suspicion as hers. They suspected that the killer would have gotten smarter from what was revealed on the podcast, that someone had seen him years ago lurking in a victims' backyard. But this was beyond the cleverness that Tara suspected. It would mean that not only did he make an effort to blend in by being a delivery worker, but he had set up a scenario that justified him placing packages in people's backyards. In doing so, he had set it up perfectly so that he could scope out Serenity's backyard. He could place the recycling bin under her window, and he would not get caught. But at the thought, Tara wondered one thing. How could he not have noticed the doorbell?

"When did you get the doorbell?" Tara asked as she handed the phone back to the woman.

She shrugged. "A few days ago." She looked at her husband for affirmation, and he nodded.

"Do you mind if I take some pictures?" Tara asked as she pointed to the video.

They both shook their heads. Tara took pictures with her phone and suddenly got to her feet, feeling as if time were slipping away. She knew now that it was possible he could've missed it. He could've scoped out the area, checking for cameras before it was even placed there. It could be the one flaw in his plan.

The man and woman stood up as well. "You don't think—" the woman started, staring at Tara with concern. She didn't finish her sentence, but she didn't need to. Horror spread over her face.

"Have you ever spoken to him? Do you know his name?" Tara asked.

The woman shrugged. "Briefly. Just about the theft. He seemed like a nice guy. I would never think…" She paused for a moment, glancing at her husband. It was clear what she wanted to say, that she would never think that he would do something like this, but everyone knew that they didn't know him well. She looked at Tara once again as her face grew tense. It was as if a sickness had suddenly hit her. "I mean, I guess I don't know him well at all. But I do know that his name is Alex."

Moments later, Tara and Warren were briskly walking to the car. Tara already had her phone open, searching local delivery service stores. There were two in the area, and Tara showed them briefly to Warren before dialing one as she swung open the door to the car.

"We'll call both. See if an Alex works there," she said as the phone rang.

Warren nodded, started the car, and then turned to her. "We might as well head to the first one," he said. "They're both close enough, and I don't want to waste any time."

Tara agreed as Warren pulled into the road, Serenity's home growing distant behind them. But as Tara waited for someone to pick up her call, an unsettling feeling washed over her. Were they about to catch the Silent Stalker and meet him face to face? Or was this all too easy?

Chapter Fifteen

The store sat in a large strip mall on a main road on the west end of Nashville. It was now late morning, and the store was not quite busy yet. Few cars sat in the parking lot, and as Tara and Warren moved closer to the store, they could see only one customer through the glass window. It had probably just opened, Tara assumed.

The man behind the counter looked up as they entered and began helping the customer at a faster pace, as if preparing to speak to them. He was tall, towering over the customer, who looked to be about Tara's height of 5'6". He wore a collared company shirt that hung loosely on him but seemed to still be too short, just barely grazing his khaki pants. He was clean-shaven, his hair fiery red. He looked young, maybe in his early twenties. Tara assumed it was the employee she had spoken to on the phone. His voice shook with nerves, showing his youth, but his voice was deep, as she would expect from someone so large. Tara had asked him a few questions, but after stuttering on a few of them, he put the manager on the phone, but even the manager could only confirm that an Alex did work there. He couldn't release any more information unless in person, where they could confirm Tara and Warren's identity by seeing their badges.

As Tara and Warren moved to the counter, the customer thanked him as he handed her back a debit card and took her package behind the counter. He looked briefly at Tara and Warren, but then his eyes focused on the customer until she was pushing the door of the store open and leaving. When she was finally gone, he spoke.

"Can I help you?" he asked. His voice shook, just as it had when Tara called. He knew exactly who they were, and Tara was now certain he was who she'd spoken to.

She held up her badge. "I believe we spoke on the phone."

His eyes widened with a flicker of surprise. It was as if even though they had spoken, he still didn't believe that they were who they said they were.

"One moment," he replied. He continued to stare at the badge until Tara lowered it.

He turned, opened a door behind the counter to a back room, and disappeared. She could hear him speaking to someone, and moments later, an older man appeared with a nametag that said *Manager* affixed to his shirt. He was much smaller than his employee, who had about a foot on him. His shirt hugged his large belly, and he wobbled to the counter. He pursed his lips, knitted his white eyebrows, and stared at them skeptically. Tara once again flashed her badge, and his face softened. His eyes darted between Tara and Warren.

"What can I help you with?"

The young employee had gone back to work. He stood a few feet behind the manager, taping up a box on a counter against the back wall, but upon his boss's question he stopped as curiosity took hold. The manager sensed it and spun around, sending him a look of warning, and his shoulders instantly slumped.

He taped the box quickly, and then his hands slid away from it. "I'm going to take my break."

The manager nodded, a slight smile forming. The employee disappeared once again into the back room and closed the door.

"I believe we spoke to you on phone," Tara started. The manager nodded. "You said an Alex works here?"

The man nodded. "Alex Debrowski."

"And does he usually deliver to Park Avenue?" Tara asked.

The man nodded skeptically. "What is this about exactly?" There was a flame of fear in his eyes.

Tara was sure he'd heard of the murders. After all, it was all over the news, and the street was mentioned heavily. It was part of their route. It had rung a bell and that Alex frequently delivered there. But it was clear he didn't want to ask outright and spark suspicion accidentally.

Tara pulled out her phone, pulling out the screenshot of the delivery driver. She zoomed in, trying to get as clear of a picture of him as possible. She held it out in front of her. It was a clear view of his tall, thin frame. And even though it wasn't a clear image of his face, it was obvious that he wasn't young, maybe in his forties, and his sharp jawline was prominent.

"Is this him?" Tara asked.

He squinted at the image. "It certainly looks like him," he confirmed, his eyes rising once again to Tara. "You going to tell me what this is about now?" he asked as his eyes narrowed. He was growing impatient. He placed his hands on his hips.

Tara pulled the phone away. "There was a murder last night at a house he delivered to yesterday." His face changed. It was as if what he feared all along flashed before him. Worry hung on his face as he opened his mouth but didn't speak. His eyes widened in concern, but he scrunched his face. "We just wanted to talk to him," Tara continued. "See if maybe he saw or heard anything that may be able to help with the investigation."

The manager nodded, his face relaxing. It was exactly what Tara wanted him to feel, because she knew depending on the nature of their relationship, he would be more inclined to speak.

"Is he here?" Tara asked.

The manager shook his head. "He actually called in sick this morning, said he wasn't feeling well."

Tara looked over at Warren. She could see his skepticism. "Do you have his address?"

The manager looked at them questioningly but obliged. "Uh, yes," he replied, moving to a computer. He spent a moment there and then scribbled it down on a piece of paper and handed it to her.

Tara thanked him, but she wasn't done. "How long has Alex worked here?"

"About twenty years. He started pretty soon after me. I was much older, though. I think he was in his early twenties."

Tara nodded. That would mean that Alex was in his early forties now, which was what she assumed. It fit the description of the killer. He had been old enough to commit the crimes twenty years ago and young enough to commit the new crimes now. Tara was growing even more suspicious.

"Do you know why he might've been placing packages in people's backyards instead of by their front door?" Tara asked.

Once again, the man's eyes darted between Tara and Warren. He was growing even more suspicious. "What do you mean?"

"We have camera footage of him going into a backyard to deliver a package. Did you know anything about that?"

For a moment, the look of confusion remained on his face but then instantly vanished as a thought struck. "Oh, yes, you mentioned Park Avenue," he said. "There's been reports of theft, so he was instructed to put them in the back."

His response seemed genuine, but Tara wasn't convinced it wasn't all premeditated. Even if there were true cases of theft and the company told Alex to place the packages at the back of homes, he could've manipulated it all to work out in that way. For a killer to have gone twenty years under the radar, Tara knew they were up against someone who thought out every detail to make his actions seem legitimate and unsuspicious.

Tara looked down at the piece of paper in her hand and thanked the manager once again, but as they turned to leave, he spoke again, and Tara stopped in her tracks.

"Look, I don't know if you guys think he did something, or what but Alex is a pretty stand-up guy. I've known him for years."

Once again, Tara thanked him, but as she and Warren stepped outside and walked to the car, Warren spoke. "For all we know, he could've been stealing packages all along to set up this exact scenario."

Tara nodded. Warren too knew that the killer they were looking for was smart, smarter than any killer they had sought together. As Tara sat in the passenger's seat and Warren started the car, the manager's words rang in her head. "Stand-up guy," she repeated. "That's exactly what the killer would want someone to think."

***

The drive to Alex Debrowski's home was long, about thirty-five minutes outside of Nashville in a more rural area of White Bluff, Tennessee. Homes were spaced miles apart, divided by wooded areas and farmland. Tara watched as each home came in and out of view, only to see another one minutes later. Each home had a large amount of property, but Tara assumed it was cheaper to live there, being so far from the city.

"Quite a commute," she said as they neared their destination, trees and homes flashing by.

Warren nodded and Tara turned back to the window. She took a deep breath. They were now ten minutes out, and she braced herself for whatever they were about to encounter. All their theories on Alex Debrowski were just speculation. It was uncertain whether they were driving up to the Silent Stalker's home, but it was definitely possible, and at that thought Tara stiffened. But as she continued to stare out the window, as the destination grew nearer, a thought struck her.

"Do you think Serenity Jackson could be the last victim?" she asked Warren. It was a thought that had surfaced before. After all, the killer had been dormant for twenty years. She wondered if he only resurfaced to kill two women that had been digging up his past. It was certainly possible that his MO had changed, that what motivated him twenty years ago was separate from his motivation now. What if all he wanted to do was keep it buried?

Warren shrugged, eyes still on the road. "It's possible," he said. "But for all we know, he was only planning to kill Chloe Waterman." He was right; it was possible. After all, it was Chloe's podcast. Serenity was just a guest, and the killer most likely didn't know that she had plans to pick up where Chloe left off. "I think it's likely that he did kill to keep it buried," Warren added. "But it's also possible that one kill could've reignited an old flame, and that's what led to Serenity's death."

A chill ran over Tara. She knew he was right. They couldn't be certain that the rampage was over, but Tara wondered if it was only the podcast that made the killer resurface. She had studied serial killers. It was very uncommon for a serial killer to stop and lay dormant, especially for so many years. There had been cases where law enforcement even thought a serial killer lay dormant, but they had only moved somewhere else, picking up in a completely different state and jurisdiction, so they were never initially seen as related. Tara knew this was different. He had picked up in the same area, so he had likely stayed there. The FBI had even worked on the case at times as a cold case but had never seen a similar pattern of crimes anywhere else in the country.

But there were other reasons serial killers would lay dormant. They could've have been placed in jail for an unrelated crime, or there were rare cases like BTK, a serial killer in the seventies and eighties who tormented women in Kansas, but the time between his murders sometimes spanned years. He was enough in control of his own desires to stop killing when he was close to getting caught, but then he resurfaced again by sending a cryptic letter to the police years later. It was believed that he missed the attention. At that thought, another hit her at lightning speed. *Maybe he missed the attention*, she thought. *Maybe he actually liked the podcast. He liked the attention, but in an effort to not get caught and to initiate more attention, he resurfaced.*

She turned to Warren. "What if we're wrong about the podcast? What if he actually liked the attention and craved more? Maybe they were partially getting too close, but at the same time, he wanted the media to talk about him again."

Warren raised his brows, contemplating, and nodded. "It's like he's saying 'you want to talk about me, well here you go.'"

"Exactly," Tara said. "He saw the excitement stirred by the podcast and wanted to blow it up into hysteria."

"That makes perfect sense, actually."

Warren slowed the car as they neared the road Alex lived on. He turned onto a quiet street. Each house sat at least a quarter-acre away from the road. Tara's heart quickened as they pulled up in front of a ranch style home that sat up on a hill about half an acre away from the road. The house was white, with dark green shutters. But even from afar, Tara could see that the paint was chipping and the roof was missing shingles. It needed work. But just as Warren turned the car off, a man came from around the house. He was dressed in a light flannel, work boots, gloves, and a baseball cap. He was holding something, and as Tara took a closer look, she could see that an axe was held tightly in his grip. He walked briskly to a pile of wood on the side of the house, held the axe up high, and sliced it into a piece of wood on the ground. He placed the cut pieces in a pile next to him.

"Looks like Alex Debrowski," Warren said.

Tara nodded. It did look just like the man in the video. He had the same tall, slender body, the same long-gaited step. He was turned away from them, fixated on the woodpile. He didn't see them just yet. Each time the ax hit the wood, a boom vibrated through the air, bouncing off the trees.

"Doesn't look very sick to me," she said. She had remembered what the manager said, that Alex

Debrowski had called in sick. But it was hard to believe that a man chopping wood with such force was unwell.

"My thoughts exactly," Warren replied.

Unease swept over her, and she turned to Warren. "Let's see what he knows." Warren nodded, but there was an unspoken understanding between them that it could be dangerous. A warning flashed in his eyes.

"Be prepared," he finally said as they both reached for the door handles and stepped out of the car.

Upon their exit, Alex continued to chop wood, unaware of their presence. His back was facing the road. The driveway ran up the side of the home to the left of him. Tara assumed he had earbuds in, protecting his hearing each time the axe hit the wood. But as they walked up his long driveway, he stopped for a moment, as if sensing their movement. His head turned just barely, and Tara was sure she saw him look at them from the corner of his eye, but it was sneakily, as if he didn't want them to notice. He placed the ax down, casually took off his gloves, and began walking to his front door. He kicked off his boots on the steps briefly and then stepped inside, closing the door behind him. Tara looked over at Warren.

"That was weird," she whispered under her breath.

Warren nodded as he stiffened, ready to face whatever they were about to. It was as if Alex had wanted it to seem like he didn't notice them, like he had finished his job and gone inside to grab a bite to eat. But why he had acted that way dangled in front of them like a carrot in a trap. They needed to know, but Tara could sense the danger. She felt for her gun, just under her shirt, hooked onto her belt, and felt some slight relief.

As they neared the end of the driveway, Tara saw that a red Dodge Ram truck sat in the driveway. There was a closed garage to the right of it, and she made a mental note of the potential escape route. They continued walking on a cracked cement pathway that led directly to the door and walked up three steps that had black metal railings on either side. Tara scanned the large bay window to the left of the stairs, but she didn't sense movement. She wasn't sure if movement or no movement was what she hoped for.

Tara opened the storm door and knocked on a dark green wooden door that matched the shutters. She braced herself and waited a moment. But there was no answer. She knocked again and waited. Again, no answer. Her eyes moved down the pathway toward the driveway, listening for the garage. But she did not hear it open. She was about to knock one last time when the sound of shuffling feet could be heard from inside.

"One minute!" they heard. It was a deep, raspy voice that Tara assumed was Alex's.

They waited, but all they heard was the sound of more movement. Every few seconds they heard a soft thud as if someone was moving a heavy box and placing it down carefully. Tara glanced at Warren, who raised his eyebrows. It was clear that Alex was doing something he found important enough to complete before anyone stepped inside his home. It sounded as if he were hiding something.

A crash echoed inside, and Tara reached for her gun, tense with anticipation.

"Shit," they heard. It was loud enough to hear, but controlled.

"Everything all right in there?" Tara asked.

"Uh, yes. I just dropped something. I'll be there in a minute."

The sound of shards of glass rang through the air, as if they were being swept and dumped into a trashcan. He sighed, then footsteps could be heard moving closer to the door, which he opened.

He stood in front of them. His eyes were an emerald green surrounded by the redness of exhaustion. He had a large, steep nose and a cleft chin that made his lips look smaller. His hair was buzzed on each side, and he wore a Tennessee Titans baseball cap.

He looked at them with confusion, but Tara could see a hint of fear in his eyes as he shifted awkwardly, moving his hand farther up the door.

"Can I help you?" he asked with a forced smile. A bead of sweat trickled down the side of his face, and he wiped it away with the back of his hand. His fingertips were covered in soot.

"We're looking for Alex Debrowski," Tara said.

The man's face flashed a slight shade of red. He immediately sensed it and spoke quickly to shift the attention. "That's me."

Tara flashed her badge, sending the redness to drain from his face. He stared at them, his eyes wide, his face white. He didn't speak. He shifted awkwardly once again, leaning slightly on the door as if in an attempt to look calm, but everything about him screamed fear.

"I'm sure you've heard about the murder on Park Avenue. I believe that street is part of your normal route. We were just hoping to speak to you and see if you saw anything."

"Uh, yeah, sure. I deliver there often." His voice shook with his words, but Tara could tell he was trying desperately to control it. He looked as if the anxiety would burst through him.

"Can we come in?" Tara asked.

The man's eyes shifted between Tara and Warren, and then he turned his head slightly, looking behind him. He nodded, opening the door and leading them into a dark, small living room that had a worn beige couch and a recliner that sat directly across the room from a flat-screen television. The walls were white and bare, but the room was clean besides some muddied boot marks on a mat by the door.

He motioned for them to take a seat on the couch. Tara and Warren sat down as he sat in the recliner.

He leaned forward. "I'm not sure how much help I can be. I never saw anything out of the ordinary, but I'm happy to answer your questions." He shook his head. "It's terrible what happened to that girl." He looked off in the distance as he said it, and Tara couldn't tell if he was being genuine or if he couldn't meet their eyes out of fear. He was holding something back, that much was obvious. She could feel it in everything he said.

Tara told him the house number. "Do you remember delivering there?"

He nodded without hesitation. "I've delivered there many times," he admitted.

"And did you ever meet this woman?" Tara pulled out a picture of Serenity from her pocket and held it out in front of her.

He stared at it a moment, confusion crossing his face. He almost seemed to relax slightly at the question and seeing her picture. *That was odd*, Tara thought.

He finally looked up and shrugged. "I never really spoke to her or anything. I think I've seen her from afar, just waving at her as she got her package and I drove off."

Tara nodded, putting the picture away. "Did you ever see anything odd? Or maybe just someone on her property?"

He pursed his lips, and again he shook his head. He leaned back into his chair, resting his arms on the arms of the chair. It was like something in him changed. He was calmer, genuinely calmer. Either that or he had fully got a hold of his anxiety to the point of being able to hide it completely.

Tara asked a few more questions, whether he ever saw anyone else with her, whether he ever heard anything odd. But at each question he shook his head.

"Look, I really wish I could help," he started with a shrug. "I just deliver packages. I just drop them off and go. I don't think I'm the help you're looking for." He leaned forward, as if ready to stand up at any moment, waiting for when they would tell him they were done. He glanced down at his phone in his lap, checking the time and then back up at Tara and Warren.

Tara nodded, but there was something odd in his body language. He seemed too eager to have them go.

He didn't say it, but it was clear that he wanted this conversation to be over.

"Did you ever see anything in the back of her property?" Tara asked.

He knitted his brows, confused. For a moment he didn't answer, but then his face loosened, as if he knew what Tara was referring to. "Oh, the theft," he started. "Um no. I dropped boxes in her backyard before to avoid the theft, but I never saw anything." Color rose to his face again. His body tensed, his fingers clenched on the arm of the chair.

There was something about the theft that was making him nervous. His eyes moved behind him slightly but then shot in front of him once again, as if he didn't mean for them to veer off. Tara looked over to where his eyes had moved. She wasn't sure what he was looking at. The wall was bare, except for a closet door. Tara wondered if that was what he had looked toward.

Tara turned her attention back to him, but he had noticed, and his face flashed an even redder shade.

"Did you ever witness any theft?" Tara asked.

He stared at her a moment, his eyes wide in fear. He started to speak but stuttered and then started over. He shook his head. "Never did. I just know customers reported it."

"And was it your idea to place packages in the back?"

His eyes shifted between Tara and Warren, panic swirling within them. He tried to relax, sitting back a bit in his chair. But his body was still tense, screaming with fear.

"I think I might've suggested it. It just seemed like the best logical option."

Tara nodded, gazing at the closet once again. She followed the edge of it to the white doorknob and down to the floor. She didn't see anything odd, and she was about to turn her attention back to Alex when something shining on the floor caught her eye. About a foot in front of the door, she spotted a jagged shard of glass.

She looked briefly at Warren, who had followed Tara's gaze and spotted it as well. They both looked back at Alex, who was now sitting at the edge of his chair.

"Did you break something?" Tara asked, motioning toward the broken glass.

He turned his head, hands still clenched on the armrest. When he spotted the glass, he froze. His eyes opened wide. An awkward laugh left his throat as he faced them once again.

"Ah, yes. Some wine glasses I bought. I...uh..." he stuttered, the redness spreading down his neck. "I was trying to clean up quick before I opened the door. A little too quick, I guess." He shook his head as if playing it off as a clumsy accident and forced a smile, but the fear was undeniable. She could smell it like it had smacked her in the face.

They sat in silence a moment, him growing increasingly agitated. He began to bounce his leg, a nervous tic. He needed something physical to release the pent-up anxiety. "Is there anything else I can help with?" he asked. Again, he forced a smile, but it wasn't genuine.

"You don't seem much like a wine drinker to me," Tara replied. "Was it a gift for someone?"

He opened his mouth but didn't speak and then closed it. He couldn't think of a response fast enough until one burst out of him. "My mother," he said. "I bought it for her."

Tara peered around the home. There was only one jacket at the door and no women's shoes. As far as she could see, there was no evidence that anyone else lived there. "Does she live here with you?"

Alex rubbed his palms on his knees. He couldn't even try to hide his fear anymore. He shook his head. "Used to," he admitted. "She lives in a nursing home now."

Tara looked toward Warren, who gave her a puzzled look. "They let her drink in a nursing home?" he asked.

He stopped rubbing his knees. His fingers clenched them instead, so hard it looked like he would puncture a hole in his jeans.

"Um, well, no," he started, shaking his head. "She just likes them. She drinks mocktails out of them."

Tara nodded. She had to admit it was a clever response, but she still wasn't buying it.

For the first time, a flash of anger crossed his face. "What does this have anything to do with what you're here for anyway?" He had had enough with the questions. The anxiety had reached a breaking point, and Tara knew that could also be dangerous. She glanced at Warren from the corner of her eye. He was now fully on the edge of his seat.

Tara stood up. Warren followed her lead. "We don't have any more questions," she said, and Alex instantly relaxed. "However..." she began again. He looked up at her with frightened eyes. "Do you mind showing us the wine glasses? With an open theft case as well, and your close proximity to the packages, we just have to cover our bases, as I'm sure you understand."

He stood slowly. "Of course," he said with a nod, but his words did not match his body language. Everything in his stance, the hesitation in his nod, and his words sent Tara's instincts on fire. He crept forward to the closet door. Tara and Warren stood behind him. They eyed each other, both fully aware that he was unpredictable.

But just before he reached for the door, he spun around. "Do you mind if I use the restroom first?" The same forced grin formed on his lips. "I'm assuming this might take a bit of time, and I really do need to go."

"It'll only take a couple minutes," Tara assured him.

He had no other choice but to nod as sweat glistened on his forehead. He turned back toward the door, his hand hovering over the doorknob. He hesitated again for a moment, sending a wave of adrenaline through Tara's body. He was going to do something, she could feel it. She watched as his eyes wandered to the shard of glass on the ground, but then his eyes shifted again in front of him. It was about a foot away from him, just to the left of Warren. But as Tara looked toward Warren in the corner of her eye, he shifted slightly, shielding the glass from Alex's path. Alex didn't even notice as he finally opened the door in one swift motion and stepped back.

Tara and Warren stared in awe at the boxes upon boxes piled ceiling-high. There had to have been at least thirty boxes. Some were very large, some smaller. Warren moved closer to Alex and gave a nod to Tara, letting her know if was okay to take a look. She moved closer, hovering over the boxes as she read who they were addressed to.

Rena Sullivan, read one. *Thomas Goldberg,* another. *Ebony Hall.* Tara stood on her tiptoes, reading the names on the boxes placed higher. All contained names that were not Alex's.

She turned around and faced him. "Do you want to tell us why you have all these boxes?" she asked.

His face was ghostly white. "I—" he started, but he couldn't finish. No words would leave his throat. He stared into the pile of boxes. He knew what they were, that he had them, but it was as if he were looking at them for the first time, realizing what he had truly done to himself. It was a look of life flashing before someone's eyes, of hope fleeing every corner of their mind.

In one swift motion he spun on his heels, heading for the front door. But Warren had already sensed it and jumped into his path. Alex stopped abruptly, momentum still pushing him forward, sending him almost tumbling. He spun around toward the now unguarded glass and threw his body onto the floor, his arm outstretched. His fingers grazed the edge of it, cutting the tips of his fingers. He groaned in pain, blood pooling underneath.

Tara saw the opportunity. She jumped on his back, holding him with the weight of her body as she tried to hold down his arms, but he was larger than her. He was heavier, and stronger. Her arms were no match for his. He let out another grunt of pain as he grabbed the glass fully in his hand. He was about to swing it behind him at Tara, but Warren's foot came crashing down right onto his hand, sending the glass into it. He screamed out in pain once again as his hand instinctually shot open, sending the glass skidding out in front of him.

"Get off me!" he screamed. His eyes shot to his hand. A piece of glass stuck out from his palm. "What the hell did you do to my hand?" Tears streaked down his face as Warren cuffed him and Tara stood up. Warren forced him to his feet. "I was going to give them back!" he screamed in between whimpers. It was a desperate attempt to gain sympathy, but Tara and Warren weren't buying it.

Warren forced him out the door, down the steps and down the driveway to their vehicle, and forced him into the back seat. Warren leaned in, taking a closer look at his hand, which was cuffed behind his back, and then pulled away, went to the trunk, and pulled out a sweatshirt. He placed it between Alex's hands. "Just hold this tight," he said to him and then slammed the door shut.

Once he closed the door, he turned toward Tara. "How's his hand?" she asked.

"Not bad. I think he'll just need a couple stitches. We'll try to be quick." He nodded in direction of the house as he began to walk toward it. Tara nodded. They needed to search the rest of the home before they took him back for questioning.

"Looks like Alex isn't the stand-up guy people thought," he said with a shake of the head.

Tara nodded. Alex had clearly been the one stealing packages. It was even likely that he had set up the entire scenario so that putting packages in the back of houses seemed legitimate. He was also clearly violent. Every piece that they had just learned about him did not meet the "stand-up guy" persona his manager had described. The impression of his character and the reality fit the mold of the Silent Stalker perfectly. But there was something about him that made Tara question it all—his nerves. Everything about him screamed fear. But as Tara and Warren made their way back up his driveway and into his home, she wondered, *Was that an act too?*

They stepped into the home once again. Right in front of them sat the small pool of blood and the glass broken in fragments across the floor. It was now late in the afternoon, and the sun was hitting the house straight on, sending fragments of light through the closed sheer curtains, catching the dust in the air. It was a small ranch, with only one main floor and a basement, built into the hill and connected to the garage.

The front door opened right into the living room. A kitchen was right next to it, almost straight across from the front door, with a cutout window connecting both rooms. The closet door sat opened, the boxes still stacked on top of each other between the cutout window and a long, thin, dark hallway that connected to the rest of the home.

"You want to start in the bedrooms?" Warren asked. "I'll start in the basement."

Tara agreed. She too knew that if he were hiding anything, that was most likely where it would be, where it would more easily be hidden. They both walked down the hallway, the old shaggy carpet crunching under their feet. Warren stopped by a closed door, opened it, and turned a switch, revealing a series of unfinished plank stairs.

"Wish me luck," he said as he quickly descended until his footsteps were barely heard.

Tara turned into a nearby room and was met by blank walls and an unmade bed that she assumed was Alex's. She quickly surveyed the room. There was one dresser that stood tall against the room, across from the bed. One nightstand with a lamp atop it, and a closet with sliding doors were directly next to her on the side of the bed. She began rummaging through everything, through the nightstand, through the closet, but all she found were his clothing and other meaningless objects like a lighter and his glasses. Tara moved into other rooms. Alex's bedroom was the only one, but Tara searched the bathroom and the kitchen, looking for anything of importance, but after she finished her search of each room, she sighed in disappointment.

"Tara," she finally heard. Warren's voice echoed up the stairs, and she followed it until she stood in a wide-open garage that was mostly empty except for something that Warren was bent over by.

Tara moved closer. She was about to ask what he was looking at, but as she moved closer, she saw. Perched up against the side of the garage sat more boxes, and as Tara leaned in closer, she could see that they too were addressed to different people. But it was one box in particular that caught her eye. It was the one Warren was hovering over. It was unmistakably addressed to Serenity Jackson.

They both pulled away, looking at each other. They weren't sure what it meant, but it now connected Alex to the victim in more ways than one. He was not just a delivery person; he was a thief. He had stolen her property. The question now was why.

"Did you find anything?" Warren asked.

Tara sadly shook her head. Warren pursed his lips in disappointment as his eyes wandered back to the box. "Well, regardless, Alex clearly has some explaining to do."

Tara nodded. Alex was clearly guilty, but the question was of what?

Chapter Sixteen

Fluorescent lights shined down on Alex Debrowski, making his bald head look even shinier. His baseball hat had been removed, revealing that what hair they had seen with his hat on was all he actually had. He was slumped over, hands outstretched in front of him, the left one now bandaged, and his eyes focused on the steel table in a trance.

Tara and Warren had just entered the room, but he didn't even bother to look up. It was as if he didn't even notice, as if his mind was somewhere else completely. As they each pulled out a chair across from him, he lifted his head for the first time. His eyes were bloodshot, as if he was struggling to hold back tears. His face was white with fear, but his body was relaxed in defeat. He didn't dare look them in the eye.

"You want to tell us why you had all those boxes?" Tara asked.

His eyes fell again to the table, staring hard at it as if he were trying to see past it. He didn't speak, nor did he plan to.

"You stole them?" Tara asked, trying to get him to respond, but his eyes still remained on the table. His lips did not move.

Silence swirled around them into a storm of tense air. He looked up briefly but then locked his eyes on the table again. It was getting harder for him to remain silent.

"What did you do in in back of Serenity Jackson's house?" Tara asked. "Did you steal those packages so that you could put them in the back of homes without question and set up a way to enter women's homes?"

At that, he lifted his head sharply. His eyebrows knitted in concern. "What, no!" he said with a shake of his head. "I would never do something like that." He looked between Tara and Warren as he spoke, but then his eyes fell in shame. "I would never hurt someone."

"Well, why did you have those boxes then?" Tara asked.

Again, silence filled the air.

Tara sighed in frustration. "If you say you wouldn't hurt someone, then you better explain why you had those boxes, because what we're thinking says you would."

He sighed, placing his elbow on the table, his head falling into his palm. He stroked his forehead hard. "I shouldn't have done it," he started as a sob left his throat. "My mom needed to go into a nursing home, but I was struggling to pay for it."

"So, you stole packages?" Warren interjected.

"Not exactly," he started. "A buddy of mine said he could help get me some money, so I told him when I dropped something off big, and he would come back later and scoop it up." He paused briefly, stroking his injured hand awkwardly. "He was selling them for me on eBay and splitting the profits."

"So then why were all those packages in your house?" Tara asked.

His eyes drifted into the corner, terror momentarily flashing within them until defeat settled once again. It was clear he knew he had already said too much, had already ratted someone out. "He needed me to hold them for him," he said, still staring at the wall, unable to meet Tara's eyes. "He got arrested on some drug charges, so he asked me to go to his house to get them before it got raided." He burst into tears. "I shouldn't have done it all," he cried. "Once people started to catch on that their packages were being stolen, I was going to give them all back, I swear." The words burst out of him like vomit. It was as if at each question, the regret at what he had done grew until it had nowhere else to go but to burst from his lips.

"What's his name?" Tara asked.

"Wesley Miller," he replied without a moment of hesitation.

Tara made a mental note of the name as she stared at him, his body slumped over, his head cradled in his uninjured hand. He seemed genuine, but Tara knew there was always the slight possibility that he was an extremely skilled liar. In fact, she was certain the killer was. But there was something about him that made her question his role. It was the way his face beamed a deep shade of red with anguish, the way his eyes widened at each accusation, the way he cried. A serial killer could be a good liar, but they always had difficulty showing emotion because most often they never felt it themselves.

Tara pulled out a picture of Serenity's backyard from her pocket and slid it across the table. It was a picture of the recycling bin placed perfectly underneath the bathroom window. Alex looked down at it, scooping the picture up, holding it to his face. He scrunched his face in confusion.

"What am I looking at?"

He looked genuinely perplexed. Tara pointed at the recycling bin, and for a moment his face lit up as if in recognition, but then the look faded. It was odd, Tara noted, but she wasn't sure if he had only just made the connection for why it might be there or if he had put it there himself and forgotten to cover his trail.

"Do you know why this recycling bin is on this side of the house?" Tara asked.

He stared at it wide-eyed, as if hoping to find the answer within the picture. When it didn't speak to him, he looked up, curiosity stirring. He opened his mouth, about to speak, a question at the tip of his tongue, but then he closed it and shrugged. He knew what they were implying, that the killer had placed it there. But he either didn't want to answer or ask for fear of looking guilty or because he *was* guilty.

"Did you see it there when you dropped the package off?" Tara asked.

He took the picture up once again and leaned back in his chair, staring at it inquisitively. He quickly placed it down, his eyes following it, and then nodded. "I think I did, actually." He leaned forward, looking at it once more. "Yeah, I did, definitely. I thought it was a weird place for a recycling bin, but I didn't pay much attention to it."

Tara shared a quick glance with Warren. He sounded genuine, but it seemed odd to her that he would even have noticed.

"Where did you leave the package?" she asked.

"By the back door," he replied without hesitation.

Tara stared at him skeptically. His reply only made her doubt his words even more. She recalled walking into the backyard, standing on the patio, and seeing the sliding door that opened onto it. It was right next to the end of the driveway. He would've opened the gate, turned left, and placed the package only a few feet away. The recycling bin was placed about fifty feet from there. It was possible to see the recycling bin from afar, but why would he even notice? It wasn't something so bizarrely unusual that it would stick out easily.

Tara looked down at Alex's free hand fidgeting with the bandage of the other. He was nervous. He was either lying because he had put the recycling bin there himself or he was lying because he didn't want it to seem like he put it there himself.

But Tara wasn't done. "Where were you last night?"

At her question, he fidgeted with his bandage even more, pulling on it until he noticed and stopped. He placed his hands in his lap.

"I was home," he said. He looked frantically between Tara and Warren, realizing that he now didn't have an alibi. But then a thought struck him. "I spoke to my mom at the nursing home; you can ask them." A glimmer of hope entered his eyes.

"What time?" Tara asked.

The hope suddenly faded, his eyes became glossed over and fell to his lap. "I don't remember exactly, maybe around eight," he said.

"How long was your conversation?"

"Maybe a half hour." He didn't look up.

It wasn't enough of an alibi, and he knew it. The murder had happened around ten thirty. Starting a half hour conversation at eight left plenty of room to commit it.

But Tara had one more question for him. She pulled out a picture of Chloe Waterman and slid it across the table. His eyes lifted and stared at the picture. He knitted his eyebrows with a tilt of his head as familiarity crossed his face.

"Do you know her?" Tara asked.

At her question, he looked up. His face fell as color drained from his skin. He stared back at her, scared and confused.

"I saw her on the news." He looked between Tara and Warren. "What does this have to do with the packages?"

Tara leaned closer and spoke. "You tell me."

He leaned back in his chair as an awkward chuckle burst from his mouth. He was quiet a moment, staring at them blankly, as if trying to make sense of Tara's words. "Look," he finally said, throwing his hands up as if surrendering, "I may be guilty of stealing those packages, but this is crazy." His hand rose to his forehead, stroking it hard as he shook his head again. "You think I'm a murderer," he said, but he was speaking to no one, only processing the information in front of him. He stared down at Chloe's picture again.

"I may break the law to try and help my mom, but in no way would I ever hurt someone."

His eyes remained on Chloe's picture. Tara studied him. He was either telling the truth or a very good actor. But he also had no solid alibi. He had been at the victim's home the day she was murdered, he was in her backyard where the killer had prepped for his kill, and he had assisted in stealing packages, perhaps to make putting them in the backyard plausible. It all added up to their original theory. But then Tara suddenly had a thought: the message on the wall. She turned to Warren.

"Do you have a paper and pen?" she asked.

Warren stared at her a moment with confusion, but then his face relaxed. He knew why she was asking, and he nodded. "I'll go get one."

He left the room, as Alex watched him leave with confusion, and returned moments later. He placed the pen and paper in front of Alex. "Heart to mold," Warren said. "Write it." Alex stared at him with even more confusion.

"What for?"

"I'm not at liberty to say what it means, but if you're innocent, it could save you."

Alex looked down, slowly lifted the pen, and wrote the words across the pad. When he was done, Tara took it and stood up. They would have a forensics handwriting analyst look at it. If the handwriting matched, they would without a doubt be able to tie him to the scene.

"We'll see if your story lines up," she said to him before turning to the door. Warren followed.

When they stepped outside the room, Warren turned to her. "We'll get the chief to look up Wesley Miller to see if his story checks out."

Tara nodded at his words.

"And who knows," he added with a shrug, "Alex Debrowski could've even been setting up the scene for someone else,"

Tara knew what he was implying, that Wesley Miller could even be a suspect. It was a theory she had even pondered herself. She nodded again. Everyone was guilty. The question was of what.

***

Tara and Warren sat in a spare room in the police station, their eyes focused on the sea of cold case files spread out on the table in front of them. Chief Meyers had already looked into Serenity's job and informed Tara and Warren that there were no coworkers of interest or that had any useful information. The majority of the workforce lived in New York, and the very few that stuck around Nashville after the move and worked remotely all had credible alibis and rarely communicated with Serenity. Tara and Warren were now waiting on Chief Meyers to check out Alex's story. They had already passed the piece of paper with Alex's handwriting off to a forensics handwriting analyst, but they wouldn't get results until morning, and they didn't want to waste any time.

"You think it's him?" Tara asked as she looked up from the case file in front of her.

Warren's reading glasses sat on the tip of his nose. He didn't look up, just shrugged. "He seemed sincere," he said. "My guess is that the packages were just a coincidence."

Tara nodded. She agreed, and the more she thought about it, the more she doubted that Alex Debrowski was the killer. He seemed too confused when they showed him the picture of the recycling bin, when he realized why they were truly questioning him, and he seemed way too nervous. It was a trait Tara seldom, if at all, had seen in the serial killers she dealt with. They were confident, even when caught, and even when trying to lie. They always failed to realize that their emotion did not match their words because they failed to feel it themselves. It was always their biggest downfall.

At the thought, Tara's phone vibrated in front of her. She looked down to see Chief Meyers' name flash across the screen. She picked up, placing it on speaker, hoping he had some news.

"What you got?"

Chief Meyers sighed. "Well, there's a Wesley Miller in the county jail, got arrested a few days ago with class E felony drug charge for heroin possession."

Tara shared a glance with Warren. Any remaining hope was extinguished. Alex Debrowski's story was checking out, and it looked like Wesley Miller had a solid alibi. "So he was locked up the night of the murder?" Tara asked.

"That's right," the chief confirmed. "We also spoke to the nursing home for Alex's mother. His story checks out. They have record of him speaking to her around 8:30 p.m. It was about a half hour phone call."

His story checked out. But there was still a huge gap of time unaccounted for. He said he was home, but they had no way of knowing that. He still had no alibi for the time Serenity was killed around 10:30 p.m.

Tara thanked him, and they were soon off the phone. It sat silently on the table, Tara and Warren just as quiet. They still had nothing solid. They still had doubt. Tara looked down at the time on her phone. It was seven thirty. Another day had slipped away, and they still had no certainty that they had found the killer. She knew this case was going to be hard, but this was beyond difficult. For a moment she wondered if they would be able to find this killer at all, but she quickly shook off the thought. *I can't think like that,* she told herself. The thought and the moment of weakness hit her like a punch in the gut until her body tensed, ready to fight even harder.

She grabbed hold of the case files in front of her, scanning them one after the other. "We have to be missing something," she said to Warren as he stared down as well, flipping through them with the same urgency. "Maybe there's a connection we're missing," she added.

Warren nodded as he stopped on each victim's case file, scanning their victim information.

They already knew the victims were all women, all with similar ages. Tara stared down at the ages. Thirty-eight, forty-two, thirty-five, forty-five. She looked over at Warren. "All mid-thirties to mid-forties?" she asked. Warren nodded. "Children?" she asked. Each of the victim's files she had checked indicated children of their own, all of different ages, all with a different number of children, but they all had motherhood in common.

Warren nodded. "All mothers," he confirmed.

Tara looked up. "It must mean something."

"But Serenity," he replied. "She's the only one that deviates."

Tara sank back in her chair. He was right. Serenity had no children. She was a widow. It was a major difference from the rest of the victims, who were all were either married or once married and had children of their own.

"But I think it's safe to say that his motive was different with Serenity and Chloe," Warren added. "I think the podcast was his motive, and Serenity was just another loose end." He thought for a moment. "In fact, I think Chloe having a child might've just been a coincidence."

Tara nodded. He was right. It could certainly be a coincidence, and it certainly seemed plausible that the killer's motive had changed from his murders years ago, but there was something that didn't sit right with her.

"It can't be a coincidence that all the cold case victims were mothers, though," Tara replied. In fact, Tara had heard a study once that about 15–20% of women in the United States never even have children. That would mean that if the killer had twelve victims, it was likely he had more than one victim that never had children. But then another thought struck her.

"And wouldn't children just make the kill harder?" After all, if a victim had children, the killer would have to watch their moves as well to know when the victim would be home alone. Tara glanced down at the cold case files again, skimming each document, flipping to next each time she confirmed her theory. She looked up. "They were all killed alone," she added. Her heart drummed as Warren scanned the case files in front of him as well.

"You're right," he replied as he too flipped through each one, unable to remove his eyes from the papers in front of him.

In each case file, the victim had been a woman, killed in her own home, alone. For many, the kids were at school, the husband at work. For one victim, the kids were at sleepovers, the husband getting a drink with a friend. Another, the kid at soccer practice, the husband out for a run. Another, the wife divorced, the child at their father's. Tara scanned through each file. No one was home except the victim. There was now no doubt in her mind that the killer was targeting mothers.

She turned to Warren. "You think he only resurfaced to put the podcast to rest?"

Warren nodded, leaning forward. He stared at the wall. "I think that was definitely part of it. But like I said before, the podcast could've excited him too. He might've wanted to stir up mass hysteria."

Tara agreed. It was the same motive for killing Chloe that they had discussed earlier in the car. He liked the attention the podcast was giving him, and he craved more. He knew that killing off the podcasters would only lead people to wonder if it were him, and it would lay to rest what they were digging up along with it.

Tara wondered if it meant that he was done, that he had resurfaced only to say that he was back and then would fade again into the shadows. But deep down, she knew that was unlikely.

"If they were getting too close, then the podcast has to have answers," she added. She pulled out her phone, searching for the podcast. They had already begun to listen to it and hadn't heard anything that sparked their interest as a lead, but as Tara scrolled through the episodes, she knew they had barely scraped the surface. There were fifteen episodes total.

Warren leaned over her, staring down at the podcast as well. "Maybe work backwards," he said.

Tara nodded. He was right. The podcast was started over four months ago. If there were something that led the killer to believe they were getting too close, it would have been spoken about closer to when the murders occurred. Tara's finger hovered over the most recent episode and pressed *play*. Chloe Waterman's voice sailed through the room.

"This is your host, Chloe Waterman," it started before Serenity's voice cut in.

"And your guest cohost, Serenity Jackson," she added.

Chloe then jumped back in. "We want to thank our listeners for your continued support. It's because of you all that this podcast exists, which has kept a light on these unsolved cases. By doing so, we hope to give these women the justice they deserve." She paused a moment. "I'm happy to say that because of the recent breakthrough we had of an eyewitness coming forward, it has reopened this case. We hope that we are all one step closer to revealing the identity of this monster."

Tara knew exactly what she was referring to. It was the teenage girl who had seen a man in a victim's backyard years ago. Tara wondered if that was the only detail the killer needed to want to stop the podcast—an eyewitness coming forward. But her ears stayed glued to her phone. There had to have been something more, something that the podcasters had said, or why wouldn't he have just killed the eyewitness? Tara listened intently.

"Right now, it seems that the Nashville Police Department is looking into a sketch, seeing if there have been any other possible sightings. But as you know, many years have passed and there's not a whole lot of information to go off of," Serenity added. "We ask that if anyone has any other clues into who this person may be, please come forward," she continued.

The podcast then broke to a quick sponsored ad, and when it returned, Chloe once again dived back in. She recounted their previous episodes, all the information that they had gathered so far. She recounted what family members of victims had said. "So far we know that the killer was certainly organized. He was a skillful planner, he's careful, he carries out the murders carefully," she said, referring to the lack of evidence left behind; the lack of fingerprints. He left no sign of himself. "He prepped for these murders. We know this from the eyewitness and from family members saying victims mentioned objects being moved in their backyard prior to their murder." Tara had also remembered those details from the case files. There were two cases where a family member had recalled the victim mentioning a garbage pail moved, a recycling bin overturned and under a window. Each time, they didn't think too much of it until it was too late.

Chloe and Serenity continued to talk about details of each case, trying to make connections. Tara and Warren continued to listen, ears glued to every word. But each bit of information was something they had already heard or had already read in a case file.

Tara fast-forwarded bits and pieces and jumped into other episodes. She then paused at something Chloe said: "The killer could've even been someone who was a frequent visitor in the community. A deliveryman, a handyman, a bus driver, heck, even an ice-cream truck driver, who knows." They were discussing that the killer had been watching his victims, that he knew when each one would be home alone. It was the same theory that Tara and Warren had discussed. Tara paused the podcast and turned to Warren.

"Do you think that mention could've sparked the killer's interest?" Tara asked. If they had named his occupation, the killer could've gotten spooked.

"It's possible," Warren said with a shrug, but they both knew it wasn't enough to go on. It was only a mention, only a theory. There was no substantiating evidence that the killer was even someone within the community. But it did make Tara wonder about Alex. In many ways, he certainly fit the profile of the killer. She mentioned it to Warren.

"He does," he agreed.

But Tara also remembered his nervousness and the doubt that swirled within her because of it. "But he doesn't meet the profile of a serial killer."

Warren nodded. "It's true," he said, throwing his hands up. "But I mean, this killer has gone undetected for twenty years. He could just be really good at faking it."

Tara nodded. She too knew that no two killers were alike, and there were always those ones that surprised everyone, like Ted Bundy, a serial killer in the seventies who was charming, handsome, and had lasting relationships but still murdered numerous women undetected. Maybe Alex Debrowski was just as surprising of a killer.

Tara and Warren listened for hours until exhaustion got to be too much, and Warren looked down at his watch.

"What time is it?" Tara asked. She was struggling to focus on Chloe's words as her mind craved a break.

Warren cocked his head back, surprised. "Nine thirty." Tara looked up in surprise. They were so invested in the podcast that they hadn't even realized the passage of time. Her stomach suddenly growled to remind her that she hadn't had dinner.

Warren sighed. "I say we call it a night. We'll have Alex's handwriting results in the morning."

Tara nodded as she paused the podcast. As much as she wanted to keep digging, she knew they didn't have any leads. It was too late to question anyone, and they needed their rest. She just hoped that Alex Debrowski was the man they had been looking for. She stood up, following Warren to the door.

As she turned to say goodbye, he patted her on the shoulder. "We'll solve this case, Tara. If anyone can do it, we can, together."

Tara forced a smile. She wanted Warren's words to make her feel hopeful, but she could see from his own unconfident smile that he was also trying to convince himself. It made her uneasy. Warren was always confident. As they walked to the parking lot, an unsettling feeling came over her. Maybe they were in over their head.

Chapter Seventeen

Tara sat at the bar of the hotel and took a swig of her Sam Adams before scarfing the last bit of pasta. It was late on a weekday, and the bar had mostly cleared out. Only a couple sat close together on the other end. They were both dressed nicely. The woman wore a flowing black dress, the man a button-down shirt. It had the appearance of a first date, but Tara could tell by their closeness that it wasn't. He pushed her tightly curled bob behind her ear and kissed her cheek and then whispered something to her, making her laugh. Her white teeth glistened between her bright red lips.

Tara turned back to her beer and took another swig. She wasn't sure why she had come to the bar. It wasn't her usual scene. She usually enjoyed her own company in her hotel room when she was on cases, especially when she was this tired. But she needed a distraction. She needed to clear her head. The more she thought about Alex Debrowski, the more unsettled feeling took hold. She couldn't help but feel that his reactions were sincere, that he truly just got wrapped up in stealing when trying to help his mother.

But there was also something else she had been thinking about—the video doorbell. Why would the killer have gone to such lengths to be unnoticed prepping for the murder but fail to see the doorbell camera? *Yes, it was installed only a few days before the murder, but wouldn't the killer triple-check?* Tara wondered. *Especially after there had been reports of theft in the neighborhood?*

The television in the corner of the bar interrupted her train of thought. It was the news. Tara had been trying to ignore it, but each time she heard "Silent Stalker," her eyes shifted back to it. A female reporter stood just outside of Serenity Jackson's home, illuminated in lights from behind the camera. She spoke. "Often a guest on the well-known podcast *Unveiling the Silent Stalker*, Serenity Jackson had been looking into the cold case murders for months with her friend, Chloe Waterman. Both have now been murdered in a similar fashion, and it's believed that the Silent Stalker is back." The reporter turned toward the house. The camera zoomed in. "The killer snuck into their homes—"

"Anything else, Miss?"

Tara broke out of her trance to see the bartender standing in front of her, pulling her plate away. He motioned toward her beer, which was now finished. She shook her head. "Just the check, please," she replied.

He nodded, taking her plate and beer, and turned toward a cash register. The couple at the end of the bar had just finished their drinks, and they stood up. The woman once again laughing at something he said as he took her hand and led her out of the bar. Tara was now the only one left, and it made her feel weirdly lonely. She missed John. It was late, the bar was closing, and it made her realize that she hadn't checked in with him all day. She had partially been avoiding it, even though she missed him. She knew she needed to tell him about her father, about the conversation they had and that it gave her more reason to look into Mackenzie James. John wasn't going to like it, especially since her reason to keep digging was due to a warning from her father. But she also knew she had promised herself and John she would be truthful.

Tara paid for her meal and made her way to her hotel room. When she finally got there, she kicked off her shoes and sat on the bed. It felt good to be back in her room. It felt good to sit on the bed. She was more tired than ever and craved sleep. It was now almost ten thirty, and she contemplated if she should even call John. *He might not even be up*, she told herself. *What's the point?* But she quickly shook off the thought. She very much knew that John was usually going to bed around now, but he always stayed up a bit later to wait for her call. *I can't avoid him forever,* she thought. It wasn't fair to him, and she certainly wasn't doing either of them any favors by letting it hang over her head another day.

Without letting another thought seep into her head, she scooped up her phone, pulled up John's contact, and pressed *send*. The phone rang a few times, and for a moment Tara thought he wasn't going to answer and that she truly could avoid this conversation tonight. But then a groggy voice came through on the other end.

"I was wondering when you'd call," he said. Tara could picture his sleepy smile and his messy hair from just waking up.

"Sorry I woke you."

"You know never to be sorry about that."

A pit formed in Tara's stomach knowing that his excitement to speak to her would soon shift. She tried to keep the light mood going for a bit longer. She asked him about his day. He had gone to his parents' place for dinner.

"They missed you," he said. "They keep asking me when we're going to pick a date." He chuckled. They both knew his mom had the tendency to be pushy, but Tara knew without a doubt that her question bothered him. "I keep telling them we'll pick one soon." He sighed. "I don't know what else to tell them."

A silence fell between them. He was prompting her for a response, but Tara knew that what she needed to tell him would dictate it.

"I know," she started. "But you know what I need to do first."

He was silent. He knew enough not to push back, that Tara needed to find closure before picking a date, but he also didn't love the decision.

"I spoke to my dad," she added.

"What, when?"

"This morning. I called him." Her words were met by silence. He was waiting for her to elaborate. Tara sighed and continued. "I was surprised he even took my call, to be honest, but the fact that he did, I just know I struck a nerve. I'm close to answers; I can feel it."

"What did he say?" John asked with a mix of curiosity and concern.

Tara paused. She knew he wasn't going to like what came next. "He told me to stop looking into it. He said it's dangerous."

"Tara," John said in a sharp warning.

But Tara shot back, "You know I can't let this go. It'll eat me alive, John. Please stop pushing back on this." The words flew out of her in one breath, and she stopped to steady herself. It was the first time she had truly gotten angry, but she was getting tired of it. She understood where he was coming from. He was worried about her. But that wasn't what she needed now. "If we want to have a future without my past haunting me, then I need to deal with it now. I need your support on this." She paused a moment. "As my future husband," she added.

John remained silent for a moment and then sighed. Tara knew she had struck something inside him. His voice revealed resignation. "All right," he finally said. "I'll stop trying to convince you otherwise."

Tara's heart leapt. Even though she had hoped for his full support, there was certainly a part of her that doubted he would be able to give it to her. But hearing him say those words shot a dose of strength through her body. "Thank you," she replied, "because I'm not sure I'd be able to do this without you."

Her words hung between them, carrying a weight that they both understood. Tara was a strong person. She could certainly dig into her past without John, but it was him and their future together that made it purposeful. She wanted to be free from it so that she could be free with John.

"What do you need me to do?"

Tara sat up straighter in surprise. She didn't expect him to take an active role in it all, but she was thrilled that he cared to do so. "You don't have to do anything," she replied. "Like I said, I just need your support."

"Well, as your husband, if I'm going to give you my support, then I'm going to help you as much as I can."

Tara smiled. *Husband.* She liked the sound of it. But her smile faded as she remembered his question. She wasn't even sure what she needed him to do, or what *she* needed to do, for that matter. They had already discussed that her father had no living relatives and she couldn't think of anyone close that she could ask if they knew Mackenzie James. But then a thought struck her.

"That photo album I got from my grandmother's house...don't we have that somewhere?"

She had taken the album from her grandmother's house when she passed away. It was originally her mother's and included pictures that Tara's mother had taken when Tara was a child. She rarely looked at it. When she was younger, she did often to feel close to her mother, but as time went by and as she grew older and became more aware of what had happened, the photo album had become a source of pain rather than comfort. Tara hadn't looked at it since she took it from her grandmother's house years ago.

"I think we keep it in the closet on the top shelf," John responded. "What about it?"

"Maybe there's a picture or something in there that might help me know where to look next." It was a long shot, she thought. But she didn't have any other options or ideas. She wasn't expecting to see a picture of Mackenzie, even though she hoped it would be that easy, but she wondered if she would maybe see someone that she had forgotten. After all, it had taken her years even to remember the detail about her past that had sparked her even visiting her father in the first place—that she had suspected that someone else was in the room the night her father murdered her mother.

"Hold on," John said as Tara heard him place the phone down and then his feet shuffling down the hall. A moment later he returned. "I'll FaceTime you," he added.

Her phone rang seconds later. A smiling John with the beginnings of a five o'clock shadow stared back at her. "You need to shave," she joked.

He chuckled. "It's nice to see you too," he replied. Tara smiled in return, and he beamed wider.

But then his eyes moved to something below the phone, and the smile faded. He flipped the camera so Tara could see what he was looking at. Staring back at her was the photo album. It was just like she remembered it, old and brown. The corners were bent. Some pages were beginning to hang too far out of the album from years of being turned and pulled.

"Should I just start flipping through them?"

"I'll just tell you when I need you to stop."

John turned to the first page. Tara's baby pictures were staring back at her. Her in her mom's arms at the hospital, her dad standing over her. Both smiling wide. A knot twisted in Tara's stomach. She scanned the others, pictures of her footprints, of her sleeping on her mom's chest at home, her mom smiling at the camera, her first bath, her first smiles, her first food.

But at each turn of the page, the pictures get darker. Her mom's smile faded. Her dad's eyes looked more bloodshot, like he had been drinking, and then leapt in time to where it looked like no pictures were taken at all.

"Slow down," Tara said. His page-flipping had picked up speed at Tara's silence.

But her command made him now flip exaggerating slow. "Is this better?" he asked cheekily.

Tara rolled her eyes. But as she looked back down at the images, her playfulness vanished. "Stop."

John's fingers moved from the pages and he hovered the phone closer. Tara focused on a picture placed between two others. It was an image of her father sitting in the backyard on a lawn chair, a beer in hand, a drunk grin on his face. Tara sat nearby in a small sit-me-up chair, grinning at the camera. Her mother must've taken the photo. But it wasn't the image of herself or her father that caught her eye. It was the person sitting across from him.

Right across from him in an identical lawn chair, holding a beer in his hand as well, sat a man. He was mid-laugh, his head cocked backward. But Tara could still see the blonde seventies mustache just below his nose, and the slightly lighter combed-over hair on top of his head. He wore a beat-up shirt that was only buttoned up halfway, revealing the hair on his chest.

"That guy," Tara said. "I remember him. He was my dad's friend." She had forgotten all about him. He didn't come around often, but every once in a while on a weekend when her dad was home, he would come over and do just what they were doing in the picture: sit and drink until the sun went down.

"Do you think your dad still talks to him?" John asked.

"I have no idea," she replied. The last she had ever seen him was when she was six years old, the year her mother was murdered. She didn't even remember his name. "I have no way of knowing either," she added, referring to whether her father still talked to him. "I do remember where he lived, though. Maybe he still lives there." She couldn't forget. She had been there a few times, just in passing. He lived across the street from them in a small red brick house. The few times Tara's father never came home, when her mother knew he wasn't on one of his work trips, when he had gotten too drunk at a bar, Tara's mother would go over to the man's house with Tara in tow to see if he was there. But he never was.

"It's worth a shot," John replied. She could hear the hesitation in his voice, but he was trying desperately to hide it. "When would you go?"

Tara sighed. She knew she wasn't going any time soon. "As soon as this case is over," she replied. At the thought, she checked the time. It was eleven. She sighed. Her eyes felt heavy, and she was suddenly annoyed at herself that she wasn't already in bed. She was exhausted and needed to be well rested for this case. "I should really get to bed."

John agreed. "Don't let it keep you up," he said. They said goodnight, but his words hung in the air. He was right; she couldn't let it keep her up. She needed sleep; she needed to stay focused on this case. But her body and mind didn't need convincing. Tara's eyes grew heavy, and before she could even turn out the light, she fell into a deep sleep.

***

The crisp, cool air swirled the autumn leaves into the air like a small tornado until they settled once again gently by her feet. Tara loved this time of year. The start of school. Carving pumpkins with her mother and apple picking. She loved the way the wind made the tip of her nose cold, but the sun still beat down, making her feel warm in between each gust.

Tara held her mother's hand, which was warm— too warm for the cold that they stood in. It was slick with sweat—a sweat only stress would cause. They walked briskly down the road in silence. They had just stepped off their yard. And as Tara looked up at her mother, every bit of happiness vanished. Her mother's eyes were fixed forward. Her jaw was clenched in anger. Tara didn't know why; she didn't understand why she was angry, but she knew that was why she held her hand so tight.

Fear bubbled up at the thought that she might be in trouble. But she didn't dare to ask. She had never seen her mother with such focus, such intensity. She replayed every detail of that morning in her head. Her mother forgetting to make her breakfast, staring into her cup of coffee as if she was lost in it, until Tara finally asked her and she threw some toast in a toaster, buttered it, and gave it to her. Tara had thought she was in trouble then too. Her mother never gave her just toast for breakfast. It was always eggs or pancakes, or sometimes something extra special. She always made a big effort to make Tara happy, but today it was as if she was barely even in the room.

Tara stared straight ahead, putting one foot in front of the other as her mother led her across the street and then to the red-brick house. Tara had never been to that house before, but she knew her father's friend lived there. They walked briskly up the steps, and her mother pounded her fist against the door.

Within moments, the door swung open. The man with the blonde mustache stood in front of them. His face fell instantly. His eyes grew wide when he saw Tara's mother's face.

"Where is he?" she demanded. "He didn't come home last night."

He already had a beer in his hand, still in his pajama pants and a t-shirt. It was still well before noon.

He shook his head. "He wouldn't like you coming over here asking these questions," he replied.

"Where is he?" she demanded again, paying no heed to his remark.

He shrugged. His voice softened. "I don't know," he replied. His eyes fell to his feet.

"You're lying." Emotion seeped into her voice. She was about to cry, but she looked down at Tara's fearful face and her body stiffened. She took a deep breath. "Please," she added.

"I don't know," he said again. He looked from Tara's mother to Tara. He seemed pained. Tara could see it too; he was lying. "But I won't tell him you were here," he added.

Tara eyes popped open but instantly squinted at the bedside light she had forgotten to turn off. She turned over, looking at her phone. It was midnight and her heart drummed. She had remembered that day, the day her mother went over to her father's friend's house. It was the first of a few more, but Tara had never thought too much about it. It was the norm for her as a child. Her father getting drunk at bar, passing out somewhere, only to return home later the next day. And then there were his work trips. It was common for her father not to be there, but she didn't understand at the time that it wasn't normal. Now, looking back, it occurred to her that those moments on the doorstep of the man with the blonde mustache were the only moments that Tara had seen her mother angry and not just scared. Tara had to assume she trusted him, that he wouldn't go in run to Tara's father and tell him that his wife had pounded on his door. Surely, that would've resulted in a beating.

Tara stared unblinking in front of her, focused on the silent television. There was a fire in her mother's eyes that day, and sorrow in the man's. It was as if something unspoken sat between them, tying them together but unable to voice the strand that laced them. *She must've suspected something,* Tara said to herself. *And he knew that her suspicions were justified.* The only question was what it was and if her mother's suspicions were true or if the truth was far worse.

Chapter Eighteen

Adeline took a sip of her wine and curled up closer under Derek's arm, resting her head on his chest. They were watching a movie, eyes focused on the television in front of them that lit up Adeline's dark living room. They were watching a movie they both hadn't seen but wanted to and they promised they would watch it together. It was the third time Derek had come over. They had been dating for three months now, but it had taken her a while to finally invite him. After all, she hadn't been with another man since Terrence, her ex-husband. It felt strange starting over; it felt somewhat wrong to have a new man in her home where her children lived and were still angry about the divorce themselves. Her children still didn't know about Derek. Her ex-husband didn't know. No one did. She only had him over when her kids were at their father's, and she didn't know when she'd even have the courage to tell them.

Derek kissed the top her head, sending a wave of warmth through her body, along with stifling guilt. Part of her wanted him to leave, the other part craved for him to stay. She felt guilty that she would once again tell him he needed to go. The movie was nearing the end, Adeline's eyes were growing heavy, and as she looked up at Derek, she saw him close his eyes briefly. She shook him.

"Don't you fall asleep on me." She laughed.

He cocked his head upright, eyes popping open, and flashed his perfectly white smile. "I'm not falling asleep," he said playfully.

Adeline smiled and sat upright, placing her glass of wine on the coffee table in front of her. She wasn't going to let him fall asleep. Not here. And she certainly wasn't going to let him get too drowsy to drive home. Her kids wouldn't be back until the afternoon tomorrow, but she just wasn't ready for him to spend the night.

"Maybe we should call it a night," she said.

Derek's smile faded slightly, but he tried to hang on to it, to mask the disappointment. It was the same reaction Adeline had seen the other two times he had come over and she had asked him to leave. She felt badly that every time he had been hopeful, and each time she crushed it the same way. He never mentioned anything about wanting to stay the night. He was a gentleman, but Adeline knew. He had mentioned he wanted to meet her kids, that he wanted to move things along with her, but each time she pushed back. She was lucky. Most men would've gotten frustrated and moved on. But Derek was different. He was patient. He understood where she was coming from. He had been divorced himself years ago, and so he understood the grieving process.

"We can get breakfast tomorrow," she added, hoping to bring forth his smile once again.

"I'd like that," he replied. He leaned over and kissed her once more before standing to retrieve his shoes.

"It'll just have to be early, if you don't mind. Like seven thirty. The kids come home at ten." She scrunched her face, revealing she too knew it was a lot to ask. It was already midnight. But she didn't want to risk her kids seeing Derek drop her home, nor did she want her ex to see. They still had yet to cross the bridge of mutual understanding that they were seeing other people.

Derek laughed. "It's early, but anything for you," he said as he grabbed his jacket and slipped on his boots.

Adeline smiled, kissed him goodnight one last time, and watched him step out in to the dark. Moments later, Derek's car was gone, silence sat heavy around her, and sleep pulled her into bed.

***

Adeline's eyes popped open. She wasn't sure what she had heard, but she knew she heard something. It was a thump, something hitting the ground. But as she stared into the darkness, listening to the silence, she wondered if it was all but a dream that had awoken her.

She listened a moment longer, but when no sound returned, her eyes grew heavy once again until they fluttered closed. But just when she was about to drift into sleep, she heard something more. The shuffling of feet down the hall. It was faint, as if the footsteps were cautiously light, but the sound was unmistakable. Adeline felt a rush of fear. She sat upright. *Could it be Joshua?*

"Joshua?" she called to her son, but no voice replied. The sound of feet stopped abruptly. Adeline stared in a panic at the open door, her body frozen. She could just see out into the hallway, but no one was there. "Who's there?" she called again, but once more she was met with no response.

A creak of a floorboard sounded just outside her door, sending a paralyzing panic through her. Her heart felt as if it would burst through her chest. She looked over at the window in her bedroom. She was on the second floor, but she could try.

She looked back at the doorframe once more, and panic seized her. She gasped, her head swirled into a haze. In front of her, taking up the size of the doorframe, stood a dark, hooded figure.

She sprang up, but he lunged at her, pinning her down on the bed. Something pierced her abdomen, and excruciating pain forced the breath from her body. Another and another until her body went numb, her vision darkened, and she didn't feel anything more at all.

Chapter Nineteen

Tara took a sip of coffee before throwing her hair up into a tight ponytail. As she turned to the mirror in her hotel room, she sighed. She was exhausted, and she looked it. While coffee helped, it failed to give her the boost she needed. She had tossed and turned ever since her dream in the middle of the night. She must've dozed back off at some point, but when she did, she had already lost the opportunity for the hours of sleep she needed.

All night, she had wondered about her father's friend, about the confrontation with Tara's mother. She wanted desperately to find him, to ask him. For all she knew, they still spoke. She just hoped he still lived in the same house. But as the obsession crept into her mind, she desperately shook it off. *Focus,* she told herself. She needed to give this case her full attention.

She sat on the edge of the bed and slipped on her shoes. She had already spoken to Warren. He had spoken to the forensics handwriting expert, and they had determined that they did not think the handwriting on the wall matched Alex Debrowski's due to a differentiation in stroke patterns. The killer uniquely curled the end of almost every letter.

Tara finished tying her shoes and sighed. They were starting over. They had no leads, nothing to go off of. She had agreed to meet Warren downstairs. They were going to expand their search for cameras, looking at everyone's yards within a mile radius of the victims' homes. It was their only hope that someone had captured something in their back or front yard. Before she headed down to meet Warren, she scooped up her phone sitting next to her on the bed. She had told Warren she would call the chief. If they were going to do such a wide search, they needed the help of as many police officers as possible.

Tara placed the call and pressed the phone to her ear as she stood up and grabbed her room key from the table in front of her. As she shut the door to her room, the chief's voice burst through the phone.

"Agent Mills," he said in a hurry.

Tara let go of the door, letting it slam shut behind her. Her feet stopped moving. She could already hear in his voice that something was wrong.

"What is it?"

"I was just about to call you. There's been another victim."

***

Tara looked down at the GPS as they neared the home. They were less than a mile away from the crime scene, which was in the Bellevue neighborhood of

Nashville. It was about twenty minutes from Serenity's home.

Tara looked over at Warren. He gripped the steering wheel, staring at the road in fury. They both felt it—the anger, the frustration, the disappointment in themselves. There was no denying it now; they couldn't stop themselves from taking blame. Another life had been lost, and they couldn't help but feel guilty.

They didn't know much yet. The chief hadn't even arrived at the scene. He was on his way when Tara called. All he had heard was that the victim's boyfriend had gone to pick her up, only to find her dead in her bed with the same wording on the wall that had been at the other scenes. It was all the chief needed to hear to want the FBI there. She was forty-two and had two children on her own.

"We should have the chief send his cops out, checking for cameras," Warren said.

Tara nodded. It was their original plan before they got called to the crime scene, but now the area to search got a bit wider. "This is more than the podcast now," he added.

He was right, and at the thought, Tara's heart sank. They had never settled on the thought that the killer's motivation was just to quiet down the noise from the podcast, but it had been their suspicion. Now, they knew without a doubt that the killer was on a new spree, and he wasn't about to stop.

He had struck another mother. It was a pattern that they were almost certain of, but Serenity still didn't fit it. But there was another pattern that struck Tara's mind as well.

"She had a boyfriend," Tara stared. "It sounds like no one was home with her. I'm assuming she's divorced or separated." It was similar to the other victims. Chloe was separated, Serenity was a widow. In many of the cold cases, although not all, many victims were separated or divorced as well.

Warren nodded. He knew what she was getting at. "My guess is it's convenience. He knows no one is home. It makes it easier to get to these women, and if they don't have a live-in partner, even better." He shrugged with a sigh, staring straight at the road as they neared the victim's house.

Tara agreed. It was her thought as well. He was looking for women who were accessible. "We should send an alert to the public to stay with a friend or a relative. Hopefully it will make them less of a target."

Warren agreed. "We'll let the chief know to alert the media."

At his words, the car neared the end of a cul de sac. Police vehicles lined the street. No news crews were there, but Tara knew it was only a matter of time before they caught wind of the story.

They pulled up to a large two-story brick home with a long driveway that extended from a two-car garage. A man hunched over, his hands on his knees stood in the front lawn, Chief Meyers standing over him with two other officers. His body shook with each hysterical cry, with each gasp for air. He wore a button-down shirt that fit snugly on his broad shoulders. Tara assumed it was her boyfriend, the man that found her.

Tara and Warren stepped out of the car, and Chief Meyers's eyes shot up and then back down to the man.

He gave the man a quick pat on the back as he stared painfully at the man whose life had clearly just been shattered, and then stepped away toward Warren and Tara. The officers closed in, trying to get the man to sit down.

"That's the boyfriend?" Tara asked as they stepped out of earshot. They all glanced toward the man with the officer, and the chief nodded. "Were you able to get anything out of him?"

The chief sighed, eyes still focused on the man. "In bits and pieces," he started with a shrug. "He was here last night, watching a movie but left around 1:00 a.m. He then came back around seven to pick her up for breakfast. Apparently, she's recently divorced. Her kids don't know about him yet, so they were going out to breakfast before they got home from their dad's."

Tara felt her stomach twist. "Do they know yet?"

"We spoke to her ex-husband. They know." His face fell to his feet.

One of the officers walked toward them, and the chief looked up. "How's he doing?" he asked.

The officer shrugged and tilted his head. They all knew that he wasn't doing well. "We got him to sit at least," he replied. Tara looked over to see the man sitting in the grass, knees hugged to his chest, hands clasping his dark hair hard as if he were pulling it from his head.

The chief nodded. "See if you can get an eyewitness report from him." The officer nodded and turned back toward the man crouched in the grass. The chief turned to Tara and Warren. "I'll show you guys inside."

Tara's stomach twisted into a knot as they walked past the witness and up the stairs of the home and through the front door that had a wreath of yellow daisies hanging upon it and a map that said *Welcome* just before it. She braced herself. She knew from the last crime scene how messy and ruthless this killer was and that the picturesque entrance was only a façade for what they were about to see. The home opened into a large white living room of vaulted ceilings with dark wood accent beams. A white brick fireplace was straight across from the front door, with two entryways on either side. One led to an open kitchen, the other to a hallway. The room was impeccably clean and neat, and it gave Tara an unsettled feeling. It was like seeing a beautiful sunset before a storm would blow through. It was satisfying but misleading in every possible way.

Forensics was already there, scanning the floor, dusting the room for fingerprints. Chief Meyers sighed again, leading them up a set of stairs to the right of the room and onto the second floor.

"Any camera on her property?" Warren asked.

The chief shook his head. "We checked, nothing." He turned into a room, Tara and Warren right behind him, but all their feet stopped short once they laid their eyes on what was in front of them. Chief Meyers instinctively looked away. Tara's stomach churned. Warren stared blankly and swallowed hard.

The victim's long, curly black hair was draped over the side of the bed. Her legs jutted out from the oversized t-shirt she had been sleeping in. Her leg twisted in the white sheets, now died red underneath her. Blood splattered on the walls and on the floor.

Tara and Warren moved closer, inspecting the victim. Tara leaned over the bed. Numerous holes lined her abdomen where she had been brutally stabbed. Her hands were stuck in a clenched position, as if they were once gripping the bed. Just above the headboard, written in blood across the white wall, was the same message seen at the other scene: *A heart to mold until it crumbles.*

Tara stepped back and followed Warren's gaze, which had moved toward an open window on one side of the bed. He walked toward it and peered out. Tara did the same. They were a story high, too high for the killer to gain access. He had to have entered some other way, Tara assumed, from some other part of the house. "Any other windows open or unlocked?"

The chief shook his head. "My guys took a look in the back too. Didn't see anything out of the ordinary. Not like the last house." He was referring to the recycling bin turned over and placed under the window of Serenity Jackson's home. "But I don't think he really needed to stage anything. The basement window sits just above the foundation. He could've easily slid in, and it was unlocked. Forensics is checking for fibers and prints."

Tara nodded, her eyes lingering on the victim. "How old are her children?"

The chief's eyes fell to the floor. "Eight and eleven."

Tara's eyes fell as well. She couldn't bear to look at the victim as the thought of the woman's children became unbearable. She was just grateful that they hadn't found her, not like the first victim's child. Tara turned on her heels, exiting the room with Warren and the chief behind her. She turned to both of them. Warren stared at her, anger brewing as he bit his lower lip and shook his head. She knew what he was thinking. Another mother was taken from her kids. They couldn't allow this to happen again.

"Let's check the backyard once more, then let's go see what this boyfriend knows," he said.

Tara nodded. She just hoped that the boyfriend was now able to speak and that he had information that could be a lead.

***

Tara and Warren stood on the front lawn, the boyfriend sitting on the ground in front of them. They had taken a look through the backyard, but just as the chief had mentioned, there was nothing that seemed suspicious or out of place. Tara took a look around her. There were neighbors out now. A couple stood at the edge of the lawn talking to the two officers, trying to get information. Every once in awhile, they peered over the officer's shoulder at the boyfriend sitting disheveled in the grass. He eyed them as well, over his hands that covered his mouth, trying to gain a hold of his emotions.

Warren nodded to the driveway. "Want to talk over here?"

The man nodded as he peered over to it. There was a car parked in the driveway, Adeline's, and at the sight of it, he almost began to cry once more, but he took a deep breath instead, steadying himself. He stood up. He was of average height, shorter that

Warren but taller than Tara. He followed them across the lawn.

Once they stood between the car and the garage in an effort to shield themselves from attention, Tara spoke. "You were with her last night?"

The man nodded as he stared at her blankly, his eyes swollen and red. He was in shock. It was like looking at a shell of a person.

"I told the other officers already. I got here around eight, and we watched a movie. I stayed till one and left. We were supposed to go to breakfast this morning," he replied.

"Did she ever mention being afraid or feeling like someone was watching her?" Tara asked.

He shook his head. "Of course, we knew about the Silent Stalker from the news, but we just never thought…" He trailed off.

Tara asked more questions. If she had noticed anything moved in her backyard, if she had mentioned anyone that seemed creepy, but at each question, he shook his head.

"Do you happen to know if she ever keeps her basement window open?" Tara finally asked. They had taken a look at the window when they were in the backyard. The chief was right. It sat just above the foundation and was about three feet by two feet. It was large enough for a person to slide through, and it led directly to a finished basement with a set of stairs to the main floor.

He knitted his brows, looking at them in confusion, but then his eyes opened wide in fear.

"You think he came through there?"

"We're not sure," Tara replied.

The man sighed, bringing his hand to his head in frustration. He shook his head. "She used to keep it open to help with the humidity in the basement. It gets damp down there pretty easily. But she told me she would keep it closed and locked once we heard about the Silent Stalker." He paused a moment, staring out into the distance. "Shit," he finally blurted. Tears began to well once more. "There were a couple times she would leave it open during the day and go close it. I always checked to make sure she did. But last night I didn't." His hands covered his face again as sobbing overwhelmed him.

Tara and Warren looked at each other. But it still did not give them much to go on. Chief Meyers was having cops search the area for cameras, Forensics was dusting for fingerprints, and scanning the home for fibers. They still didn't have a lead. They needed to talk to the people who knew her best. They needed to talk to her family.

Chapter Twenty

Tara and Warren pulled into the driveway of the ex-husband's home in Fairview, a city within Nashville about a half hour from the victim's home. It was another large farmhouse, with a large, protruding porch. The house was white with black shutters and a black matching door.

Tara exchanged a quick glance with Warren as he turned the car off. He sighed. The family already knew that they were coming. The chief had given them a heads-up, but it didn't lessen the difficulty of the situation. Talking to a victim's family was always hard, but with children involved, it was especially heartbreaking.

"Let's just hope we can get them justice," Warren said with a nod.

Tara nodded. It was the least they could do. She just hoped the family was ready to speak too and that what they said provided a lead.

Tara stepped out of the car, and Warren followed as they made their way to the front door. She knocked, and within moments a man answered. He wore black-rimmed glasses that sat on a straight, thin nose. His eyes were red, the skin around them swollen from crying. He stared blankly at them for a moment as the weeping of children could be heard behind him. It was as if for a moment it didn't register who they were, or his mind had drifted somewhere else completely, until Tara flashed a badge. At the sight of it, he closed his eyes for a second and took a breath he had forgotten to take. He nodded and opened the door wider.

"Come in," he said as he led them into a large mudroom with dark hardwood floors and light gray walls. A long white bench lined one portion of the wall, coat hangers above it, and upon the bench sat two duffle bags. Tara had no doubt that they were the kids', packed and ready to go back to their mothers. But now, time stood still.

Tara pulled her eyes away, but the man had caught her gaze and looked at them a moment, sadness once again washing over him like a wave pulling him under. But then his eyes turned toward the other room, to where the muffled crying was coming from, and he straightened up, the emotion washing off his face just as quickly as it had appeared.

"One moment," he said to Tara and Warren as he raised his finger in the air and walked into the living room. Tara and Warren could see two young boys sitting on the couch. One was curled in a fetal position while the older one stroked his back, wiping tears from his eyes with his other hand.

The father crouched in front of them. He lowered his voice. "The FBI are here," he said. "We need to tell them all we know so they can find who did this.

Can you be strong for Mom?" he asked. He choked up slightly at the end, but he swallowed the emotion hard.

The younger boy sat up. The crying stopped. They both nodded in unison. The father leaned in, pulling their heads toward his in a huddle, and kissed their crowns. One last cry burst through the mouth of one of the children, but then he whispered something to them, and they both nodded again.

He pulled away and stood before them, the children's eyes wandering to the entryway where Tara and Warren stood. They stared at them in bewilderment, fear dancing in their eyes. They looked lost, broken. Every few seconds the youngest's lip would quiver as he stifled tears.

The ex-husband waved Tara and Warren into the room. The room was of average size but felt tight with the number of people and the layout of furniture, centered around a coffee table. The two boys sat on a couch, their father in a chair at the end of the coffee table. A loveseat sat directly across from him. Tara and Warren took a seat on it.

A stifling silence sat heavy in the room as all three sets of eyes peered at them.

"I don't think we got your name," Tara started.

The man's hands clutched the end of the armrest, and he pulled himself forward slightly with a startled look. It was as if it was against his character not to introduce himself, and he was startled that it had gone unnoticed by him. He relaxed slightly and sighed. He knew he didn't understand anything about himself now. "Ernie," he replied. He then gestured toward his children. "Joshua," he said, motioning to the youngest, "and Eugene," he added, motioning to the oldest.

Both boys' eyes fell at the mention of their name. Both had sandy blond hair that hung just above their eyebrows. They looked very similar, except the older was larger. For the first time, Tara noticed that the oldest was wearing a soccer uniform. He still had shin guards on and long socks. The number twelve was patched onto one side of his chest. But his uniform was clean. It had no marks of dirt or grass, revealing that he had never made it the game.

"Do you mind if we ask them a couple questions?" Tara asked the father.

He shook his head, his eyes falling to the ground. He knew it was necessary, but of course he didn't love the idea.

Tara turned to the boys. She needed to be delicate. "Did your mom ever mention anyone recently? Maybe someone that she saw outside near your house?" It was clear that the killer had been watching his victims. He knew when they were home, when they weren't, and when they were the only one in the house.

The youngest sniffled, wiping a tear from his eye, and looked at his older brother, who was struggling to hold back tears too. He shrugged and shook his head.

"Did she ever have anyone over? Maybe someone working on the house or outside?"

Again, they shook their heads in unison.

"Did she ever mention seeing something outside or inside the house that might've been moved or not in its right place?" Tara asked. She remembered the overturned recycling bin at the last scene. It was likely the killer had somehow tried to set up this murder as well for easy entry and departure.

Once again, the boys shook their heads, and Tara's hopes sank. But then the youngest perked up. "She was wondering where my ice cream pop went once. We got it from the ice cream truck, and I was supposed to save it until after dinner, but it was gone."

At the mention, the oldest couldn't hold his tears any longer. "That was me. I ate it," he burst out. The sudden guilt and not being able to ever confess it to his mother sat heavy on him.

The youngest stared blankly at him. Tara assumed he would normally throw a fit, but instead he leaned in, wrapping his arms around his brother. "It's okay," he said. "I'm not mad."

The father stood up and wrapped his arms around both his boys. He turned his head back to Tara and Warren. "I think they've had enough for today."

Tara and Warren both nodded. They were only able to ask a few questions, and the answers did not amount anything, but they understood. "We'd like to be able to talk with you in private too," Tara added.

The father nodded and then tried to console his sons before shuffling them out of the room. Moments later, he returned but walked straight into the kitchen, poured himself something, and sat back down in his chair. He took a swig of what looked like gin.

"I hope you don't mind," he said when he placed the glass down. "I don't usually drink, and definitely not at this time, but I need something." Muffled crying trailed through the house from upstairs, and he took another swig.

He didn't seem like an alcoholic. Tara certainly knew how to spot one. There were no open bottles anywhere, no glasses left finished. He wasn't drunk, and he sipped his liquor slowly.

"Did you and Adeline still talk?" Tara asked.

He sighed. "No more than what concerned the kids." He paused for a moment, swirling his drink. "There really wasn't much else to talk about. I mean, we're divorced." The mention caused him to wince.

"Did the boys ever mention anyone to you? Maybe someone she had spoken to? Or someone that she seemed afraid of?"

He shook his head and shrugged. "I mean, we all didn't even know about her boyfriend. If she was scared of anyone, she'd probably shield that from the kids too."

Tara asked him a few more questions—if the boys ever mentioned someone they were afraid of, if he ever sensed fear from them or their mother, if he knew if anyone ever did work on her house. But each time, he shook his head.

When they finally exhausted their efforts, Tara and Warren thanked him. Moments later, they stood in the driveway, walking to their car. Tara turned to Warren, but he didn't even notice her movement. His eyes were focused in front of him, his face twisted in concentration. He looked desperate for answers, as if he were searching every corner of his mind for connections and theories. She was about to snap him out of it so they could figure out what their next move should be when his phone rang.

Life sprang to his face as he fumbled in his pocket. He looked at the name flashing on the screen as he swung open the car door, took a seat inside, and pressed the phone to his ear. Tara got in the car as well.

"Where was it?" he asked. His eyes were wide.

Tara's heartbeat intensified. *A lead,* she thought. *They found something.* She could see the hope spring life into his face.

"We'll meet you at the station," he added. He hung up and swiftly started the car. He started backing out of the driveway as he spoke to Tara. "They found a fingerprint," he said. A smile seeped onto his lips.

***

Tara and Warren sat in the station, waiting for the fingerprint to be run in AFIS system to see if anyone within it matched the fingerprint found in the home. It was a partial fingerprint, but the fingerprint expert had determined it was enough to deem a person a match if found. And it was where it was found that spiked Warren and Tara's interest. It was found on the outside of the basement window.

Tara looked down at the cold case files. They had been waiting for two hours and contemplating theories in the meantime. Another mother had been murdered. They were convinced it meant something and that Serenity was just a loose end from the podcast.

"Maybe someone who has had relationship issues," Tara proposed as she sat back in her chair, her eyes drifting momentarily to the door, hoping to see movement. She looked back at Warren when there wasn't any.

Warren shrugged. "That would bring meaning to the message," he replied, referring to the one written in blood at each crime scene. Tara repeated in in her head. *A heart to mold until it crumbles.* "He could be someone who had failed relationships and wanted to seek revenge on all women as a result."

Warren nodded again. "Or it could have something to do with some sort of childhood trauma," he proposed. "That could be why he's seeking mothers."

It was a valid point and one that Tara had thought about as well. Each woman could be a surrogate for his mother as he lived out a desire related to his childhood. As Tara looked back down at the case files in front of her, a knock sounded on the door. Both Tara and Warren spun in their seats to see the fingerprint analyst swing open the door and stand before them. She was short, with straight shoulder-length hair and bangs cut evenly just above her dark-rimmed glasses. She held papers and stared at them with a satisfied smile. Tara stiffened.

"We have a match," she said as she placed the papers down in front of them.

Tara's eyes darted to them to see an image of a man staring back at her. His hair was ruffled, his eyes sunken and tired-looking, a sheepish grin in his stubbly face. It was mug shot.

"He's a handyman. He was in the system for domestic violence, arrested twice now, both within the past six months. The most recent was a few weeks ago."

He was clearly a violent person. He was violent toward women. And the sudden increase of violence at home would correlate with the increase in violence elsewhere. It was something they had discussed before, that sometimes serial killers went dormant if something within their personal life was fulfilling their desires, but now what if it wasn't?

"How old is he?" Warren asked.

"Forty-four," the analyst replied.

Tara scanned the criminal report. He was the owner of Handy Shultz, located in East Nashville. He had owned the business since he was eighteen.

Tara thanked the analyst. She nodded and left the room. Tara pointed out the details on the report to Warren. "He's owned this business since before the first cold case crime occurred," Tara said. It didn't seem like a coincidence. It would give the killer easy access to his victims. "It would make sense why he knew so much about his victims, and when they would be alone," she added. "He'd easily be able to scope out his opportunity."

Warren nodded, but he was staring at the cold case files in front of him, quickly scanning each one before moving to the next. It was as if he was searching for something. He didn't blink, his eyes were so steadily focused.

"What is it?" Tara asked.

At first it was if he didn't hear her, but then he spoke, eyes still scanning the papers. "Handy Shultz. I saw that somewhere," he replied. He slid a case file closer to him, reading it quickly, "Here," he said. He pointed excitedly at a line on the paper. He pushed it toward her, and she looked down to read it. *Handy Shultz*. It was written as the employer of a victim's husband. Tara looked up.

"You think they worked together?" she asked.

Warren nodded. "Looks like it. I say we give him a call. But first we should call Adeline's boyfriend. He might know if she had a handyman working on the house. He might be able to shed some more recent light on him."

Tara agreed, pulled out her phone, and dialed the boyfriend's number, placing it on speaker. He picked up promptly.

"Did you find something?" he asked without even a hello. He must've had Tara's number saved. She had given it to him and told him to call her if he remembered anything of importance.

"Not quite," she replied. She didn't want to get his hopes up, and he sighed. "We just wanted to ask you a couple questions. Do you know if Adeline had anything fixed within her home recently?"

"I already told you. She hasn't had any work done to her house recently," he replied.

"Does the name Handy Shultz sound familiar?"

He paused a moment. "Yeah, it does, actually." Tara and Warren shared a look. They both could feel that they were on the brink of something. "Why do you ask?"

Tara ignored his question. "Do you know why it sounds familiar?"

The man sighed. "A few months ago, there was a leak in her basement from a pipe. I recommended it to her. I've heard good things about him."

"Did she ever say how she felt about him? If she got weird vibes from him at all?"

He thought for a moment. "Not in particular. She said he seemed nice, I think. But..." he paused a second. "I do remember that he complimented her

224

looks. Said she was pretty or something, and it made her feel a bit uncomfortable." He paused again. "Why, do you think he has something to do with this?" His voice was laced with fear. It was fear of guilt, that he had recommended this handyman.

"We're just covering our bases right now," Tara replied. "We don't have any definitive information."

The man sighed again. Tara exchanged another quick glance with Warren. As much as they wanted to give him answers, they knew that they needed to keep any information confidential for now to protect the investigation. Last thing they needed was the victim's boyfriend knocking on the handyman's office in a rage, tipping him off. Plus, fingerprints could last up to forty years on a nonporous surface such as a window, and they had no way of determining how long it had been there. For all they knew, it was simply there because he had done work in the basement.

Tara thanked him. "We'll let you know as soon as we have any information," she said. The phone call ended, and Tara turned to Warren. "Should we try the husband of the cold case victim?" Warren nodded as he entered the number into the phone.

Tara stared down at the case file. A picture of the victim stared back at her. Her name was Victoria Monet. She was thirty-five and strikingly beautiful. She wore hoop earrings, which were popular in early 2000s. They peaked through curly dark brown hair that framed her high cheekbones. She smiled with perfectly white teeth, her lips crimson. She was the third victim of the Silent Stalker. She was home alone while her husband and kids went on a camping trip without her. It was supposed to be a weekend of relaxation. She was killed the Friday night after they left. Her body was found two days later by her husband. Luckily, the kids hadn't yet entered the home.

Warren placed the phone on speaker. It rang a few times, until a man picked up.

"Is this Luis Monet?" Warren asked.

The man hesitated. "Who's asking?"

"I'm sorry to bother you," Warren started. "This is Agent Frank Warren and my partner with the FBI. As I'm sure you've heard, the Silent Stalker case has been reopened. We were hoping we could just ask you a few questions that might help the case."

The man sighed. "I mean, if it's really going to help the case," he replied. There was a hint of sarcasm, of doubt. He sounded defeated yet numb. Tar knew it was from years of wanting justice, only to be disappointed, knowing that his wife's killer still walked free, and that each year gone by was another he should never have been given. "Just give me a moment," he added before placing the phone down. They could both hear heavy machinery in the background, as if he were at a construction site. He said something inaudible to someone, then the sounds grew quieter, as if he were walking away. "I'm just at work, so I can't talk long," he finally said.

Tara got the sense he felt this was a waste of time. She was certain it was a defense mechanism. He didn't want to get his hopes up. After all, his wife's murder had been left unsolved for close to twenty years.

"From our understanding, you used to work for Eddie Shultz at Handy Shultz?" Warren asked.

The man was quiet for a moment. It wasn't a question he was expecting. "Yes, I did," he finally replied.

"And how long did you work there?" Warren asked.

"About three years. I quit a few months before my wife—" He couldn't finish his sentence. "You know what I mean." Tara could hear the flicker of a lighter and then him taking a puff off a cigarette.

"Why did you quit?" Warren asked.

The man let out a long exhale. "Why are you asking me all this?"

"We're just covering all our bases," Warren replied. "He did work at another victim's home."

The man took another drag. And then another. It was as if the question had a sparked a sudden anxiety. "You don't think—" he started but stopped himself. Tara knew what he was going to ask. But he also knew not to jump to conclusions. "I quit because I caught him sneaking a picture of my wife undressing when he was doing work at my house one day." Anger boiled through his words. "He was a womanizer, I knew that about him, but I never would've thought he would do something like that. I couldn't work for him after that."

"Where was she when he took the photo? And where was he?" Tara asked.

"She was in the bedroom. He was outside, peeking through the window. He was helping me put a new door in. I quit right on the spot. What I really wanted to do was punch him in the face, but I didn't want to do that in front of my wife."

Tara and Warren shared a look. Victoria was killed in her bedroom. They both knew that he could've either been taking pictures of her or of the room to plan. Or both.

Tara and Warren thanked him as they both stood from their chairs. They had a lead. Tara's heart fluttered with hope, and as they left the room, she wondered if after twenty years, they were finally going to unveil the Silent Stalker.

Chapter Twenty One

Tara and Warren arrived at a townhouse in East Nashville. Thick bushes lined the front porch of the grayish blue home up to where a cement pathway led to the front steps. Warren pulled the car in front. There was a Subaru parked in the driveway, and Tara could see light shining through the shades of the windows on the porch. She turned to Warren, but his eyes were focused on the house, tilting his head as if he were trying to see around it.

"It looks like they have a fenced-in backyard," he said, still staring out the car. Tara could see the cedar fencing. He turned to Tara. "We need to be aware of everything, every sound, every movement." He spoke urgently, as their lives depended on his words, and Tara knew there was a good chance they could.

She nodded. She knew what he was saying: if Eddie Shultz was home, there was a good chance he would make a run for it or do something rash. They needed to be prepared.

They stepped out of the car. Tara felt for her gun, making sure it was fully concealed under her shirt as they walked down the path and then up the stairs to the door. Purple perennials sat in two pots on either side of the door, with a mat that said *Home, Sweet Home* in between them. It gave Tara a strange feeling. It felt like they had painted a fake smile on the face of their home.

Tara knocked, and without any hesitation the door swung open and a woman stood before them, but she stopped the door from opening more when she saw who they were. It was as if she was expecting someone else. Her face fell and scrunched in confusion. Her hair was dyed platinum blonde in a short pixie cut. A long floral dress hung on her petite shoulders and swept the ground, exposing the lotus flower tattooed on her upper arm. And Tara could just make out a small studded nose ring that reflected in the sunlight. But there was something else about her that Tara's gaze lingered on. The skin around her eye was swollen and purple. It was the look of a fresh bruise.

The woman shifted uncomfortably at Tara's gaze, angling her body into her home, as if to hide what Tara saw, but no matter which way she shifted, the bruise was still exposed. "Can I help you?" she asked. She looked around them fearfully, but Tara sensed it wasn't fear for them. It was for whoever else she was expecting.

Tara flashed her badge, and the woman's eyes widened as she took a step back. "Is Eddie Shultz home?"

The woman looked back in forth between the two of them. Her lips parted, staring at them in complete shock. Her face tightened. "Is everything okay?"

"We think he might be able to help us with an investigation we're working on. Is he home?"

The woman hesitated a moment but then shook her head. "He's off today, but he had a gig down at a bar in town. He plays guitar."

"Well, would you be able to talk to us then? Maybe you can help us."

She tilted her head, contemplating the question. Her expression was mixed concern, curiosity, and fear as her eyes darted around where Tara and Warren stood. "Is this about the Silent Stalker case?" Tara wasn't surprised she had asked. It had been all over the news, updates on every morning, noon, and evening show.

Tara nodded. "We've been asking residents for any information on possible sightings," she replied. It wasn't the full truth. Tara wanted to pick her brain about her husband, but it was true that they lived only a couple of blocks from Serenity's home. It wasn't incorrect that they had been asking around the neighborhood. The chief currently had his officers doing exactly that.

"I don't know if that's a good idea," she started, but her words were interrupted by her phone, which had suddenly beeped. She reached for it on a table next to the door and read a text across the screen. As she read it, she instantly relaxed. She texted back and then looked up, the tension in her face erased as well. "Actually, I suppose it's okay." There was a hint of nervousness in her voice, but she continued. "I'd like to help as much as I can. Anything to get that creep off the streets." She shrugged. "I'm just not sure how much help I can be." She turned on her heels, waving them into her home. Tara got the sense that she truly did want to help. But there was something that had made her hesitate. It was fear, and Tara assumed it was the same fear she felt before she received the black eye. Tara knew abuse; she had lived with it, each quirk of fear. It was the same fear her mother had. The same hesitation. It dictated her every move. And it all made Tara even more suspicious of Eddie Shultz.

The woman's floral dress swayed with each step, sweeping the dark hardwood floor. They stepped into a living room with an open floor plan, an island counter, and bar stools separating them from the kitchen. They took a seat on a large sectional that surrounded a black-painted brick gas fireplace. Just above sat a large walnut slab mantle with decorative candles on each end, a television centered and anchored above it. The room was immaculately clean. Each surface had a perfect shine, as if not a speck of dust sat upon it. The rug beneath their feet was a perfect white. Everything within the room was purposely placed, no jackets strewn over the chairs, no purse on the counter, and no sign of children. It was the one thing that stuck out to her most.

"I almost forgot to introduce myself," the woman said with a forced smile as she sat on the other end of the sectional. "Susan Shultz," she added, facing them with her legs crossed and her hands hugging her knee. Her perfectly pedicured toes poked out under her dress. Tara knew why she sat there. It was an effort to give her eye a much-needed break from their glares and skepticism. While they could still see it, she was now angled toward them, with the side of her face facing the wall. She felt more comfortable, and she sat up straighter.

"Did your husband ever mention that he did work on Adeline Brown's home?" Tara asked.

She cocked her head back at the question, as if it had slapped her in the face. "The woman who was murdered?"

Tara nodded.

"Uh, no." She shook her head. There was panic that Tara saw momentarily flare in her eyes, but she stifled it. "He doesn't like to watch the news," she added. "Says it's too depressing." Again, she flashed a forced smile, but it was quick and brief, as if it was too difficult even to hold it.

"So I'm guessing he never said anything to you about the house or something that might've seemed off to him?"

Again she shook her head as she uncrossed her legs and then crossed them again. It was clear she was growing uncomfortable. "Look, I don't really want to answer questions about my husband. He can answer those himself."

Tara nodded. She understood, and she didn't want to torture Susan by unloading questions that would instill fear, making her afraid of her husband's reaction if she answered them.

"Did you happen to see anything odd in your neighborhood the past few days? Maybe something that just felt off to you? A person you've never seen before? Someone acting strange?"

Again she shook her head. Tara asked her a few more questions. If she noticed anything out of place in their backyard within the past few days, if they heard anything on the night of Serenity's murder. But at each question, she shook her head.

"Do you have any children that might've seen something?" Tara asked.

At the question, the woman's hand instantly left her knee and fell in her lap as she began to run one hand over the other, hard. Tara was certain the question had made her uncomfortable. Her face fell, her eyes focused on her lap as well. She shook her head.

"We don't have any kids," she said. Her eyes stayed fixed on her lap as silence sat heavy in the room. She sighed.

"I'm sorry, I didn't mean to upset you—" Tara started. The woman's head instantly shot up. She waved away the words, shaking her head.

"Don't be," she started. "We've tried to get pregnant for a long time. I just kept having miscarriages." She tried to look at them as she said it, but she couldn't. Her eyes pulled away, staring at the floor once again.

"I'm so sorry," Tara said.

"I'm sorry as well," Warren added. He leaned forward in the couch, staring at her with compassion.

She didn't speak. She nodded, emotion rising. For a moment, it looked as if she were about to cry, but then she took a deep breath. "It never gets easier saying it," she said. A smile peeked through her sadness. "It's been really hard for my husband. The constant getting his hopes up and then the loss. It's put a lot of strain on our relationship."

Tara nodded. It seemed like the perfect storm. Marriage trouble, depression, and anger. It was all enough to take someone over the edge. "Did he do that to your eye?"

The woman's hand instinctively went to her face as she slunk back in her chair. It was as if she had forgotten all about it and had suddenly realized that she was fully exposed. She opened her mouth to speak, but the rustle of keys in the door made her head spin around.

The door opened, and a tall man wearing a t-shirt and jeans that had the stains of hard work stood before them. He was large, with salt-and-pepper stubble and a sharp nose that led down to his lips. He shot his head back in surprise at the sight of them.

"What's going on, Suz?" he asked. He held a guitar case and placed it down carefully at his words.

Susan instinctively stood. "I—" she started, looking between Tara and her husband. Tara could see the total fear in her eyes.

Tara held up her badge. "We were just hoping to speak with you. As I'm sure you know, there's been a few murders around Nashville, and we just want to talk to anyone who has had contact with the victims just to help piece together their timeline."

He shrugged, crossing his arms as if they had no reason to be at his home. "And you think I can help?" He walked right past them into the kitchen and grabbed himself a glass of water. Tara couldn't tell if he was trying desperately to act like he didn't care that they were there, or if he truly didn't.

But she found it difficult to believe that he didn't know who they were talking about. Even if he hadn't watched the news, it was spoken about everywhere, it was on every television outside of his own home, in every bar. He had to have known that Adeline Brown was a victim and also a woman he had done work for.

"You did work on one of their homes. A leak in the basement?" Tara told him the address.

She saw him pause for a moment. The glass held to his lips, but he didn't sip. His eye momentarily popped wider as his hand gripped the glass harder. But just as quickly as the moment of fear surfaced, it vanished. "So?" he said. "I deal with a lot of leaks in basements."

He turned to the fridge and began rummaging through it.

"I saved you some dinner," Susan blurted from the couch.

His back turned, he waved his hand, brushing off her words like they were nothing. She slunk back in her chair.

"Well, I'm sure it's not everyday that your customer is murdered," Tara replied. "Her name is Adeline Brown." She stood, reached in her pocket, pulled out her picture, and slid it across the island counter to him. He pulled away from the fridge and stared down at her.

At the sight of her, his face loosened, fear washing through his eyes, but then he curled his mouth into a scowl and pulled away. He shrugged. "I think I remember her. Not much to remember, though. It was a quick job. I fixed it and got out of there."

He moved across the room with his water glass in hand and sat down on the arm of the sectional, right next to his wife. It was as if he had forgotten that he was getting something to eat out of the fridge. As he sat, he looked over at his wife. An unsettling smile crept onto his lips, and she cowered. Her gaze shot to the floor.

Tara couldn't help but notice the physical hierarchy. Sitting on the arm of the chair, he was slightly elevated above her, and she was close enough to him that he towered over her. It was as if he was purposely trying to intimidate her, to say just how angry he actually was that she let the FBI into his living room.

He crossed his arms and stared at Tara. "Are we almost done here?"

Tara nodded as she reached again into her pocket, pulling out a picture of Victoria Monet, the woman murdered years ago whose husband had worked for Eddie. "Does she look familiar to you?" She slid the image across a large coffee table between them. He stood, grabbed it, and backed up to his seat. His eyes were glued to the image. At first he stared at it with confusion, as if he recognized her but couldn't pinpoint from where. But then his eyes opened wide, and heat rose to his cheeks. He remembered her. And he remembered what he had done. Tara was sure of it.

He looked up, his face suddenly stoic. "What about her?"

His wife carefully leaned into her husband, trying to catch a glance of the image. It was clear that she too had sensed her husband recognized her. But he sensed her movement and pulled the image away. His eyes stayed locked on Tara and Warren. It was the first time he had given them his full attention, and in doing so, he didn't realize how much he had just revealed. It was as if he were trying to stare down a predator about to attack him.

"From what we understand, you worked with her husband, correct?"

He squinted, almost as a warning. Anger swirled in his glare. But he didn't answer. His wife looked up at him, sensing the tension, but his eyes still remained on Tara.

"We know you were at their house too prior to the murder. Did you maybe remember anything from then that stuck out to you?"

His wife's eyes moved back and forth between them. Her brows knitted in concern. "Eddie, what are they—"

"Shut up!" he yelled.

She didn't speak another word. Once again, she cowered back.

His words pierced Tara. It took everything within her not to say something, not to correct him.

"What the hell are you accusing me of, huh?" he asked. His body was tense, now at the edge of the armchair, his hands tightly resting on his knees.

His wife sat at the edge of her seat as well. Her once crossed legs were now anchored to the floor. She stared bewildered at her husband and then at Tara.

"We know you took pictures of Victoria Monet years ago when you did work on her home."

Redness burst to the surface of his skin, his eyes unwaveringly focused on Tara's. But it wasn't embarrassment; it was anger. And his stare felt like a warning. She was going too far.

"Eddie, what's she talking about?" his wife asked, her voice shaking. The tension thickened into a stifling fog. It was too much for her to bear.

He didn't respond. His gaze was still set on Tara. He stared her straight in the eye, but it only fueled Tara's determination. She knew she was on the brink of something.

"We found your fingerprint on Adeline's basement window. Were you taking pictures of her too?"

He only continued to stare at her, the redness now turning a shade of purple. He shifted even farther to the edge of the arm of the couch. Tara sensed Warren moving closer to the edge of his seat as well. They both knew he was unpredictable.

"Do you know why your fingerprint might've been there?" she asked. "I believe you were doing work on a leak, not a window. Am I right?"

Again, he didn't answer. The silence spread like a warning through the room. An awkward smile seeped on his lips, a chuckle burst from his throat, and he casually reached for his glass of water on the coffee table. His behavior had shifted from denial to aloof and detached. Tara's pulse vibrated in her ears. He was going to do something. She could feel it.

She watched as he drank, as he pulled the glass away, as he slowly lowered it. Too slow.

In one swift motion, he chucked the glass at them. Tara and Warren instinctively shot up as glass shattered before their feet. The wife jumped up. She screamed. Eddie Shultz spun around, charging to the door. Tara and Warren bolted after him, but he was already fast ahead. His boots skidded across the wooden floor as he tried to stop his momentum as he got to the door. He grabbed the knob, swinging the door open. Tara and Warren were close behind him. He dashed onto the porch, about to jump down the steps, but Tara threw herself forward. Her hand grazed his shirt on the way down, but just as she hit the ground, she grabbed hold of his ankle, sending him tumbling forward, thumping down each step.

Warren jumped over her and down the stairs. Eddie tried to scramble to his feet, getting on all fours, but Warren straddled his back, sending him flat once again. Warren cuffed him.

"You all right?" he shouted back at Tara.

She was already standing, brushing off her knees, and nodded. Warren forced Eddie to his feet. He stood up, defeated, and Warren forced him to the car.

Tara sensed a presence behind her and spun around to see Susan Shultz standing in the doorway. Her hand hovered over her mouth, her eyes wet with tears. "I don't understand," she said, her voice soft like a whisper, as if she weren't speaking to anyone. Her eyes were fixed on her husband being pushed into the back of the vehicle.

"It might be a good idea if you stay with someone for a few days so you're not alone, until we have more information," Tara replied.

Susan didn't speak. She nodded slowly. She was in shock, and Tara couldn't help but feel sorry for her. They had struggled with fertility for years, she had just learned that her husband was taking photos of other women and that it was suggested he was connected to a string of murders as well. It was a lot for someone to digest. "We're going to have to search your home," Tara added.

Again, Susan didn't reply. She didn't protest. She took a seat on a rocking chair on the porch, near the purple perennials, and pulled out her phone. "I'll call my sister." But again, it was as if she was speaking to no one, only speaking out loud, trying desperately to process what just happened and formulate her next steps.

Warren slammed the door of the car and briskly walked back up to the porch until he stood before Tara. They locked eyes, and Tara nodded in the direction of Susan, letting Warren know she was within earshot. They stepped farther down the porch, and Tara glanced at Susan once more. She spoke into the phone, her eyes still unwaveringly focused on the car, on her husband.

"I don't trust her sitting out here alone," Tara whispered.

Warren raised his brows and nodded. He didn't either. He sighed. "I'll call for someone to take him in. In the meantime, go search the place. I'll hang out here," he said.

Tara nodded. She was surprised. Normally, she would've been the one to hang outside while Warren searched, but the fact that he had trusted her enough to take the lead herself showed just how much he trusted her. In fact, Tara had felt like an equal for quite some time now; she hadn't even thought much about it. He would always be her mentor. He would always have more experience. But he now trusted her judgment fully. He didn't question her abilities. And she too was beginning to feel much more confident in herself as an agent too.

She turned to the house and swiftly entered. Susan's gaze still didn't waver. Tara searched the living room, in side table drawers, in drawers on the television stand, but didn't find anything except books and magazines, all neatly placed. She looked through the coat closet, pushing the coats apart, scanning through a sea of shoes underneath. Nothing. She scanned everywhere in the room and then moved to another. She walked down a short hallway into the bedroom. It was large, with high ceilings painted gray with a white shiplap accent wall, against which the bed was pressed. Large windows that looked out into the backyard filled the room with sunlight. Tara searched the nightstands. She found glasses, a television remote, ChapStick, but nothing of substance. She searched the closets, the drawers.

As she rummaged through the clothing, Tara heard the sound of a police vehicle in the distance, until it was just outside the home. Moments later, footsteps sounded down the hallway.

"Tara!" It was Warren.

"In here," she yelled. His feet pounded down the hall until he stood before her.

"Anything yet?" he asked.

Tara sat on her heels, her gloved hands still in the drawers. She shook her head, disappointed.

"Did you search this room yet?" He nodded in the direction of a room across the hall. Tara shook her head, and Warren quickly disappeared into it.

Tara continued to search. But when she still didn't find anything, she stood up. She knew it was unlikely she would find anything in the bedroom anyway. His wife didn't know. Tara knew he would most likely keep the pictures he took far away from her. Her heart sank at the sudden thought that they wouldn't be here at all. She knew the best place to hide the pictures would be at his office, which his wife most likely didn't frequent. But as she stepped out into the hall, she heard Warren.

"Tara!" he called. She followed his voice into the room across the hall.

It was a small, tight office. Papers were scattered over the desk, where a computer sat in the sea of it all. The sun shined through a large window, reflecting on a cloud of dust that had spread through the air from Warren's search. It was clear Susan didn't go in there much, if at all. The difference in cleanliness from the rest of the house spoke volumes.

Tara's eyes fell upon Warren, sitting on his knees on the floor, his back to her, facing an open closet, hovering over something in his hands. As Tara moved closer, he spun around.

"We got him," he said.

Tara stared down at the two images in his hands, held out over a pile more at his knees. One was older and torn, but Tara could just make out the brown, short, curly hair, the slim figure, the long neck. It was Victoria Monet. And in the other, a different woman sat on a yoga mat upright, stretching her arm across her body in only a sports bra and leggings, the profile of her face facing the camera. But Tara didn't have to think twice about who it was. She had seen that room before. It was a basement. It was a picture of Adeline.

***

Eddie Shultz ran his fingers through his messy brown hair, digging his fingers into his skull. Tara and Warren had just entered the interrogation room, and he still had yet to look at them. His face was tense with fear as he stared at the table underneath him. He didn't blink. He knitted his bushy brows. It was as if her were concentrating, trying to see through the table. Tara couldn't help but notice that it was a big change from his confident attitude earlier. At his home, he had barely given them the time of day, but now it was clear it was all a façade to mask his true fear. But now he was caught.

Tara and Warren both pulled out a chair across from him and took a seat. He still didn't look up until Tara slapped two pictures down on the counter.

"You want to tell me why you have these?"

He lifted his head slowly, peering at the images, already fully aware of what was in front of him. He didn't speak. His eyes just lingered on them as he bit his lower lip. Tara and Warren had gone through all the images. They didn't see any of the other victims, but there were a total of twenty-six pictures.

"And all of these?" Tara asked again. She dumped the envelope of the other images out onto the table and spread them across so he could see. In each image, a woman was in her home. In her bedroom, in the bathroom, in a basement. Some fully clothed, some not at all, but each picture had something in common. They were taken while the woman was not looking, either through a window or a cracked door.

Again he stared at them, his face growing a shade of red as his eyes darted from one image to another, until he couldn't bear to look at them anymore and his gazed moved to the corner of the room.

"Is this why you ran from us?" Tara asked, pointing repeatedly at the images. "Or are you hiding something more?"

He turned to her and winced, shooting his head back in confusion. He shook his head. "I don't know what you're talking about." But there was something in his eyes that told her otherwise.

Tara pulled the pictures of Adeline and Victoria out of the pile. "You don't know that these two women were murdered?"

His eyes shot to the table again as he ran his fingers through his hair once more, pulling at it with frustration. He sighed and looked up. "I know how bad this looks, but I swear, I had nothing to do with that." He stared Tara dead in the eye. His were now red and watery, but Tara couldn't tell if it was all an act. He didn't seem surprised when they mentioned the murders. He had either heard about the murders and connected the dots on his own, or he knew because he was guilty.

"Why was your fingerprint on Adeline's window?" Tara asked again.

He bit his lip hard, his eyes falling once more to his lap as silence lingered in the room. Tara was about to ask him once more, but he suddenly lifted his head, threw up his hands in defeat, and let out a frustrated grunt. "I took a picture on my way out, all right?"

"When?" Tara asked.

He sighed again, letting his back slam against the chair, unable to look at them. He knew he had to explain himself. The pictures were right in front of them, and his fingerprint was on a victim's window. He was clearly guilty. The question was of how much.

He was either in the wrong place at the wrong time purely by coincidence or he was the murderer they had been looking for all along. Either way, in order to prove that he wasn't guilty of murder, he needed to explain the pictures, and he knew it.

He gritted his teeth and swore under his breath. He looked up. "I saw she had workout gear on when I was leaving. I kind of figured she was going into the basement, which is where all her equipment is. So I went around back and snapped a picture."

He said it casually, as if it was something innocent. It was as if *just snapping a picture* was what he had told himself over and over again each time he had the desire.

"And what? You just get off on these pictures? Or are you really scoping out an entry point?" Tara asked.

His face scrunched in confusion. "What? No!" He knew what Tara was suggesting. "I may take pictures when I shouldn't, but I'm not a damn murderer!" He slammed his fist on the table but then pulled it back, staring at it as if surprised by his sudden emotion. He took a deep breath, trying to regain his composure. "Look, I know how this looks. I may take pictures when I shouldn't, but I swear, I would never murder someone." He stared Tara straight in the eye.

"But you'd clearly hurt someone, right? Like your wife's eye?"

His eyes instantly fell. "I'm not proud of that. We've had a tough couple years."

Again, Tara's blood boiled at his response. *A tough couple years.* The words lingered in her mind. She knew it was the same reasoning he had told himself and probably his wife for why he hit her, as if it somehow in a way it slightly righted his wrong. *Could he have told himself something similar for why he murdered women? That they had dressed too provocatively, that they shouldn't stand in the window or have a man in their house alone?*

"Did you ever hit any other women?" Tara asked.

Heat rose to his face. He was about to slam his fist again but stopped himself, clenching it hard instead. "I know what you're accusing me of. I'm no murderer," he replied through gritted teeth.

It was clear he was angry, but Tara was uncertain if it was because he was being accused or because he was caught. He looked like a cornered dog, ready to protect whatever hid in his mouth.

"Where were you two nights ago?" Tara asked.

He rubbed his stubbly chin hard. "At home, with my wife," he replied, once again unable to look at them. He knew it wasn't a solid alibi, and after all his wife had just learned, Tara knew he doubted she would even confirm it.

Warren suddenly stood from his chair, staring down at him. "We'll see what your wife says," he replied.

Eddie didn't look up. His fists clenched tighter. Tara could see on Warren's face that he didn't trust Eddie's excuses. He nodded to the door before turning on his heels and headed toward it. Tara followed, wondering if once and for all, they had captured the Silent Stalker.

***

Tara and Warren stood outside the interrogation room. It was now late in the evening, but the hustle and bustle that would normally die down at this time was still in full effect. Everywhere Tara looked, the station showed signs of a high-pressure case. Police personnel walked briskly up and down the halls, phones rang nonstop, and talk of another stakeout sailed through the station.

Tara lowered her voice. "You think it's him?"

Warren stared at Eddie through a small window in the door. Tara followed his gaze. He sat with his head in his hands, trembling as if he were crying. "It would be a pretty big coincidence."

He was right. It would be, capturing pictures of two of the victims in the rooms that were used as a possible entry point into their homes. But there was one part that made Tara ponder. "Why wouldn't he have pictures of all the victims, though?"

Warren turned toward her. He shrugged. It was a question he was clearly grappling with as well. "Maybe we haven't found them. Or maybe he didn't get the chance to take one for every home. Maybe he went on memory."

Tara nodded. He was right, it was certainly possible. At the thought, Chief Meyers caught her eye. He stared straight at them, his feet pounding the floor as he walked briskly. Warren turned toward him as well.

"How did it go?" he asked when he was finally within earshot.

"He's certainly guilty of taking those pictures," Warren replied. They had already filled the chief in on what they had found and who Eddie was. "It would be a pretty big coincidence," he repeated.

The chief nodded. "Well, if you have any doubt, I have something you might want to see."

Tara and Warren shared a quick look. They knew the chief had sent his force out to look for cameras.

Without another word, the chief waved his hand and turned on his heels, signaling for them to follow him. They followed him down the hall into a room where an officer with salt-and-pepper hair sat in a chair by a computer. He stood up and gave a satisfied smile, making his cleft chin even more apparent.

Meyers introduced them. "Officer Delacruz found something about an hour ago on a camera a street over from Serenity Jackson's home."

Tara stared at the computer. It was video that was paused and showed a backyard surrounded by a white vinyl fence. The camera was angling down, as if it were attached just under the roof of the house. A light shined down into the yard, casting a spotlight on the ground underneath it.

The chief signaled for the officer to show them. He sat again at the computer as they all hovered over him. Tara watched intently. At first, they saw nothing, just the rustle of trees at each gust of wind and a cat stalking through the yard, but then the officer abruptly paused the video. "There." He pointed at the corner of the screen. Tara squinted, leaning in closer, and as she spotted what he was gesturing toward, her heart began to pound.

Just behind the yard, where their fence met a neighboring fence, a dark figure could be seen propping himself up over it until he disappeared on the other side. Tara asked him to zoom in. He replayed it once more, and she watched again as the man positioned his arms on the fence, pulled himself up, and disappeared on the other side. He was standing on something, and Tara tried to make out his appearance, but it was too difficult. He wore a black hood, black pants, his face and body completely shielded. There was no way to tell who it was.

"How far is this from Serenity's house?" Tara asked.

"Eight houses away," the chief said. "He must've climbed through all those yards. There's a major street two houses after the one he climbed to. He must've been heading there."

"Did you search the area?" Warren asked.

The chief shook his head. "I have a whole team there right now, searching the yards, but it's been difficult because it's so dark out. They're going to regroup in the morning."

Tara felt renewed hope. She knew there was a good chance they could find something, a fiber, a fingerprint, anything he dropped or left behind. She hoped that just as he made the mistake of missing the camera, he had made others along the way. She stared at the video, now paused, and zoomed in. It was hard to tell, but the man seemed relatively large, thin, with broad shoulders. "His body type does look similar to Eddie's," she said.

Warren nodded, with a bit more certainty. "Let us know as soon as you hear anything," he said to the chief and the officer. They nodded in unison.

Moments later, Tara and Warren stood in the hallway once more. It was now nine thirty. Tara could feel the weight of the day bearing down on her.

"We're not going to know much more until the morning," Warren admitted. He was right. There was not much more they could do, and it was looking more and more likely that Eddie was the guy they had been looking for.

Tara and Warren called it a night, and as Tara walked to the car, she wondered if tomorrow morning would be the end of this case after all.

Chapter Twenty Two

Pictures flashed before Tara's eyes on the muted television as she held her phone to her ear, waiting for John to pick up. He had asked her to call him, and Tara was excited to let him know that she thought the case would soon be over.

"Tara." She could hear his smile as he said her name, and one burst onto her lips as well.

They spoke for a moment, John recounting his day. His parents had stopped by for dinner. "My mom left some wedding magazines for you," he said. "I told her we have enough already, but she didn't listen." He chuckled, and Tara laughed too.

It was very like his mother. She was growing impatient, waiting for them to pick a date, to start planning. It was her little push. But Tara also knew the things she did were deeply out of love as well. She was excited for them to get married, for Tara to be part of the family, and for that, a satisfaction Tara had always wanted to feel as a child burst inside her. It was the feeling of having family.

"How's the case?" John asked.

Tara's thoughts halted, and the feeling dissipated. "Good," she started. But she couldn't find it within herself to say what she had wanted to, that she was hoping the case would soon be over. That tomorrow morning they could potentially be able to link the killer with solid evidence depending on what they found during the search. That they might already have the killer in custody. Something made her stop.

It was that feeling of family. Of all the families that had now lost that feeling by losing a mother at the hands of the Silent Stalker. It was the realization that those children would forever lead a life in search of it once again. It sat like a pit in her stomach, and she couldn't help but question if she truly was bringing them justice. If they were focusing on the right person, or if someone else was still out there.

"You all right?" John asked. She had been quiet too long.

"Yeah," she replied. "These cases just get to me sometimes, that's all."

John didn't reply. He understood, but he had always felt like Tara's cases were another world of hers that he got glimpses of but struggled to relate to. He never quite knew what to say, and rightfully so. "Are you any closer?" he asked. He had to say something, but Tara knew what he really wanted to ask for were details she couldn't reveal.

Tara sighed. "We might be. I'm not sure yet. We'll know more in the morning."

Again, silence lingered between them until John spoke. "Well, I miss you," he said. "You should probably get some sleep." John knew better than to get his hopes up; a case could take days or weeks, and a potential break in the case could mean everything or nothing in regards to when Tara would be coming home. But he was right—she should get some sleep. It was now close to eleven, and her eyes felt heavy, her mind swirling in a daze of overuse.

Tara and John said their goodbyes, but as Tara hung up, she thought once more of the doubt that had seeped into her mind. Were they putting their focus in the right spots? She had remembered Eddie in the interrogation room, his horror when he thought they were accusing him of murder. And she still couldn't quite wrap her mind around his motive. *Why did he only have pictures of two of the victims, but not others? Why did he not choose to murder the other women in the pictures he took? And why would he want to kill them anyway? Just because he was angry at women and snapped?* Something about it tasted sour. The murders weren't sexually motivated, so why the pictures of the women? She remembered Warren's theory that maybe he was taking pictures of the room, but then why take pictures while they were in it? Wouldn't that just make it more difficult? One last thought ran through Tara's mind. *What if Eddie Shultz isn't the killer after all? Are we just looking for evidence to convict him when the real killer is out there?*

Tara stared at the television. But at each spiraling thought, she tried desperately to push back. She knew what these thoughts did to her: they pushed her to do something rash. Each time, she had let doubt seep so heavily into her mind, she got herself in a dangerous situation, and there was no way she was going to be that stupid again.

At that thought, Tara let exhaustion sweep over her. She turned out the light and switched off the television, the darkness pulling her under into a deep sleep.

Chapter Twenty Three

Light flooded through the sliding glass doors of the kitchen, meeting the complete darkness of the night sky. And just at the edge of the lawn, where it touched the forest, he stood there, letting the darkness swallow him.

This wasn't the first time he had stood here. In fact, he had done so many times before as he studied her habits, her hours, her family's habits. She was a nurse, an ER nurse to be exact, and he had sat here other nights, waiting for her to get off her shift, waiting for her to get home, and waiting for a time when she would be alone.

He had missed last night, but it was okay because he knew the opportunity was forthcoming. She had three children, all under the age of ten. He could just see them now, protesting in the living room beyond the kitchen, not wanting to go to bed. They never did when their grandmother watched them, which she did three nights a week while their mother worked a night shift. She was a widow. No husband. No boyfriend. But the children and grandmother were an even bigger obstacle. It was why he had waited so long, studied her so meticulously. But the children were also why he was here in the first place, why he had chosen her. He had witnessed the sadness in their expressions more often than not. He had watched their mother scold them unprovoked, frustrated at the life she had created. He had watched the despair wash over them each time. He knew they questioned why this life had chosen them. But most of all, he knew what they felt too well. It burned from a scar within him.

His body tingled with excitement because he knew the time was coming when he could have her alone. He had heard her speak of it, on the phone to friends, to her mother, to her children on the way to the bus. This weekend, she was going away. A bachelorette party, he had overheard. Her children were staying at her mother's for the night, and there would be almost a full day when they would be gone and she would be home alone before she left. The thought made a smile creep onto his face.

Her home was the easiest of all the women, its yard surrounded by woods and located within the Bellevue neighborhood of Nashville. He knew her habits, how she tried to keep her windows closed and locked because of what had been circulating on the news. But how each night, an hour after she would go to bed, she would crack the window ever so slightly because she was warm. It was also what would pull her into the kitchen around the same time for a glass of water and then to the bathroom. Only later the next day would she realize that she had left it open for half the day already. She would lock it, only to repeat the cycle again that night.

Her home was a split-style ranch with a porch just outside the kitchen on the second floor and stairs that led up to it. Her bedroom window was on that floor as well, and just in the left-hand corner of the porch. *It's too easy*, he thought with another smile.

He stared at the home awhile longer as the grandmother placed a child's cup in the sink and spotted the clock above it. He watched as her face shifted, and he imagined her voice grew stern, her arms waving as she attempted to shuffle the children to bed for her final attempt. The children finally obeyed, and they all disappeared down the hall. Lights were turned on and then off in the children's rooms until the grandmother returned fifteen minutes later, poured herself a cup of tea, and took a seat at the kitchen table in total defeat. She closed her eyes a moment, as if she might drift off, but then a sound in the distance jostled her awake, and her daughter ascended the stairs. She wore blue scrubs, her brown hair straight to her shoulders, her bangs just brushing her brows. She was small and petite and could almost be mistaken for a child at this distance.

They spoke for a while, she poured herself a cup of tea too, and when the grandmother finally finished hers, she gave her daughter a kiss on the forehead and said her goodbyes. Moments later, the mother sat alone, cupping her tea in both hands, staring into it, becoming lost in it, until exhaustion wrapped around her. He could see it pulling her under each time she almost nodded off, at each flutter of her eyes. She stood up, turned off the light, and went to bed. *It will be her last time*, he told himself with a smile. He stared at the home a moment longer, rage burning within him. *Her children will be better off,* he thought as he disappeared into the dark.

Chapter Twenty Four

Tara sat on her hotel bed, upright, her legs crossed, staring at the wall in front of her. Chloe Waterman's voice sailed through the room, as it had done for the past few hours while Tara's ears remained glued to the podcast emanating from her phone.

It was now six thirty in the morning, and the sun was filtering into the room, sending a blanket of light across her lap. She didn't know how long she had been sitting there, only that she had awoken while it was still dark, her mind fixated on the case, on Eddie Shultz. She knew she had told herself to let it go, but she couldn't. It sat in her mind like a splinter, growing more painful each time she turned a blind eye.

There was something about him. His complete mortification when he learned that they were accusing him of murder, the lack of images of all the victims, only showcasing two out of thirteen. And it was also the images of the women, taken in a sexual light, undressing, barely clothed. Tara couldn't ignore the fact that the images seemed sexually motivated when the crimes did not.

She had been listening to Chloe Waterman
recounting each case, each crime scene, each failed
lead. But there was one mention that had stuck out to
her. Tara had paused it and replayed it over and over,
and did so once more. She listened to Chloe's voice
intently. "Each victim was alone at the time of the
murder. They were widows, divorcées, or had
husbands that were away. Law enforcement believed
that widows and divorcées were highly targeted due to
convenience. But they also all had one thing in
common that in my mind seemed to debunk that
theory. They all had children."

Tara paused it. She was right, and it was something
that Tara and Warren had discussed before. They
already suspected that the killer had a different motive
for killing Chloe and Serenity—that it was to put an
end to the podcast. But Adeline did not have any
connection to the podcast whatsoever. It was clear that
killing Chloe and Serenity had rekindled his old
hunger. It was what led to Adeline's murder. Adeline
had children, and Tara was convinced it was connected
to what made her a target. *But why choose women with
children then? If the killer is looking for convenience,
like law enforcement originally assumed?* she
wondered. She knew what Warren would say. Maybe
the killer wanted a challenge, but not an impossible
one.

But then another thought occurred to her. There
was one piece of the puzzle they were missing. One
piece of the puzzle that knew the first two victims
well: it was Chloe Waterman's daughter. Her father
had originally refused to let them speak to her, and
Tara didn't quite know where it could lead, since she

was a selective mute, but by not speaking to her, Tara felt like there was a large gap in their investigation. She remembered what Rick had said. Chloe was acting odd; she wanted a surveillance system. If anyone knew what she was afraid of, it would've been her daughter.

She looked down at her phone. It was now 7:00 a.m. Chief Meyers and his officers were probably out now, re-searching the area where they had caught the killer on the camera. But she couldn't just sit back until they found something. She picked up her phone and called Warren. She knew she had a habit of second-guessing when others thought the case was coming to a close, and Warren hadn't always been supportive of her thought process. But she also knew she was usually right.

On the second ring, he picked up. "Were you up too?" he asked. His voice was raspy. He sounded tired, and Tara's beating heart subsided. It was clear that he was up too, that he had reservations as well.

"Something's just not sitting right," she replied.

"It's not for me either," he agreed. "The more I think about it, the more I can't help but think that Eddie was just in the wrong place at the wrong time, doing the wrong thing."

Tara took a sigh of relief. "We never spoke to Chloe's daughter," she reminded him. "She knew both of the first two victims. There could be something there that we overlooked."

"It's worth a shot." Tara knew what he meant. It wouldn't be easy. Not only was she a selective mute, but last time they had asked to speak to her, her father refused. They were going to have to work hard at convincing him to let them speak to her, and they were going to have to work even harder at getting any information from her.

But another aspect of Warren's words stuck out to her too. His willingness, his trust, his lack of doubt. It was another reminder that Warren's respect for her as an agent had grown, seeing her less as a rookie.

"You're not going to push back on this?" she asked.

Warren chuckled. "Not today. It's about time I listen to you."

Tara beamed with pride. But Chloe's daughter soon seeped into her mind, and her smile faded. Her face tightened in determination. If Warren had doubts too, it only solidified her own feelings, and talking to Chloe's daughter felt even more urgent.

***

Warren drove into an underground garage of a hotel in North Nashville. It was where Rick was now staying with his daughter.

"I guess Fiona's husband must've come back on his business trip," she said as Warren parked. When they were there, Fiona had said her husband was in Chicago.

Warren pursed his lips and shrugged. "I can only imagine how that all went," he replied. The husband didn't know about the affair. Tara wondered if he now knew. But given that Rick was staying at a hotel, Tara assumed the husband had learned of the affair and didn't want him staying there, or Rick couldn't bear to tell him and take advantage of his hospitality at the same time.

"Either way," Tara said, "the fact that he's at a hotel without her doesn't look too good. But it's probably better that way."

Warren nodded. He knew Tara was referring to the child. It was hard enough processing her mother's death while also processing the fact that her father had a budding relationship with her mother's friend. The thought made Tara's blood boil. It seemed incredibly self-centered that he would even seek shelter at the home of the woman he was having an affair with.

Tara and Warren walked out of the parking garage, around the building, and into the hotel lobby. They walked briskly across the marble floor and into the elevator. Warren had already spoken to Rick. He had reluctantly agreed to let them speak with his daughter. It seemed now that they knew about the affair, he wasn't as concerned about them speaking to her. It was another example of just how self-centered he was, caring more about his secrets than the psychological welfare of his child. It gave Tara another jolt of anger, but she swallowed it. She needed to be understanding and kind if she were to have an effective conversation with his daughter.

Once they got to the fifth floor, Tara and Warren stepped out, scanning the room numbers until they came across 508. Tara knocked.

They could hear the television blaring in the background with some sort of children's cartoon. Within moments, they heard the door unlock. It swung open to reveal Rick standing before them. His face stony, he stared at them blankly. Even though it had only been a few days since they last saw him, in comparison, it was as if weeks had gone by. Dark shadows hung under his eyes. His once combed-over hair now lacked the sleek shine of pomade and stuck up every which way. His once clean-shaven face now had thick black stubble. He sighed and nodded, opening the door wider.

They stepped into a room with two queen beds. The daughter was sitting on one, curled up by the pillows in her pajamas, staring at the television. Her eyes moved to them briefly but then turned back to the show she was watching, and she curled her legs in even tighter.

It was a bright, sunny day outside, but no one would ever know by being in the room. The curtains were pulled together tightly. The only illumination was from the ceiling light, making the room feel suddenly stuffy.

All three of them stood close to the door, and Tara turned to Rick, keeping her voice low.

"Does she know we're here to talk to her?" she asked. Her eyes drifted to his daughter and then back to Rick.

He sighed and nodded. "I tried to prep her the best I could. She won't stop staring at that television, though. It's all she's wanted to do since we got here. But after all she's been through, I just can't take away the only thing that she's finding some comfort in." His eyes drifted to his daughter.

Tara nodded. She understood. She remembered when her own mother died, when she went to go live with her grandmother. She had watched her favorite movie probably fifty times: *The Lion, the Witch, and the Wardrobe.* It was like it gave her mind a much-needed break from the trauma. Like she could be somewhere else completely in her head. Tara knew the television was an escape for the girl.

"We can connect you to a child psychologist if you need one," Tara suggested. But Rick shook his head.

"She has one she sees regularly. She trusts her already."

Tara and Warren nodded in unison. "Do you have somewhere else to stay eventually?" Warren asked as he looked around the room. They both knew they weren't going to go back to their house, where his daughter had a traumatic experience, and they assumed since they were staying at a hotel room, they weren't planning on staying with Fiona either.

He sighed again and nodded. "My brother lives in Georgia. We're going to stay with him while we sell the house and look for another." He paused a moment, his eyes falling to the floor. "After Chloe's service."

"Is Fiona going with you to Georgia?" Tara asked.

Rick's eyes stayed on the ground as he slowly shook his head. "It didn't work out," he confirmed.

Tara nodded. She was about to say she was sorry to hear that, but she stopped herself. Because in reality, she wasn't. Even though Chloe and her husband were separated, he was still seeing her best friend, and she knew that if the daughter had found out, it would've negatively affected her in some way.

She stared again at the daughter. "Is it okay if we speak to her now?"

Rick nodded as he dragged his feet across the floor to the bed. Tara and Warren followed behind. He sat down close to her. "They're going to speak to you now, okay?" he said, his voice merely a whisper in her ear, but all she did was nod. Her eyes were still locked on the television. He moved away from her and gave Tara and Warren a skeptical nod with a raise of his brows as if to say *good luck* and then sat on the other bed.

Tara and Warren sat on opposite sides of the bed, the girl's eyes still transfixed to the television. Her short black hair was curly and unruly, framing her face. It was as if she was trying to hide behind it.

"Felicity, we just want to ask you a couple questions, okay?" Tara said.

The girl didn't look at them. It was as if she didn't even hear their words. "Did your mom ever seem afraid of anyone?" Tara asked. Felicity didn't speak, she didn't blink, just stared at the television. "Maybe someone outside your home that shouldn't have been there?" Tara added. Again, her questions were met by silence. Tara glanced at Warren.

"I know this is hard, Felicity," he added. "We just want to make sure that whoever hurt your mom doesn't hurt anyone else. If you answer our questions, it could really help us find who did this."

Tara and Warren braced themselves, hoping that maybe his words would cause a reaction, but again they did not. Hope slipped from their fingers.

Tara and Warren locked eyes again. He pursed his lips and raised his brows as if to tell her it was her turn. Tara took a deep breath. She knew that if she were going to get anything out of this girl, she had to speak in a way she understood.

"You know, I lost my mom too when I was about your age. In a very similar way," she said. Felicity

267

glanced at her a moment in the corner of her eye and then returned her gaze in front of her. But it was all Tara needed to know that she was beginning to listen, that Tara was headed in the right direction. "I know how scary it is, how alone you must feel. And I know you just want to push it all away, that you don't want to think about it. But I also know that the longer you do that, the longer it hurts." Tara paused. The words flowed from her as if she were speaking to her younger self. They were the same words she had said to herself, just never out loud. "I know you don't see it now," she added. "But it is important to you and your mom that the person responsible gets caught and put in prison where he belongs."

The girl's eyes fell. She didn't speak, but Tara was certain she had struck something. Her eyes then fell on Tara, and she gave her a slight nod before scooting off the bed, grabbing a coloring book on the table by the television, and sitting back down in front of them. At first Tara was confused, but then she watched as the girl turned to a blank page, held a crayon, and began to draw. When she was done, she pulled away, facing the pad of paper toward them. Tara and Warren both looked down as her father hovered over them in confusion.

Upon the paper, the girl had drawn a large truck outside a row of homes. A window was cut out in the truck, and a face smiled from inside, holding something out in his hand. Two women stood before it, a big smile on their faces as well, and a smaller girl, who Tara assumed was Felicity.

"Is this you?" Tara asked, pointing to the girl. She nodded. "And is this your mom?" Tara pointed to one of the women that was holding the girl's hand. Felicity nodded again.

Tara looked at the other woman. She had a large belly, and Tara's heart thumped against her chest as it occurred to her who it was. "Is this Serenity?" Tara asked. Again the girl nodded. Tara shared a look with Warren. He saw it too, the round belly on the stick figure drawing under a long dress. "Was she pregnant?" Tara asked. The girl once again nodded. Tara's heart pounded even harder. She wasn't sure what it meant.

Suddenly, Rick stepped closer. He stared down at the picture and then at his daughter. "Honey, Serenity wasn't—" He stopped himself.

Tara and Warren stared at him as confusion crossed his face and then his eyes abruptly grew wide and his jaw dropped.

"What is it?" Warren asked.

"There was probably a good five months I didn't see her. It seemed every time I went to the house, she had just left. I never really thought about it until now."

Tara stared once again at the drawing. Serenity was not pregnant when they met her, but now it seemed she had been at some point. *Could she had lost her child or put him or her up for adoption?* Tara wondered. *Could the killer have been targeting mothers all along?* Her thoughts ran wild. She and Warren knew without a doubt that the podcast resparked the killer's rampage, but they had thought that his motive for killing Chloe and Serenity was only tied to his desire to keep the podcast buried. But now Tara wondered if killing them satisfied a deeper motive, one that was connected to them being mothers.

Her thoughts solidified like a puzzle that had just become whole. But she knew there was something else in this picture. She stared down at what was in the stick figure in the window's hand. *Is it an ice cream cone?*

"Is this an ice cream truck?" Tara asked. The girl looked at her, eyes wide, as if pleased that Tara understood. She nodded. "Did you get ice cream from this truck often?" Tara asked. Again the girl nodded excitedly, but then she grabbed hold of the crayon and abruptly crossed out the two women and herself.

Tara stared down at it, confused. For a moment, she didn't quite know what the girl meant by it, but then a thought struck her. "You stopped going to it." Again, the girl nodded excitedly. The smiling ice cream driver still stared back at them. And then another thought popped into her head. "Did your mom tell you to stay away from this truck?"

Again, the girl nodded without a second thought, sending a shiver down Tara's spine.

Tara stared down at the drawing one last time. She remembered Chloe's words from the podcast that the killer could be a frequent visitor to the community. *Could Chloe have sensed the killer was in her community the whole time? That he was posing as an ice cream driver, studying his victims?* And then another realization came. Adeline's sons had mentioned an argument over ice cream that they had gotten from an ice cream truck. *Could the killer be an ice cream truck driver, studying his victims?*

Tara suddenly jumped to her feet. She thanked Felicity and her father and turned to the door, Warren already on her heels.

When they finally got to the hall and were out of earshot, Warren spoke. "We'll need a list of ice cream truck drivers in the area who frequent Chloe's street." Tara nodded as they waited for the elevator. When it finally arrived, Warren shook his head. "An ice cream driver. Who would've thought?"

Chapter Twenty Five

The clock ticked steadily above the door as Tara and Warren waited patiently in a room in the police station for Grace, the secretary of their FBI division, to call them back. She was in the process of searching for ice cream truck drivers in the area, narrowing it down to ones that frequented Chloe's street. The police had also looked into Serenity being pregnant, speaking to adoption agencies, confirming at a hospital that the child had been born. Tara and Warren had learned that she did in fact have a child that she had given up for adoption. Kiara, Serenity's sister, had even confirmed that there was a six-month time frame after her husband's death when Kiara hadn't seen her. She had thought that Serenity was just so overcome by grief that she pushed everyone away. But now they both knew that it wasn't just grief—it was to hide her pregnancy. No one knew if the baby was her husband's that passed away or someone else's, and now they would never know. That piece of the puzzle died with Chloe, the only person who knew Serenity's secrets.

But now Tara knew that her suspicions were correct. The killer had been targeting mothers all along. She stared at Warren, who sighed with a phone to his ear. While they waited for Grace, they had been doing their own research, calling up past witnesses, speaking with family members of victims, trying to get any information on the driver.

Warren hung up the phone again. Each person they had called did not remember a particular ice cream driver that stuck out in their mind, but the family members of three separate victims did remember that the victim and her children used to get ice cream at a truck once in a while. But as for the driver, none of them could give a description. After all, it had been years, and if they didn't see the driver as peculiar, there was no reason why they would pay any mind to what they looked like and remember it years later.

"I wish we knew a bit more." Tara sighed as she scanned the list of family members they still could try calling. "Like why did Chloe not want her daughter to get ice cream there anymore? He must've done something to make her suspicious."

Warren shrugged. "He could've been hanging around at odd hours. Maybe asking some pointed questions about her podcast."

Tara nodded. But she couldn't help but feel they were missing something. That there was something else Chloe knew that heightened her suspicion.

Tara stared down at the list in front of her once more and scooped up the phone, about to place another call. But just before she dialed, the phone rang in her palm. Grace's name lit up across the screen. Tara showed the phone to Warren. She quickly picked up.

"What do you have?" Tara asked.

Grace sighed. Tara could hear her typing. "I did a lot of digging. Luckily, with ice cream trucks there's not a whole lot of companies or drivers, so I was able to narrow it down pretty quickly." Tara's heart pounded. "There's a guy by the name of Joey Foster. He's been driving a truck for twenty-three years. He's in his late forties. I spoke to the company he works for. Chloe's street is his route."

Tara glanced at Warren. She could see the same glimmer of hope in his eyes. They both knew he was likely the driver they were looking for. After all, how many ice cream drivers could there be on one street? But they wouldn't know anything until they met with him.

"Did his employer say anything about him that seemed alarming?"

"Nope," Grace replied, her fingers still typing as if in a hurry. "But I definitely have something you need to see. Check your email."

Tara exchanged a confused glance with Warren before pulling up her email on her phone. There was an email from Grace. Tara opened in, revealing a link to an article. She clicked it, and her eyes opened wide at the headline. *How one mother's selfless love became a selfish scam.* Tara held it out for Warren to read. She scrolled to see a picture of a smiling young boy sitting in a wheelchair with his mother hovering over him, her hands on his shoulders endearingly. They looked happy and hopeful. But Tara scrolled on.

Violet Foster was seen as the ideal mother, one who relentlessly cared for her terminally ill son. She had quit her job, becoming a full-time aide, and had worked tirelessly to make sure her son was given everything he needed. For years, the Fosters story had garnered an overwhelming amount of attention and charitable donations, from trips to Disney World to paid medical expenses, food, and even their mortgage. But what no one knew was that Violet Foster's son was never actually sick at all.

"Oh my God." Tara gasped, her hand hovering over her mouth. Warren stared at the article, his eyes wide.

"Pretty crazy," Grace finally said. "I did a bit more digging too. Found some more articles. Apparently the son, Joey, thought he was sick too. His mother had been giving him small doses of arsenic to make him appear sick. A doctor finally caught on and informed authorities. When the son found out, he tried to toss an open bottle of bleach at her."

"That's awful," Warren replied.

"Where's the mother now?" Tara asked.

"She had a heart attack when she was serving out her sentence ten years ago."

It suddenly all made sense. Targeting mothers, why Chloe suspected him too. She must've known who he was all along. She must've seen the articles. She must've made the connection. That his victims were surrogates for his own mother, living out his biggest desire to kill her over and over again. And then, suddenly, the message surfaced in Tara's mind, written in blood above each victim. *A heart to mold until it crumbles.* It was a message about his mother, what she had done to him. Tara tuned to Warren.

"He's living out his desire over and over again," she said. "Each time, killing his mother."

Warren's eyes stayed locked on her as he quickly got to his feet. "Grace, text us the address you have." He grabbed the keys, swung open the door, and Tara followed, a mixture of unease and satisfaction flooding through her. They were about to catch the Silent Stalker. Once and for all.

***

Warren pulled the car in front of a small ranch home with brick siding and put it in park. The home sat back slightly from the road, separated by the long grass of a lawn that desperately needed to be mowed. It was now midafternoon, and Tara had hoped on the ride over that someone was home. She spotted an old beat-up silver Toyota sedan in the driveway and a light shining through the bay window in front of the home. But as she stared at the home a moment longer, an unsettling feeling swept through her and dropped like a pit in her stomach. She knew very well who could be home, who they could be about to face, and her blood ran cold.

She turned to Warren, but his eyes were already locked on her. He gave her a nod of warning. "Brace yourself," he said as he reached for the car door and stepped outside. He didn't need to say much more. They both knew that they were entering a possibly very dangerous situation, and they could be meeting someone highly unpredictable. They needed to be aware of everything.

They walked briskly up the concrete driveway and followed a brick pathway to the front door. Warren knocked. Within moments, the main door swung open and a woman appeared behind the storm door, glaring at them through the screen. She was wearing a baggy t-shirt and sweatpants. Her frizzy graying hair just brushed her shoulders and was partially tucked behind her ears. Tara could smell the cigarette in her hand even before she witnessed her smoking it.

"Can I help you?" she asked skeptically before taking a puff of her cigarette and smothering it in an ashtray next to the door.

"Is Joey Foster here?" Tara asked.

"Why?" she asked, her eyes still on the ashtray as she finished putting out her cigarette. She looked up.

Tara held up her badge, and the woman jerked her head back in surprise. "We're investigating the Silent Stalker murders, and we think your husband may have communicated with some of the victims as an ice cream truck driver. We're just trying to piece together as much information as we can get, and any witness helps." It wasn't a lie; they knew he had interacted with two victims. He did hold information. She just didn't disclose that he was a suspect. But Tara needed to step carefully. She already had the impression that this woman would take some convincing not to feel threatened.

She stared at them for a moment and narrowed her eyes, unsure if she should trust them, But then her eyes fell, and she shook her head with a shrug. "He ain't here," she finally said.

"Do you know where we can find him?" Tara asked.

"Beats me." She sniggered. "And I don't really care where he is. We're in the process of a divorce."

She was about to shut the door, but Tara spoke quickly. "Ma'am, if you don't want to help us find your husband, then can you please at least help with any information regarding these murders?"

The woman stopped hesitantly and slowly creaked the door open more. "What do you need my help for?"

"Can we come in?" Tara asked.

The woman thought for a moment and then obliged, opening the screen door and letting them into a dusty, carpeted living room that reeked of cigarette smoke. The once white walls were now gray with the soot of continuous cigarette smoke damage. It was a small room with just a couch and two reclining chairs, centered around a mounted television. Tara had to refrain from instinctually covering her nose as the woman motioned to an old floral couch. Tara and Warren took a seat, sitting just at the edge.

Tara pulled out an image of Chloe, Serenity, and Adeline. She held each one out for the woman to see. "Have you seen these women before?"

The woman stared at them and shrugged. "Just on the news."

"What about your husband? Did he ever mention them to you?"

The woman crossed her legs and leaned back in her chair, knitting her brows in confusion. "Why would he mention them to me?"

Tara was silent a moment. "Mrs. Foster, have you seen your husband much lately?"

Again, the woman snickered. "Like I said, we're getting a divorce. He's looking for a place. He comes here at night, sleeps on the couch, but that's it. He's never around other than that. And once he gets home, I go in my room and lock my door. So no, I don't see him much." She looked between the two of them. "Is he in some kind of trouble?" she asked, leaning forward slightly in her chair. She smirked, almost in amusement.

Tara shared a look with Warren. They both knew that her anger toward her husband could very well work in their favor. Tara took a deep breath. "We have reason to believe he might've communicated with one of the victims on more than one occasion, and for some reason she avoided him after that."

The woman sat back again, recrossing her legs. For a moment, fear flashed across her face as if she had fused two thoughts together, but it vanished just as quickly, an opportunity burning in her eyes. "I wouldn't be surprised if that son of a bitch was connected to those murders somehow," she sneered through gritted teeth. Her eyes welled, but they weren't tears of sadness or fear. It was anger held on for too long. It was as if she had finally spoken a truth that had held her captive. It was a bold statement to make.

"What makes you say that?" Warren interjected.

The woman sighed, trying desperately to gain her composure. "He's not right in the head," she replied, her eyes locked on the floor as she shook her head. "He's been distant for a while, and then once I wanted a divorce, something in him snapped." She looked up, meeting their eyes. "He's been walking around here like an empty vessel. Then one day I said something to him about it, and he tried to throw a pot of boiling water at me."

"And you still live with him?" Tara asked. It was hard to believe that anyone would live under the same roof as someone who tried to cause such deep physical harm.

She sighed. "I don't have much money. He said he was finding a new place. I was waiting until he was out, then we could sell the house and I could move on with my life. For now, I just lock my door when he's home."

Tara's pulse raced. If they were right, if Joey was the killer, then this woman had no idea how grave of danger she was in.

Warren sat forward in his seat. "Do you know of anywhere else he spends a lot of time? Maybe a basement, a garage, or somewhere not at the house at all?"

Without a second thought, her eyes drifted to the kitchen next her, staring out the sliding glass doors that opened onto a porch. "The shed," she said under her breath. "He's been in there a lot lately when he's home."

Tara and Warren followed her gaze. They could see just beyond the porch in the fenced-in backyard. A small wooden tool shed sat in the corner of the property.

"Do you know what he does in there?" Warren asked.

She shook her head, her eyes falling to the floor. "I'm not allowed in there. And after all the threats he's made, I honestly just want him the hell out. I don't care enough to look in there." There was something in her eyes that spoke a truth her words couldn't. She was scared to look in there. Not only scared at how he would react, but also of what she might find.

"Can we take a look?" Tara asked.

For a moment, the woman stared at them, contemplating. She grabbed her phone on the coffee table and checked the time. She sighed. "He shouldn't be home for a while, so I guess it's all right." She looked between Tara and Warren. "To be honest, if this in anyway helps keep him away from me, then I'm all for it." She stood, waving a hand for them to follow her.

Tara and Warren trailed behind as she walked through the kitchen, out onto the porch, and down the two steps into the lawn. The grass was just as overgrown in the back. Overgrown flowers lined the cedar fence and overflowed from the flowerbeds next to each door of the shed. They crept toward it, and each time they grew closer, Tara's instincts heightened. She could feel in every bone in her body that something was in that shed.

When close enough, Tara noticed a padlock wrapped around the doors. She pointed to it. "Do you have the—" She didn't even need to finish her sentence. The woman had turned her back to them, moved toward the side of the shed, picked up a small rock, and reached in a small hole underneath it.

"I watched him through the window once," she said as she handed them the key.

Tara grabbed hold of it. It felt like a weight in her palm, but she moved quickly, not wanting to waste any more time. She jammed it into the lock, turned it, and pulled the lock off. She swung the doors open.

She instinctively took a step back. The shed was dark, and it took her eyes a second to adjust, to find the light and pull the cord for it. It felt like the blood drained from her body. Mrs. Foster gasped. Warren stiffened beside her. Inside, layered upon each wall, were dozens of pictures of women. Tara stepped inside, scanning the walls. They were all of the recent victims. She could see Chloe, getting into her car in her driveway, another of her entering her house, bringing her daughter to the bus stop, grabbing a cup of coffee at a coffee shop. Each picture was taken without her being aware. Tara scanned the rest. Pictures of Serenity and Adeline all in similar settings, all oblivious. But then Tara stopped on a set of a few more of a different woman. One she did not recognize.

It was woman in scrubs, leaving a hospital, getting into her car, walking down the street with her children. Tara pointed at it.

"Do you know her?" she asked Mrs. Foster.

She moved closer, still staring in shock at everything around her, her face a few shades whiter. For a moment she stared at the picture as if she didn't know what she was looking at first, but then her eyes grew large.

"That's Ana," she replied, her eyes still stuck on the image. "Why does he have a picture of Ana?"

"Who's Ana?" Warren asked.

She was silent a moment, as if in shock, unable to speak.

"Mrs. Foster, who is Ana?" Tara repeated.

Her eyes darted from the image as she turned to Tara and Warren. "She works at the hospital. She's a nurse. I work the desk. She's a good friend of mine."

Adrenaline pumped through Tara's body. "Do you know where she lives?"

"Uh…" The woman's eyes drifted again to the picture. She was having difficulty making sense of it all, and each time she stared at the picture, she got lost in it for a moment until she remembered where she was and what she was doing. She turned to Tara. "I drove her home a couple times. She lives in Bellevue. Actually—" She pulled open her phone, opened her GPS app, and went to her recent destinations. When she found the address, she held it out to them.

Tara thanked her and took down the address. When finished, she turned to her. The woman stared at her, eyes wide. "You better get out of here," Tara warned her. "Go stay with someone. Get away from this house." She paused, glancing at the images once more. "Your husband is much more dangerous than you know," she added as the rest of the color drained from Mrs. Foster's face.

Chapter Twenty Six

Ana closed her eyes, taking a sip of her wine and savoring it. The house was quiet; her kids were gone. She couldn't remember the last time she had a moment to herself, to relax. It almost felt strange and wrong, but each time she had that thought, she forced it from her mind. *I deserve this*, she reminded herself. *I need it.* It seemed silly when she really thought about it. She was a single mother raising three children and a full-time nurse. For years, she had given all of herself to everyone around her. If anyone deserved one day to herself, it was her.

Ana placed her glass down on the bathroom sink, stared at herself in the mirror, and smiled. She was wearing makeup for the first time in she didn't know how long. She was too busy to think of appearances in marriage and afterward, and she had only worn it on special occasions. But as she stared at her perfectly curled lashes, her red lips and blemish-free skin, she wondered why she didn't make more of an effort. She felt beautiful; she felt like more than somebody's mother or nurse. She felt special.

Ana lined her lips a touch more, smoothed out her chocolate-brown hair, and put two diamond stud earrings in her ear. She stared at herself once more, but her phone vibrating pulled her eyes away. She grabbed her phone, staring down at a text. *One hour?* it read. It was the maid of honor in the group of the bachelorette party she was about to attend. A flurry of yeses were sent in reply. Ana texted the same. She was looking forward to it. Once in a while she would go out to dinner with a friend, but she couldn't remember the last time she had been to a bachelorette party. Claudia was the last woman in her group of friends that wasn't married, and to be honest, Ana never thought she would. It had been a total surprise to her and to everyone in their circle when she finally found someone and began taking steps to settle down.

Ana stared down at her phone once more, the flurry of texts continuing. She was meeting them in an hour at a restaurant in town, which meant that she needed to be out of the house in thirty minutes. The realization sparked a fire under her. She was still in her robe and had yet to even pick out an outfit. Ana checked her makeup one last time, quickly tucked the contents back into her makeup bag, and tossed it in the cabinet under the sink. It was time to get dressed.

She reached for the doorknob, but a large thud stopped her in her tracks, and Ana's heart instinctually pounded. She waited a moment. It sounded like something or someone had hit the floor forcefully. *Maybe one of the kids forgot something? Maybe it's Mom.* The thought momentarily eased her, but her instinct was stronger. She waited, listening, and as each second went by without another sound, she breathed a bit more easily. *It's nothing*, she told herself. *Maybe a painting fell. I'm being ridiculous.* She relaxed as she shook off the fear and reached for the doorknob once more, swinging it open.

But another sound creaked in the silence and then stopped. Ana's heart pounded once more.

"Mom?" she called, but she met no response. Panic washed over her. *Did I lock the window?* She had always locked her bedroom window, especially now with the murders. But she had forgotten whether she did this morning after she had it open briefly for some air. Her blood suddenly went cold. "Hello?" she called again.

Silence sat heavy in the air, but it felt wrong. It felt suffocating. Someone was there, she could sense it. Another creak of a footstep was heard closer, and an unmistakable sinister laugh barreled down the hall, hitting Ana right in the gut.

Chapter Twenty Seven

Tara and Warren stood on the doorstep of a split-level ranch. They had called for backup on the way. Chief Meyers had instructed his officers to be discreet, not to raise suspicion, and to wait until there was a signal needing assistance. As Tara looked around them at the desolate street. She didn't see any sign that they were there, but they couldn't wait, and as Tara looked next to her, she was relieved that she and Warren had each other.

Tara opened a glass storm door and knocked on a dark blue wooden door behind it. There was a car in the driveway, and light flooded through the small window at the top of the door. Someone was home. But it was now the second time Tara knocked, and still no one had answered.

Tara glanced at Warren. It didn't sit right. Why would someone be home but not answer? Warren's face tightened in concern. He nodded at the door once more, telling Tara to try again. She knocked. "Hello?" Tara called this time. "Ana, are you home?"

Again her attempt was met by silence, but they waited, listening. Still, not a sound.

"Maybe we should try the back?" Warren whispered. Tara nodded. But just as they turned down the stairs, her hand gripped the railing. Her feet halted. She had heard something, and it sent a shiver down her spine. She glanced at Warren. She could see he heard it too. He stiffened. They didn't move; they barely breathed. They didn't make a sound. Every piece of them listened for what they had thought they heard.

For a moment there was silence but then the same sound hit them like a bullet. It was a whimper, a woman's cry, and then a thud against the floor. She cried out again. Tara and Warren spun around, pulling out their guns in one swift motion.

"FBI, open up!" Tara screamed, her gun held steadily in front of her.

Her words were met by no response, the whimpering continuing.

Warren pushed her aside, swung open the glass door and with all his power, kicked the door, and it swung open.

The whimpering stopped. The room opened into a living room with a sectional and chairs creating a divider between the long farmhouse dining room table behind it. It was an open-floor plan, and the kitchen could be seen just behind the dining room table. But as Tara and Warren looked around, they didn't see a source of the sound.

Tara and Warren glanced at each other. There was a long hallway to the right of the kitchen, and Warren nodded in that direction. He continued down it, Tara following behind. They each cautiously looked in each room, their guns held out steadily in front of them. They looked in two bedrooms that seemed to be children's rooms, but still no source of the sound. As they got to the end of the hall, Tara spotted the bathroom door. It was wide open, but splinters of wood littered the ground, and as Tara moved closer, she could see a large dent in it, as if someone had kicked it open. Her heart pounded as her eyes fell to a broken wine glass by her feet, splayed in fragments on the white carpet now tainted with red.

Tara looked toward Warren, making sure he saw it too, but he only stared straight ahead. Tara followed his gaze to another room just at the end of the hall. The door was ajar, and light flooded from it, out into the hallway. Tara crept slowly behind Warren, their backs flat against the wall as they inched closer and closer to the door. They could now hear another muffled cry emanating from the room, and Tara's heart beat harder.

They reached the doorframe. Warren turned to Tara, gave her a nod, and Tara knew what he was about to do. He spun around, his gun stretched before him, and propelled his body, centered in the door. But then his face changed. The muffled crying grew louder. Tara thrust herself in front of the door as well and then froze as her mind swirled into a haze. She saw Ana first, her eyes pleading for help as a knife was pressed firmly against her neck by the gloved hand of a man behind her. He was dressed in all black. His face was weathered and clean-shaven. He gave Tara and Warren a daring smile.

Tara and Warren lowered their guns, hands in the air as they slowly entered the room, careful not to set him off.

Ana's mouth was stuffed with something, and she closed her eyes, trying to stay calm as tears flowed down her cheeks.

"Joey, you don't have to do this," Tara said. Her eyes were glued to his knife, which had already broken the skin on Ana's neck. A smear of blood sat just above it. "If you let her go, we'll let you get away." Tara's biggest priority was Ana. She of course didn't want him to get away, but if she could save Ana's life, then so be it for now. They could give him a head start.

His laugh filled the air with a sudden chill. "You think I'm stupid? You'll come right after me."

Tara sensed Warren's movement beside her. It was slight, but she knew what he was doing, making sure he had a good grip on his gun, ready to point it at the right exact second. Tara needed to keep him talking. She needed to keep his eyes on her. Joey's eyes started to drift to Warren.

"We just want Ana," Tara burst out. "Whatever you want us to do, we'll do. Just hand her over."

He stared at her a moment with a sheepish smile. He was skeptical, but she could see the consideration. He tilted his head. "What if you stay here, I take her a half mile into the woods, then I let her go."

Tara didn't trust it. She shook her head. "I can't let you take her," she replied. "But I promise we won't go after you. Leave her here, and we'll give you time to get away." He didn't reply, just stared at her, contemplating. "How much time do you need?" Tara asked. "An hour? Two hours? You have our word, we won't go after you."

His eyes drifted to the open window, still considering his options. Tara stiffened. Her heart pounded. In one swift motion, Warren raised his gun, sending one shot off aimed at the side of Joey's head. But he had sensed it, ducking as the bullet whizzed passed it, hitting a pillow on the bed and sending a cloud of feathers into the air. Ana let out a muffled cry as he tossed her to the ground and jumped at the window. He pulled his head through, his chest grazing the window frame as he pulled his body forward. But Tara sprinted forward, grabbed his leg and jerking his body back into the room. He spun around, swinging the knife, slicing wildly. Tara ducked but not far enough, the knife grazing her shoulder. She fell back on instinct. He jumped on her, forcing her flat on the ground as he raised his knife once more.

A shot rang through the air. Joey bellowed in pain, his wrist bleeding profusely. Warren stood with his gun eye level. He lowered it, ran to them, and quickly cuffed Joey.

Just then a door in the distance burst open. An officer called to them.

"We're in here," Tara yelled, grabbing hold of her shoulder, which was bleeding.

Three officers ran in to the room and stopped dead in their tracks as they saw the scene, their eyes wide.

"Call an ambulance," Warren demanded. Tara turned toward him. He had taken a bed sheet, wrapping it around Joey's wrist, which was still bleeding profusely. The officers nodded in unison.

Tara scrambled to her feet and over to Ana, who was sitting on the floor, bewildered. She had pulled out what was stuffed in her mouth, but she couldn't speak. She stared around the room blankly, in total shock, her hand still at her throat.

Tara wrapped her arms around her. "He can't hurt you anymore," she whispered into her ear as Ana's cries burst forth. Tara helped her to her feet, ushering her out of the room, away from the killer. And as they stepped outside into the fresh air, Tara realized that the killer and this case were now behind her.

Chapter Twenty Eight

Tara sat in the back of the ambulance as an EMT wrapped her shoulder. It wasn't deep. He had just grazed her, luckily. *We were all lucky,* she told herself as she finally took a much-needed deep breath. The ambulance with Joey Foster had already put on its signals and sped away to the hospital. The injury to his hand was serious, but certainly not life-threatening, and Tara was glad of that. Death seemed too easy. It would've been a quick end to years of terror, but it would've only resulted in moments of suffering when he had tormented families for years, having them live in the nightmare of not seeing their loved one and knowing that the killer was still out there. The thought made Tara's blood boil. He had spent twenty years free while others' lives were forever changed. She wanted him to suffer, to rot in prison where he belonged.

"You should be good now," the EMT finally said, snapping Tara out of her trance. She thanked him as he hopped out of the vehicle and left Tara alone. She stared out in front of her, her eyes locking on the other ambulance, which sat on the street, just outside the home. It was where Ana was being checked for any sign of trauma, for any injuries, and Warren stood just by the back doors speaking to her and an EMT. She couldn't hear what they were saying, but Warren smiled at Ana, nodded at the EMT, said his last words, and backed up as the EMT shut the doors from inside. The ambulance rumbled to a start and took off down the street.

Warren's phone rang, and he picked it up, placing to it his ear. He spoke for a moment and then locked eyes with Tara, the phone still to his ear, and walked up the driveway to her. Tara already assumed who it was—Reinhardt, and when Warren got close enough, he confirmed it.

"He wants to speak to you," Warren said as he placed the phone on speaker.

Tara leaned forward. "Another great job, Mills," Reinhardt said. She could hear the true thrill in his voice. He was impressed and satisfied, and it caused a smile to instantly burst onto Tara's face. Warren patted her on the back. "We can now officially close this cold case. You're going to help bring a lot of families some closure," Reinhardt continued.

He was right. For the first time in twenty years, the families who had lost their mothers, sisters, wives, would no longer have to live in fear that the killer still walked free. They wouldn't have to feel the anger and the pain that no one had paid the price of taking such a precious life. If he had never resurfaced, he probably would've died an old man, getting away with it. She had wondered why he even resurfaced at all, why he had taken the risk. But now she knew. It was the podcast stirring up the attention that he craved deep down, and it was his failed marriage and issues with his wife. It all created a perfect storm for his urges to grow to the point of suffocation.

"I'm going to get you guys a flight back home tomorrow," Reinhardt continued, snapping Tara out of her thoughts.

But at Reinhardt's words, a new thought surfaced. She thought of the families, the pain they had reexperienced in this case that had reopened. But she also thought of the tears of joy in having the killer finally behind bars. It made a desire bubble up inside her. She too wanted the freedom of closure, to unveil all the pieces of her past. She needed to get her questions answered. She needed to find out who Mackenzie James was once and for all.

She locked eyes with Warren. He gave her a questioning look. Tara leaned forward, speaking into the phone. "That won't be necessary," she said. "There's something I need to take care of in New York."

Chapter Twenty Nine

Tara stood on Pine Avenue in Walden, New York, her car just behind her as she stared at the home that still gave her nightmares. The small steel numbers marking the house as 72 still hung next to the front door above the black mounted mailbox. The same white metal storm door with a large window cutout still hung on the hinge, with the same wooden door behind it. But at the same time, it was different. The roof was now green with moss, the shingles chipped and rotting. The wooden porch where her mother used to sit and watch her play was swollen and rotted with chipped paint. And a *For Sale* sign was staked in the lawn.

Tara had looked up the house online a couple times before out of curiosity. It had had multiple owners since her family lived there, but each family only lived there a couple of years at most. Tara could only assume that they soon moved once they learned from people in town what had occurred in their living room.

Staring at the home sent a strange feeling over her. It was the only place she had known her mother, the only place she had felt her love, the only place she had her hugs and her kisses and her home-cooked meals. She had almost forgotten how many positive moments she had experienced in that home. They were always overpowered by tragedy. But now, standing before it, she felt a sudden closeness to her mother she hadn't been expecting to feel.

Tara closed her eyes briefly and took a deep breath. She was doing as much for her mom as she was for herself. To bring justice, to move past the tragedy that had so long clouded her mind.

Tara opened her eyes and turned down the street, focused on the house of her father's old friend. She could see it just across the street, a few houses down. It hadn't changed much. It still had the same brick siding, the same cement stairs. They had a newer front door, a newer roof, but everything else on the house and on the street felt eerily similar.

Tara only hoped that things were still as similar as she needed them to be, that he still lived there. She crossed the street. It was still a quiet road with barely any traffic, just a car every ten minutes or so.

As she neared the lawn, she stopped for a moment. *Is this crazy? What if he doesn't even remember me?* But she quickly pushed her thoughts aside. *Of course he's going to remember you. He was friends with your father who murdered his wife across the street.* She shook her head at her absurd doubt. Everyone who still lived on this street and those that moved there after would know who she was if she said her name and which house she had grown up in. Stories like that had the tendency to settle into the foundation of the past. Nothing like that had happened here until it did.

Without another thought, Tara trudged across the lawn, up the steps, and rang the bell before she could even second-guess herself again.

It didn't take long for the door to jostle open, and a man to stand before her. He was visibly old now. His cheeks hung beside his bulbous nose, his skin weathered and his hair gray. It was him; she was sure of it. But unlike the drunk she had known from her past, he was dressed nicely in a button-down shirt and khakis, his hair combed with a pomade shine.

He stared at her curiously. He didn't recognize her. "Can I help you?"

Tara opened her mouth, and for a second, no words left her throat, until she forced them. "Tara," she said, "My name is Tara." His face contorted even more into confusion as he tilted his head slightly. "Tara Mills," she added.

At the name, his eyes grew wide. He stared at her, looking her up and down as if searching for something to make the connection clearer. "Richard Mills's daughter?" he asked. Tara nodded, and again his eyes widened. A smile formed on his face. "You look good!" he said. Tara gave a slight smile. She knew most people had probably assumed she'd be a drunk or drug addict by now with all she had experienced.

He continued to stare at her as confusion settled in. "I didn't think I'd see you on my doorstep when I came to the door." He chuckled, but there was a fear of the unknown in his eyes. He knew she wouldn't have just come over to say hello. After all, the only memories Tara had of him were that he was a drunk who reinforced her father's alcoholism. He stiffened, as if ready to take a beating, but then spoke. "Did you want to come in?"

Tara was surprised, but she obliged. She would much rather have this conversation inside anyway. He led her into a small mudroom and then into a living room just beside it. It was clean and tidy, with a brown leather couch and gray armchair, sitting across from each other and atop a beige hand-woven rug. Tara couldn't help but notice the lack of beer cans that she would've expected. A dog sat atop the couch, and he looked up as they approached, tail wagging excitedly. He was old-looking, his brown thin coat now white around the muzzle.

"Do you mind dogs?" he asked. Tara shook her head. She moved closer and scratched his ear until he settled once more, curling back into a ball and dozing off to sleep.

Tara took a seat. The man sat across from her on a chair. She felt embarrassed, but she still didn't remember his name. All she had remembered was that he was friends with her father. "I'm so sorry, I always knew you were friends with my father, but it's been so long, I couldn't remember your name." She felt heat rise to her face, but he only smiled warmly.

"Raymond," he replied. Tara nodded, the name sounding somewhat familiar. "What brings you here?" he asked, sitting back in the chair.

Tara didn't know how to start the conversation, whether she should just dive right in or carefully approach. But as she met his eyes, she could see concern. She needed to just ask. "I'm trying to find someone, and I was hoping that you might be able to help," she started.

He nodded, but he had lost his smile. His hands gripped the arms of the chair.

Tara could sense he expected her to ask something, which only made her think that he did hold information. "Do you happen to still talk to my father?"

He relaxed slightly as he shook his head. "I haven't spoken to him since you all still lived here, before—" He stopped himself, but Tara knew what he meant. Before the murder.

"Do you know anyone who still might?"

Again, he shook his head. "I don't speak to anyone that we used to hang out with back then. The day your father got taken away in handcuffs was the last day I picked up a drink. And given that all our friends basically lived at the bar, I don't speak to them no more."

Tara nodded again, hope suddenly diminishing. She stared at him a moment, wondering now if this was all a waste of time, a waste of a trip.

"Who is it that you're trying to find?" he finally asked.

Tara was quiet a moment. The dog placed his head on her lap, and she stroked his ear once more. *You need to just let it out*, she told herself. She looked up, her eyes meeting his. "There's this woman whose been visiting my father. I'm trying to find out who she is." Raymond's face went white. His hands clutched the arms of the chair harder. He knew exactly who she was speaking of, Tara could sense it like an intoxicating smell. "Her name is Mackenzie James."

He stiffened. His hands gripped the chair so hard, Tara thought he had ripped holes where his fingers lay.

He was silent a moment, as if letting it all sink it, wondering how to respond. Tara was about to ask if he knew her when he finally sighed, letting the tension out of his body like a popped balloon. "Did you ask your father?"

Tara nodded. "He wouldn't tell me."

Raymond looked off to the side, staring at the floor, shaking his head. "There's something you need to know," he told her, looking at her dead in the eye, "but I can't be the one to tell you." He flinched as he said the words, knowing very well the disappointment they would cause. Tara wanted to scream at him. She had come all this way. He knew something. How dare he deny her that information? But then he stood, left the room briefly, and came back with a paper and pen. He scribbled something down. "She lives a couple towns over, with her mother," he added. He handed Tara the piece of paper. She looked down at the address written across it. "You need to hear it from Mackenzie James."

Chapter Thirty

Tara swallowed hard as her fist knocked steadily on the door of Mackenzie James's mobile home in Montgomery, a town over from where she had come from. She had thought on the way over about what she would say, how she would approach this, but she still wasn't sure. And at this point she was fed up. She wanted answers, and she wasn't leaving until she got them. That was all she knew for sure.

There was a car in the driveway, and a light was on. Tara was certain someone was home. But it was now the third time she had knocked, and still no one had answered. She knocked again. A curtain moved in the window and then quickly fell. Whoever it was knew she was there, and Tara could only assume it was Mackenzie.

"Open up, Mackenzie. I need to speak to you," Tara demanded. Anger boiled in her voice, and she waited a moment. The door stayed closed. She was about to call out again when she heard someone unlock it, and the door opened just a crack.

Mackenzie's deep brown eyes peered at her with a warning glare. "How the hell did you get my address?" she demanded.

"It doesn't matter. We need to talk."

Mackenzie laughed. "Oh, do we?" she asked sarcastically. "Get off my property."

"Let her in, Mackenzie." An unknown voice sailed through the room behind her.

Mackenzie's face fell. She turned toward the sound. "But—" she started.

"Just let her in," the voice said again, more demandingly. It was a woman's voice, and Tara assumed it was Mackenzie's mother. Confusion settled in. *How does she know about me?*

Mackenzie turned back to Tara, scowling, and sighed. She opened the door and rolled her eyes. "You can take a seat over there," she said as she pointed to a chair in the living room. A woman sat on a couch next to the chair, her legs curled under her, staring a television mounted on the opposite wall. Tara took a seat as the woman turned off the television.

She turned to Tara and sat upright, anchoring her feet on the floor. She was probably in her early sixties. Her hair was tied back in a tight ponytail, accentuating her gray roots that had grown out from her dyed blonde hair that started halfway across her head. She wore sweatpants and a long t-shirt. She didn't smile; she just stared at Tara, looking her up and down as if studying her.

Mackenzie still stood. "I really don't think this is a good idea. He wouldn't want us to—"

The woman held up a hand. "She deserves to know. And if he won't tell her, then that means we have to."

Mackenzie's face tightened in anger as she crossed her arms, still standing.

"Tell me what?" Tara asked. She could only assume that the man they were referring to was her father.

"Who we are," the woman responded. Mackenzie groaned angrily and stormed out of the room. Tara's eyes followed her. "Don't mind her; this hasn't been easy for her either."

Tara stared at her, trying to make sense of her words. She was dancing around something, and Tara still couldn't see what it was. She wanted so desperately to know, to see, and she could feel it just at the tip of this woman's tongue.

The woman sighed. "I'm Samantha James," she started, confirming in Tara's mind that she was in fact Mackenzie James's mother. "I'm sure your father's never mentioned me," she added with an eye roll. "But I was with your father for a very long time."

Tara stared at her in confusion. Her thoughts ran wild, too fast to grasp any of them. "When?" It was all she could think to ask.

The woman sat back in her chair. She looked tired and oddly calm. It was as if what she was saying didn't phase her anymore, like it had exhausted her for so long that it now just rolled out of her mouth without any force. "In high school," she replied. "And after." She paused a moment, staring Tara dead in the eye. "I was with your father when he met your mother, and I was with your father when he was with her too.

Although I had no clue." She shook her head in disgust. "Or that he got married, that he had you."

Tara felt like the air had been kicked from her lungs. She couldn't speak. Thoughts raced through her mind. The work trips, being out all night, her mother angry. It all made sense now. *He was living a double life.*

"Did my mom know?" Tara asked.

The woman curled her legs up underneath her once more and shrugged as if she had just told Tara some neighborhood gossip. "I doubt it," she replied. "I mean, I didn't know."

Silence sat heavy in the air as Tara recalled when her mom used to storm over to the neighbor's house, demanding to know where her husband was. It was undeniable that she suspected something, but Tara doubted she knew the truth.

Tara didn't know what else to ask, what else to say. She just sat there, staring at this woman in confusion.

"Mackenzie's not your only half sibling, by the way," the woman added. "I have two other kids."

Tara felt sick to her stomach. Of course, Mackenzie was her sister. She had to be. Tara had been so focused on processing the information she was given that she didn't even think about the possibility. But now it sat like a brick in her stomach.

A sudden rush of footsteps barreled into the room. The woman sat upright, her face tight with fear. She held out her hand, a signal to stop.

"Don't!" she yelled.

Tara whipped her head around. It was Mackenzie. Tears welled in her eyes, a knife in her hand by her side. But she just stood there, staring at Tara, her eyes gleaming in pain.

"She's a victim in all this too, Mackenzie. She didn't know," her mother added.

But Mackenzie still just stood there, staring at Tara like a vulture staring at an injured rat, waiting for it to die. Tara sat on the edge of her seat. She was off duty, but luckily she still carried her gun. It sat just under her shirt and brought Tara some comfort, even though she in no way wanted to use it. Mackenzie was her sister, after all. The thought made her head spin.

"It's your family's fault," Mackenzie spat through gritted teeth. Tears flowed from her eyes. She gripped the handle of her knife harder.

Her mother stood up, moving toward her. "Mackenzie, put the knife down."

"No!" Mackenzie yelled, slicing the air in front of her like a warning, and her mother took a few steps back.

Tara stood, backing away from her as well. "I didn't know any of this," Tara reminded her. "But your mom is right. I had just as much of a right to know this as you did."

Mackenzie only narrowed her eyes more. "Your family ruined ours! Don't you see that?" she screamed. "Your mom got what was coming to her."

Tara's blood boiled.

"Mackenzie!" her mother screamed, but the warning had no effect.

Mackenzie only cried louder, running her hands through her hair in frustration, the knife still in her grip. "You didn't want to listen. You didn't want to stay away. You come here stirring up more trouble, opening up old wounds." She gasped for air between sobs and then stared Tara dead in her eyes. "I should've killed you too, just like I did your mother."

Tara stared at her, everything darkening around her. The room began to spin. She wasn't sure if she had heard right.

Her mother stared at her too, mouth wide open in horror. "You don't mean that," she said. "It was your father, it wasn't—"

"That's what he wants you all to think," Mackenzie shot back. The knife was still clasped tightly in her hand.

Tara couldn't speak.

"Please, put the knife down," her mother pleaded again. She reached for it, grabbing hold of Mackenzie's hand as her eyes stayed focused on Tara. But Mackenzie swung at her, pushing her mother away from her with her other hand. She stumbled backward, and Mackenzie lunged at her, hitting her mother in a rage, the knife skidding across the floor.

Tara jumped on top of her, pushed her off her mother, and tackled her to the ground. Mackenzie tried to claw at her, to bite her, but Tara, slightly larger, held her down and cuffed her.

"Call the police," Tara instructed the older woman as she ran into the other room.

Mackenzie burst into incontrollable sobbing. Tara looked down at her. She still couldn't quite grasp what she had heard. She was her half sister, but she had killed Tara's mother. It was the answer to the question she had always wanted. The night of her mother's murder, she had sensed that someone else was there with her father, in a corner of the room Tara couldn't see from the hallway. The person was intentionally shielded. Her father had purposely stood where Tara could see him. Now she knew. It was Mackenzie in that corner. She must've been no more than a teenager. And Tara's father, Mackenzie's father, had taken the blame.

As Tara waited for the police to arrive, an overwhelming mix of feelings swept over her. She finally knew the answer to her nightmares. Her mom finally had justice. But there were also answers that she never imagined, that her father lived a double life, that Mackenzie James was her sister, that she had two other siblings.

Her father was even worse a person than she had ever imagined. He hadn't just ruined her life or her mother's—he had caused all of this. He had caused Mackenzie's pain, which caused Tara's mother's death. He had caused everyone around him pain. And after all this time, he still tried desperately to hide his secret from Tara. But as she sat there, staring at Mackenzie's sobbing, she realized one thing. She now had the truth. The one last thing he tried to keep from her, and for the first time, she had won.

Epilogue

One week later

Tara sat at her kitchen table, sipping her coffee, staring down at the wedding gowns in the wedding magazines in front of her. She had flipped through every page, looking for inspiration on floral designs, and dresses, and themes. She had finally gotten into the excitement of it all, and she had to admit she was enjoying it fully. She couldn't wait to go dress shopping, to look at venues and pick out everything else pertaining to the wedding. They still hadn't picked a date. They wouldn't be able to until they decided on a venue and knew what dates were available, but they had decided on a month, June, which was now nine months away. Tara smiled at the thought of a June wedding. She had always wanted to get married in the early summer. But there was something else about that month that felt special to her. It was her mother's birthday month. And after all Tara had been through lately, after all the pain she had dug up, she wanted to honor her mother in a much more positive light—

drawing a connection in life rather than in death. John fully supported the idea.

She heard his footsteps come down the hall and into the kitchen, and Tara slapped the magazine shut.

He laughed. "Seeing what dresses you're looking at in a magazine is not the same thing as me seeing *your* dress," he said as he poured himself a cup of coffee.

"It just feels wrong." She smiled.

John leaned over her, kissing her on the forehead. "It's nice to see you so happy."

Tara smiled. She *was* happy. Finally, after so many years, she had some closure. Mackenzie was now in jail, awaiting a trial. She had confessed even more details during questioning. She was sixteen when she killed Tara's mother. She had found out that day and had actually gone over to Tara's house to confront their father. But when he wasn't home, her rage ignited into a fire when she saw Tara's mother. As a teenager, Tara could only assume she saw Tara's mom as the root of her problem. She attacked her, and Tara's father came home in the middle of it and took the blame.

It still made Tara angry. Her father's lies, the pain he caused. She couldn't help but feel anger toward Mackenzie too, but deep down she knew that if it wasn't for what her father did, Mackenzie never would've been driven to that point, and her life too would look much different.

"You all right?" John asked.

Tara was staring blankly at the closed magazine. She nodded and smiled. She was okay. Her past was behind her. But then a thought seeped like venom into her mind, one that she had pushed out time and time again over the past week. Her father was getting a retrial, and Tara knew there was a good chance his sentence would be reduced. She knew there was a good chance he would soon walk free. But that wasn't the only part that concerned her. He had spent his whole life protecting Mackenzie, but now, Tara had exposed it all. It was enough to take him over the edge. He was angry, and Tara was certain she would now become the target of it.

NOW AVAILABLE!

ONE LAST LIE
(A Tara Mills Mystery—Book Four)

Women are being brutally murdered in Boulder, Colorado, their bodies stuffed into the trunks of their cars, and they all have one thing in common: they were meeting someone for a date that they met online. It's clear a serial killer is at large, and FBI Agent Tara Mills is quickly on the case. But she soon learns that none of the women were meeting the same person, or so it seems, because none of the victims' dates can be tracked down either.

As Tara digs deep into the world of online dating, and as more women turn up dead, she soon realizes that the killer's web is larger than she ever imagined. With the killer always one step ahead, taking on a new identity and leaving no trail, Tara fears she has finally met her match.

Tara is pushed to her limits. But with the secrets of her past finally resolved, she hopes she can finally lay it to rest and focus wholeheartedly on the case. But when she learns that her biggest nightmare is yet to come, she fears that she has only made things worse for herself, for her fiancé, and for their future.

Book #5 in the series will be available soon!

BOOKS BY SARAH SUTTON

TARA MILLS MYSTERY SERIES
ONE LAST STEP (Book #1)
ONE LAST BREATH (Book #2)
ONE LAST UNVEIL (Book #3)
ONE LAST LIE (Book #4)